THE PANTOMIME MAN

THE PANTOMIME MAN *By* RICHARD MIDDLETON Author of The Ghost Ship &c. ◡ ◡ ◡

Edited, with a Foreword, by
JOHN GAWSWORTH

Introduction by
LORD ALFRED DOUGLAS

WILDSIDE PRESS

First published August 1933

The Frontispiece is an enlargement
of an hitherto unpublished snapshot,
the property of Henry Savage, to
whom we are indebted for his cour-
teous permission to reproduce it.
                                R. & C.

PRINTED IN GREAT BRITAIN BY R. CLAY & SONS, LIMITED
BUNGAY, SUFFOLK, FOR MESSRS. RICH & COWAN, LIMITED
27 MAIDEN LANE, LONDON, W.C.2

CONTENTS

A DIARY OF YOUTH

TALES AND FANTASIES

A POET'S HOLIDAY

THE PANTOMIME MAN

LITERARY PAPERS

OCCASIONAL PIECES

A DIARY OF YOUTH

JOURNAL OF A CLERK

This Journal, begun by Richard Middleton in his twentieth year, when living at home with his family at East Molesey and working as a clerk in the service of the Royal Exchange Assurance Corporation, contains, besides personal references to his sister Margaret and the aunt whose cottage at Farnham he often visited, allusions to Charles, a fellow-clerk, and William, Lily and Elsie, youthful friends in whose company he was wont to spend the freedom of his week-ends.

Saturday, April 25th, 1903.

A Saturday off. I got up remarkably early seeing it was a holiday and went up to town. I went to Lambeth and found Lily expecting me but William was out. So I was made to sit down and listen to a long and painful story about the next-door woman who has committed suicide. She took two doses of poison and then cut her throat, probably under the influence of the poison, as it would be a very unlikely thing for a woman to do otherwise. She has a husband whom I saw smoking a cigar in the street, apparently not much distressed, and three little children. She lost a baby just before Christmas. It is very hard luck on the children. One of them, a little button (Stevenson!) of about six years of age, was always knitting in the window whenever I passed. And I had got her name, Lenny, from William with a view to sending her anonymously a set of knitting needles. But Lenny has gone away to her aunt's, so she will not get her knitting needles now. Lily's mother spoke very feelingly about it all. Said how she missed the sound of her neighbour moving about next door and calling the children. It rather shocked me to hear Lily speaking of the thing quite lightly, but of course she is too young to understand. William came an hour late, so after some recriminations we went by train instead of by tram to Richmond. However, Lily seemed to enjoy the train ride and I diverted myself by pointing out to her all the objects of interest on the way. When we got to Richmond we went to a shop and bought some cakes. It is curious in a lad of his class that William should be so very self-conscious. Or perhaps he is narrow-minded. When the three of us are together Lily and I are like a couple of rather irresponsible children. It is William who suffers. It is rather a pity—for, as I am always telling him, when he really is grown up and has *real* responsibilities he will wish he was a child again. From Richmond we took the tram to Kew. Lily did not like it much but it is only a short journey. It seems that she was on a 'bus in London and the driver, who was the better for liquor, drove them into a lamp-post. So her fear of trams and 'buses is fairly natural. It will soon wear off. We went into the gardens and it was pleasant to see the dear little Cockney lie down on the grass and roll about. What a pity it is that all children are not brought up in the country until they are sixteen. A Reform of that sort would be a big thing indeed and the details would be terribly difficult, but it would be a splendid feather in the cap of any Government. And the improvement to the race! No more stunted minds and bodies. But how many of these children would wish to return to the city when it was time to work in earnest. And what would the parents say? I fear that Reform belongs to Utopia.

While we were sitting there and munching cake and chocolate, (Arcadian meal!) a long-legged bird of some sort, I dare not give it a name, for they have a number of foreign birds of various sorts in Kew Gardens, came walking across towards us with the greatest sangfroid, and to Lily's great delight consented to eat pieces of macaroon which he swallowed whole. When he had had enough he strode off with the same calmness. Whatever he might be, he was certainly a philosopher. We then went into the different greenhouses, and Lily in a child's way, fearing the termination of her pleasure, kept asking if there were any more. Fortunately there are a good many at Kew. We especially liked the great palm house with a delightful corkscrew staircase at each end, and I think one of us would have been quite contented to run up and down it for the rest of the afternoon. But then, there were also the orchid houses to see, full of strange blooms, come from all over the world to please the eyes and nose of a little seven-year-older, and great red lilies, and a lemon hanging on to a tree, and tame goldfish in the water, and a peacock willing to hold up his tail (till further notice if he had but an audience to look at him), and peahens (less glorious and no less vain) chasing the sparrows, and the sparrows, humble but unabashed, stealing cake from the peahens, and funny foreign little ducks, and a black swan, and lots of little children running up and down the slopes, and other children playing hide and seek amongst the trees, quite oblivious of the labels informing them that most of these trees belonged to foreign countries. We had our work cut out to see them all in the time at our disposal.

As the afternoon wore on, we went and had a look at the river: and then back again to the gardens and had tea on a marble-topped table in the open air. And the silly waiter only spoke French. However I didn't try him with any of mine. Then we walked up to the pagoda, shut-up and desolate, and then out on to the road. We walked towards Richmond and passed a house where there was a reception after a wedding with carriages coming up, and carriages going away, and the front rooms filled to repletion, for it was not a very large house. We looked over a wall on to the recreation ground and saw a lady shooting with a bow at the bright-coloured targets. And Lily, with the lack of sympathy for each other that is peculiar to her sex, clapped her hands every time she missed. After that we walked on to the station and just caught a train back and got with great bustle and excitement into an empty carriage. And so back to London. Lily in a kindly mood, leaning out of window and saying good-bye to the porters at every station—who good-naturedly answered her. And then home and good-bye, with vague promises for next Saturday. I had a bad cold in the head, so I went home instead of going to the theatre. I read W. Besant's book on *Rabelais* and liked it much.

Monday, April 27th, 1903.

To-night is one of those splendid nights when I am jolly and so everything else seems jolly too. Looking out of the window in the train I caught a pleasant glimpse of a real home—quite typical. It was an upper room, almost an attic, in one of a row of dingy little houses. But the sun shining on them and flashing on the window-panes and lighting up the rooms made them look quite delightful. And in this little room there were a working man, shirt-sleeves and corduroys quite proper, and his good wife, like most English women well figured and with a pleasant expression, sitting down to tea. The man was pouring out and the woman was spreading butter on the loaf. In the background there was a white counterpaned bed. Now, I have no doubt the butter was margarine and that the man blew down the spout of his teapot, when it failed to pour properly, but in spite of that, it all seemed pretty and fit and homely. At the station here I saw a pretty little child with nice twinkling legs, showing a dainty morsel of laced petticoat, walking with a man fat and objectionable to look at, but who was evidently her father. And suddenly this man turned to her and began talking the best and most enjoyable of child's talk. Real nonsense, genuine nonsense, the kind of nonsense that represents the whole art of conversation with children. So I passed on—wrong in my judgments—but pleased nevertheless. In the photographer's window among the portraits of statue-like children and grown-ups, like nothing, lay a little tabby kitten fast asleep. It was a pleasant contrast, all in favour of the kitten: Photographs and Life.

Last night I wrote an essay, quite brief, on the necessity of ambition, especially to the profession of Clerks. It was grandiose and ridiculous and if I ever had the strength of mind to tear up anything I should tear up that. But I think I meant what I wrote on the subject all the same.

The little sketch I have written above of a little home is rather typical of the trend of my thoughts at present. (I see it is quite impossible to avoid egotism in a journal.) This trend or leaning seems to be towards the simple. The one thought which is waiting expression in my mind, at present, is that of a man and a woman, in love, on a desert island in the tropics.* The sea comes rippling in on to the coral bar, the island is richly vegetated with palms and orchids, and strange green undergrowth. Some of the trees hang over the water almost touching their reflection, like a maiden kissing her image in a mirror. The weather is always fine and through the arches formed by the creepers, hung with pendants of blossoms, brightly coloured birds

* The original germ of this, as yet untraced, story is to be found one might suggest in the island tale, *A Manuscript out of the Sea*, written by Middleton for inclusion in his *Sunshine and Rain*, Christmas, 1902.—J. G.

and insects flit and float incessantly. And through it all, he and she wander, day after day, together. And at night they can stretch themselves side by side on the yielding grasses and look upwards at the star-set canopy which cloaks the heavens from their sight. They would know neither hunger nor thirst, heat nor cold, and the island would be called the Garden of Love.

I am only assured of one thing. That Garden is neither at Hampton Court nor at Lambeth. I must go further afield to find it.

Tuesday, April 28th, 1903.

Out of the train to-day I saw a number of children swinging on ropes round a pole in Surbiton Recreation Ground. A very pretty sight. It is too bad that I must always pay for my good spirits by a subsequent attack of melancholy. Now yesterday I felt really jolly, so to-day I am in the midst of woe, and am only fit to stroll round the house with a melancholy face, a sulky kill-joy. And neither good spirits nor hump can be explained by any exterior influences that I can see. It is dreadful that my happiness should always be limited by a saving clause that I shall presently be miserable.

Wednesday, April 29th, 1903.

Received a copy of *The Cranbrookian** which set me thinking of my school days and filled me with inspiration for some verses. But by the time I got home devil a bit of it remained, so I suppose I must scratch in this instead. I have a curious study for an amateur of human beings sitting next to me now. He was moved into our department with the reputation of a lunatic (he is sixteen). But as far as I can see he is nothing out of the common, except for one

---

* The Magazine of Cranbrook Grammar School, where Middleton studied, c. 1898–99.—J. G.

thing. He is utterly unable to speak the truth. I have met many liars but never a one who lied absolutely unconsciously before. And the pity of it is he otherwise seems a nice little chap and has a pretty semi-pathetic laugh.

Lord, I've got the hump and so can write nothing.

Later.

This is a precious fine place this world and full of precious fine people, from kings to clerks and directors. But in one respect we are all equal. Within the reach of us all there is a means to bring us up or down, I know not which, to the level of the best of them. And no human being can deprive me of this power. And all the king's horses and all the king's men cannot bring me back to punish me for lèse-majesté. There are no extradition laws in Hell. Out on thee for a blasphemous knave! but the burden of Life presses hard on me to-night, and God knows why. As far as I know there is no reason except that I was happy the day before yesterday. I suppose there is a dead level of patient existence allotted to us in this life, and if we so far forget our places as to be happy we must pay for it later. God, what stuff! Lord, what fools we mortals be! Here am I, come home and had no supper, to be sulky and unpleasant, tearing my heart and mind and dancing just out of reach of unanswerable questions, and out there somewhere is stinking London, Lily in bed asleep, dreaming perhaps, happy certainly; and yet some folks would deny wisdom to a child. Which is the wiser, a fool drivelling on paper or a child—asleep? Oh, sleep it is a gentle thing, beloved from Pole to Pole. And there is my bed, white, inviting. And I may not sleep for another two— three hours. Other people may sleep at nine—ten o'clock. Why is my rest time fixed after one? Perhaps thinking in an eternal and infernal circle, about Lord knows what, gives me a sort of mental giddiness. And this I have to overcome before my brain may rest. For one's brain never does rest except in sleep. Always thinking and never a penny the wiser or better. Rather the worse, for after a time one's brain seeking for fresh food begins discussing those things which we should accept without question. So as a rule I am the ordinary (work on weekdays, play on Sundays) Christian, but to-day my brain has been at work and so to-night I am a fool. Am I to be blamed for the sayings of my heart or in my heart? At all events they do not corrupt others. Oh for a madhouse cell or—sleep. Good-night.

Thursday, April 30th, 1903.

I am pretty well recovered from yesterday's melancholy, but I haven't got much to say for myself.

I have always had a fondness for jotting down little notes or landmarks to provide pleasant recollections later. I have got a little diary here for 1901 full of these notes, mostly monosyllabic. Only two years ago and yet they strike me with an extraordinary freshness. *Jan.* 21, 1901. *Entered the office!* Thus briefly. I know now that it meant a good deal. *Feb.* 5. *Went to Alice in Wonderland.* I went to it exactly twenty times during the run. Cherchez la femme? *April* 15. *Two months' grace.* Even now the office do not like my handwriting. *April* 24. *Old Boys' dinner.* My first dinner-party! *April* 27. *Sweet smiler.* There—is a nice inviting note! But it only refers to a little girl in Slater's whom I drove nearly into hysterics by making grimaces. But when her mother turned round to look at me, I was as grave as a judge. *May 2nd. Embankment— pale. May 3rd. Still pale!* Cherchez another femme. Pale occurs nearly every day for a month. *Sat. May 25th. Holiday begins* 1.30. That also meant a good deal. *June* 12 *return to work. Went to Waterloo and "The Bells."* Good old Irving! *June 20th. Handwriting much improved. Accountant. Decr. 31st. Saw the Old year out.* I went to the theatre ninety-seven times in this year. There is an interesting entry in another diary: "*To-day I am out of debt for the first time since I went to Merchant Taylors' nine years ago.*" So much for footprints on the sands of time. I really think that twenty, or thereabouts, must be a very susceptible age, that is as regards formation of character. Just lately I have changed so much that I am almost ignorant of the workings of my own mind! It is like making a new acquaintance. And I can almost feel my character developing while I write!

Friday, May 1st, 1903.

I am thinking of writing a treatise to prove that the well-known legend of the Pied Piper is another descendant of the solar Myth. The sun being the Piper who summons children to play. Pied being doubtless a reference to sun-spots.

Saturday, May 2nd, 1903.

I left the office at 1 p.m., met William, Lily and Elsie outside Terry's Theatre and took them to "The Girl from Kays'," a poor musical play at the Apollo. Elsie, who is Lily's cousin and a year her junior, I met for the first time though I already knew her by sight. She is a pretty little thing with dark ringlets and unlike Lily will probably be pretty when she grows up. We had a good time in the theatre with ginger-beer, sweets, and so forth, and my new acquaintance was sitting on my knee, a pleasure which I must have forgone if she had been of maturer years. After the play we went down to the Embankment Gardens and had tea or rather milk at the Automatic Buffet. The food is eatable and it is a good place for children who like putting

c

in the pennies and pulling the handles. I was sorry to see that Lily wanted to do all this and almost wept when her cousin was given some pennies to put in. In fact Lily was at her worst the whole day, both sulky and selfish, while her little cousin, against whose habit of "asking for things" I had been previously warned, behaved very well indeed. But I notice that both at her own home and at her aunt's the child is kept in a state of constant repression, so I suppose they really will spoil her temper in time. William bought both the children gold-fish, for which I was sorry as they are sure to die and be the cause of tears. We all went home to tea at Lily's, who flew into a violent and almost speechless rage because her kitten was removed during tea. After tea there was music, in the course of which Elsie came very prettily and naturally across and gave me her flower for a button-hole and after that I wished them good-night. I took the tube to Shepherd's Bush and came home by tram for the first time. The night was fine and it was quite a pleasant change after the train, all the shops being lit and busy for Saturday night, the butchers selling their viands by a sort of Dutch auction, violently gesticulating with fragments of steak, and the good housewives standing round watching critically for a bargain for their lord's Sunday dinner. Passed a brass band playing outside a public-house, passed ever so many houses all lit up and romantic, passed the river black and desolate—and so home.

On the whole a very satisfactory day, but I am sorry Lily behaved so badly: However, we all have our off days: old and young alike.

Sunday, May 3rd, 1903.

Margaret has just been playing Gounod's *Faust* to me so I am afraid I cannot write much. Music can do just what

it likes with me. Raise my spirits, or perhaps easier de-
press them. And Mozart smiling down from over the
mantelpiece helps to fill my mind with visions of men
dressed in knee-breeches, silk stockings, embroidered
waistcoats, satin coats, ruffles and powdered wigs, ladies
all wonderful in silks and satins and lace, and I fear, paint
and powder, rooms lit with hundreds of candles, burning
in silver candelabra, the room furnished with gilded tables
and chairs with slender legs, and the tall mirrors on the
walls reflecting and re-reflecting this mass of moving
colours. It must have been a splendid spectacle. Or the
music changes and I see some quiet country church, at
night with the lights all lowered for the sermon and hear
the hushed rustle of the congregation, and watch the
shadows flicker up the stone pillars to the intricacy of oak
beams in the roof. And with such things in my head I
must to-morrow thrust a desk into the pit of my stomach
and scratch mechanically for a living. *Eheu*! But I must not
end on a sad note to-night. William sang *"Ora pro nobis,"*
which is a better song than most of its kind, last night, but
just at the critical point he came to the word "grievous"
and made three syllables of its grieve-i-ous and so——.
Poor William! But with everything he is a happier and
better boy than I am. Poor Dick. He generally means
well. *"Ora pro nobis."*

Monday, May 4th, 1903.

I went to tea with Charles, of my office, at his diggings
at Upper Tooting. He is a very decent sort but much
madder than I am. He has very nice diggings, so I was quite
envious. A nice light, square little sitting-room with plenty
of pictures and photographs on the walls, a sufficiency of
neat furniture and last, but not least, an aviary containing
two canaries, a bullfinch and a linnet. And when the dear

old London sun that makes everything so beautiful came in at the window and lit up the room and started all the birds singing I felt that but for the expense I should like to set up lodging of some sort myself. I am but a cross-grained companion for my family nowadays, so I am afraid they would not mind much. But I will be cheerful again one day. Charles and I got talking about our madness till it got quite dark and then the landlady's little girl, a child of four years old (also called Lily), came in and talked to us. She is the most forward child of her age I ever met and she sat on the sofa in the dim light, chattering away at the top of her voice, and shaking her fair clusters of curls from side to side for the sake of emphasis. Talking now to the birds fidgeting sleepily on their perches and now to us. And ever and anon, by way of punctuation, letting out a shrill ripple of laughter that made me glad to hear it. Then she ran away as suddenly as she had come, leaving my mind in a strange confusion of black dollies and kitties, saucy dickies and doggies, letter-boxes and Santa Claus. They came in and lit the lamps and we had supper. A boy's meal of lamb and mint sauce, currant cake and coffee. Charles, who has been making rather a fool of himself in some ways, showed me some nice manly letters of advice from his elder brother, an officer in the army. I had thought the writing of such letters was a lost art. Charles told me his brother was not quite a plaster saint though! After supper we went for a walk past the asylum where some old ladies were pacing up and down the caged-in walks. To my mind their ages makes the sight more melancholy. Fancy coming so far for that! Charles' case is rather interesting. His father is an army officer and a V.C. who was thirty years in India but has come home to be paralysed. His mother, who seems to be a dear old lady, is of the old school and thinks theatres wicked and so forth! He showed me a little book she had given him in which to enter particulars of the sermons he heard every Sunday. There has been no entry for a long time now. He is very young. He told me, almost too frankly, a good deal of the family history, which is the old story, much pride and little money. As far as I can gather his family are a little annoyed with him. But he is only sixteen and suffers, like me, from nerves. What can they expect?

Tuesday, May 5th, 1903.

My nerves are all rotten to-day.

Wednesday, May 6th, 1903.

I can write nothing.

Thursday, May 7th, 1903.

My spirits are still very low. I suppose it is the result of the typical spring weather we are at present suffering. I went to Charles' place again to-day. His landlady's husband (why not landlord?) had a violent quarrel with his brother (who is also his partner in an ironfounder's business) while I was there. The sound of their voices raised in anger: "Get out of my place," etc., came up the passage very curiously what time the woman kept up an even monotony of passionate speech to which neither of the men seemed to pay the smallest attention. They are in financial difficulties, which seems a pity as he is a good-natured little chap, while she is distinctly pretty and puts up with Charles' singularities very well.

Friday, May 8th, 1903.

I sent a couple of poems off to-day to *The Lady's Magazine*. They are both pretty feeble and will no doubt return in due course, like all the others. I bought a halfpenny paper off a boy in the street and told him quite truthfully it was my last coin; it seemed to amuse him but I don't suppose he thought it was a fact. However, I can no doubt borrow from somebody till the 25th of this month, when the labourer gets his hire. I am still fearfully off colour and cannot write for toffee.

Saturday, May 9th, 1903.

Probably the first weekday, and certainly the first Saturday, since I have been at the office, that I have literally spent nothing during the whole day. Because I had literally nothing to spend! Yet I read the first volume of Forster's *Dickens* and was not so unhappy as I should have expected. I find nowadays that the only books I really take much delight in reading are those which treat of the lives and letters of authors. Previous to this I have been reading Moore's *Life and Letters of Lord Byron* and before that the *Life and Letters of R. L. Stevenson*. Of the three, Stevenson, Byron and Dickens, Stevenson certainly wrote the best letters and, I think, had the strongest personality. In this respect I am rather disappointed with Dickens. For neither the man nor his letters seem to come up to his books. I am also afraid this passion for reading the lives of famous men is merely another form of that horrid thing, curiosity. But I should rather hope that it springs from a desire to emulate their example and gather fame. Though, one cannot find a receipt for writing good books, as one finds a receipt for cooking a pork chop—by searching in the authorities. It is a thing that must be there to start with, and which must be carefully tended and encouraged like a hot-house plant. I don't think I have written anywhere in this journal my real reason for writing it, having, as under the circumstances I must, a very monotonous and uneventful life to chronicle. I gather from the fact that I carefully avoid writing anything really private in this book that I am really writing with a view to its being ultimately read by other people. When I started it a fortnight or so ago I merely meant it to be a slight record of my thoughts and impressions which might be amusing or even useful to me in future years. For recognising, as I must, that at present my most cherished phrases are solecisms and my most studied efforts are immature, it seems better that instead of endeavouring to express half-formed views on paper in the form of stories and poems I should give my time to gaining experience, either by reading good books or observing such happenings as take place in my neighbourhood. And at the same time I can note in this book little things, the smaller and more intimate the better, which are the result of this experience, and which otherwise would have been distorted and made untrue in the effort to feed an unready and unpractised pen. These hopes of doing something better one day might strike a reader as being egoistical and conceited, but since they give me an aim towards which I can direct my efforts—and since this tendency is certainly in an upward direction—they can work for nothing but my good.

Sunday, May 10th, 1903.

In the intervals of writing I always get up and look out of the window, which is one of the casement variety. Sad on a wet day but perfectly splendid on a fine one like to-day. The road lies in front. Is there anything more splendid than a dry white road? Across the way the fruit trees all a-bloom are just trembling in the breeze. And the Spring is here. Cocks crowing. Dogs barking and birds singing —and down below Margaret is playing some soft music on the piano in the drawing-room. And it flows out of her window and in through mine, softly and pleasantly. At this moment I can thoroughly understand what is meant by *joie de vivre*.   I have lunched and so my stomach and, thank goodness, my digestion are silent. My ears are lulled with a thousand pleasant sounds. For my eyes there are the fruit trees white and green across the way. For my nose there are the wallflowers in the little garden below sending a continuous wind of sweet old-fashioned odour straight up to my casement. And for my taste, and everything else that requires soothing, there is my pipe, and the little blue wisps of fragrant smoke that slide from the bowl. So I am beautifully, lazily happy, and the good old sun smiles down and fills up all the corners. And just about four-and-twenty hours ago I was something more than miserable. And nothing has really changed but I, myself. The flowers and the birds and the sun were the same yesterday as they are to-day. But I am contented and grateful. And that makes a world of difference.

I feel that I ought to put in here some description of myself which would certainly be of interest to me at some future date. But what do I know? The chief thing that strikes me is the astonishing meanness of my inmost mind against which my reason and my conscience are always struggling with more or less success. When I do a generous thing they have won a victory. When I do a selfish action it is my own natural self that is coming out. I know also that I am morally a very weak man and, like most weak men by the way, I have a habit of covering my mouth with my hand presumably to hide the tell-tale droop. I am at times too conceited and at times too humble, never vain, but always thinking a great deal too much about my own mind and doings. In others I dislike chiefly the defects that are most prominent in my own character. I have an unsatisfactory habit of thinking the right thing and doing the wrong one. I am always watching myself and consequently am inclined to behave as though I was always walking the stage. I am very fond of little girls, rising four to fourteen, but this is traceable to the almost Germanic sentimentality by which I am swayed. Otherwise I am not at all attracted by petticoats. I am thoroughly indolent in my habits, greedy in my eating and often thoughtless in my conversation. So much for my faults. As to my qualities I have at most times a great fund of good humour and an excellent temper, and, if a sound conscience is a quality, I never do a bad action without immediately and violently regretting it.

Monday, May 11th, 1903.

I have been working overtime and am too tired to read so I must try and write a little. I have just been having another look at Dickens' masterpiece: *The Christmas Carol.* It is astonishing the amount of good the reading of that little story does me. And if I could only remember to look at it when I am in the blues I think I should speedily be cured. For sad though it is I would scarcely fail to contrast the real sorrows of the Cratchit family and the gallant good way in which they bear them with my own imaginary and baseless grievings and the maudlin manner in which I tackle them. And the whole tale always leaves me more patient, and with a firm-set realisation of the wisdom and necessity that underlies the simple trials with which we are faced on this earth, and with that philosophical love for one's fellow-creatures and endurance of their petty failings (mingled with a hope that they may similarly forgive ours) which can alone make us happy and lead us finally to the place where we may rest. "God bless us everyone." So says Tiny Tim with his little crutch and his little wasted limbs supported in a frame of iron, and so should say we, more fortunate, but often of less patient bearing, who can walk whither we list and enjoy the beauties of a far-stretching earth. Would that I, with my reasonless complaints, could lay that saying to my heart and make it my watch-word and my guide through life. The Spirit is willing but the flesh is weak. Oh, God help thou mine unbelief and "bless us, everyone."

Tuesday, May 12th, 1903.

What a jolly place London is with all its little ones! It is fine again to-day, so looking out of the window in the train I saw all the untidy sunny alleys full of children. Dancing to the barrel-organ, laughing, singing, running, jumping, swinging (a skipping rope tied to two area-rails makes a very good swing), here rattling off in play the poetry they have been taught in school, there running up and down a ladder that some careless bricklayer has left against the wall of a new house. But in mischief, or out of it, always laughing. I am frightfully fond of children. I know nothing nicer than looking into the eyes of a pretty little girl and trying to catch the madcap thoughts that slip to and fro within. Thoughts are frozen words. But my little rascal tries to melt as many as she can, for her tongue is never silent. And if you only look hard enough, until you almost fall inside among the shelves full of busy little brains, you will be able, but only for a short time, to slip back to that golden age of childhood which you had thought to have left behind for ever.

Wednesday, May 13th, 1903.

I have been meditating this evening on the very great waste of time that my work at the office necessitates. De-ducting the hours spent in sleep and meals, my day con-sists of only about fourteen hours. And of these my office demands no less than half. I know that these are very easy hours as offices go, but I am now at that very critical stage

when the mind is just awaking to its powers and when it
is gaping wide to gather in all the knowledge it can. In
other words I am just learning to think. And I have to
give seven hours a day to work which wearies my mind
but which never satisfies it. What would I have? I suppose that there is within the breasts of us all, even of those
who appear most successful, the picture of some idyllic
existence which we would have preferred to the actual
state in which we live. And mine? Such as it is, here it is.

.   .   .   .

I live in one small square room at the top of a mean
house in the middle of a mean street. Such a house and
such a street as Dickens would have loved to describe.
Full of mud and decayed vegetables and cats and barrows
and old paper and rags and broken bottles and children.
And, above all, there must be children—children everywhere—crawling on the pavement, paddling in the gut-
ter, skipping in the road, swinging on the railings, jumping on the steps, hiding behind the doors, peeping out of
windows; everywhere children moving; and in all the
other places moving children: laughing, crying, singing,
whistling, chattering, screaming, calling; all noisy. Even
in my little room the edge of the window-sill is polished
bright by the fingers of vanished little ones who lived here
in the past and who had to stand on tiptoe clutching the
rounded edge before they could look out and see the
world. It is a nice bright day and the sun darts through
the window and lights up a few shelves filled with my
books, tattered and torn as befits the companions of a
lifetime. Or it is a winter's day and I have a fire burning
briskly in my little grate, spitting occasionally, as a
chance snowflake finds its way down the short chimney
to the glowing coals. Or it is night and the comfortable, sociable light of two candles flickers from my old

bronze candlesticks and by means of its deceptive and local brilliance makes my room, so small by day, appear to lose itself at the end of a noble series of chambers and corridors all wrapped in a mist. Or it is raining and I hear the rain tapping incessantly on the panes and making the room the cosier by comparison. For, be the weather what it will, my room must always be pleasant. And I am grown so attached to it that it has become as much a part of myself as my hand or my nose. Like the best sort of friend it is not talkative itself but it is always willing to listen sympathetically to my confidences. Sometimes, of an evening, a pretty little lady with golden brown curls comes to pay me a visit and to redden her little face with the glow of the fire, sitting on a footstool at my feet and ever and anon turning two eyes big with wonder at the magic delights of fairyland, to look up into my face and to give me a pretty picture of the best sort of fairy. The fairy that peeps out of the eyes of little children. When I tell her this, she shuts her eyes and the fairy goes to bed. Soon she goes too. And then I take down some dear old volume that perhaps graced the hand of some pretty lady two hundred years ago, and go, myself, to wander in other lands. And somewhere in the house someone is playing the piano and the sound is faintly borne to my ears. No doubt the instrument is crazy and out of tune, the performer inexpert and the music vulgar and catchy, but the distance and the softness alters all this and I hear rather those vague strains that are running in the player's mind than the crude notes that are produced by his fingers. And here, in short, you have my ideal existence. A solitude broken only by the chatter and laughter of children, lit by the flicker of a glowing fire or the grateful rays of a London sun, with tobacco and good books for companions, with the intricate life of the street presenting an ever-varying picture for my eyes, with

the dim notes of half-forgotten tunes ringing ever in my
ears. A place not utterly removed from Life and its interests but yet sufficiently guarded from the rush of humanity
to allow of quiet thought.

> When all is done and said,
> In the end thus shall you find,
> He most of all doth bathe in bliss
> That hath a quiet mind:
> And, clear from worldly cares
> To dream can be content
> The sweetest time in all his life
> In thinking to be spent.

Had he his way, with Nicholas, Lord Vaux goes Mr.
Richard Middleton.

Friday, May 15th, 1903.

Yesterday I went to see some acting at the Cripplegate
Institute and so was too late home to write anything.

I have been looking at the ideal existence I sketched for
myself on Thursday. It is again and again brought home
to me how the wise man of to-day must always think the
man of yesterday a fool. And this is another instance. My
beautiful plan makes no mention of exercise and betrays
not the very smallest particle of unselfishness without which
any life would be a failure. For all the sweetest enjoyment
arises from giving pleasure to other people. Another point
is that I am not at all certain that I should really enjoy a
life passed entirely in town. But of this I can say nothing,
for I am alternately torn between the pleasures of an attic
in the slums and those of a little cottage in the Surrey
woods. And if I am to-day a rustic, I shall certainly be a
cockney to-morrow.

If my energy suffices to keep this journal going long
enough I shall work some of it into a book that I am at
present planning. This book will be supposed to be a

journal kept by a clerk in a bank or some such place stretching over some two or three years. He has been educated at a public school among gentlemen and finds himself suddenly thrust among a number of fellows, mostly good but a few bad. He has some slight literary leanings himself, with which of course they can have no sympathy. He is sensitive but very anxious to be popular like all sensitive people. He will live in lodgings by himself and his only true friend will be an elderly gentleman, of much wisdom and experience, who lives on the floor below. His journal will have an introspective turn but not too much. Not nearly so much as this. It will narrate a number of things he notices and experiences and will end in one of two ways. Either with a girl, who teaches him the common-sense philosophy that he lacks, or else on a note of failure, with his incorporation into the main body of clerks. Of course a lot of the incidents will be autobiographical, but I do not intend to make my hero in any way a picture of myself.

Saturday, May 16th, 1903.

A Saturday off. I went via the bookshops to Lambeth and fetched William, Lily and Elsie and we went to Ludgate Hill Station and took the train for the Crystal Palace. The children amused themselves on the way down by choosing houses for their parents to take, chiefly with a view to nice gardens. And, as they pointed out, whenever you were dull you could run out and look at the trains running at the end of the garden. The Crystal Palace on our arrival was fairly swarming with children, and it seemed, on purchasing a programme, that there was a Sunday School Choir Festival due to take place at 3.15. In the meanwhile the children were diverting themselves on swings, merry-go-rounds, water-chutes, electric launches, and running in and out of fifty side-shows. A room full of distorting

mirrors was especially popular and my own children insisted on going to it twice. They also liked the moving
staircase and the merry-go-round but they would not venture on the chutes. A thing, that pleased me very much,
happened while the children were at one of these places
under William's care. Two little girls evidently belonging
to the Sunday School contingent came up and asked me if
I knew where they could get some water. I told them I
did not know but that they could get ginger-beer at Lyons'
places in the Palace. As I had guessed, they had no money,
so I gave them a shilling and sent them off confused but
happy, while I walked on feeling glad, not that they should
think me rich or generous, which I am not, but that a
shilling should still be able to give so much pleasure both
to the giver and receivers. I must confess that I did not
much enjoy the side-shows (I must have got blasé since
the days of my childhood when the Palace was to me indeed a Palace of Enjoyment); but my time was to come.
For in the afternoon the children sang. There were five
thousand of them, all children with the exception of perhaps thirty men to provide the basses, and they filled the
great Handel Orchestra from the bottom right up to the
far-away top. Five thousand little bodies all fidgeting with
their music, some in white, some in colours, some in black,
giving the appearance of a vast piece of tapestry waving in
the wind. Presently the conductor came in to a sound of
applause and they stood up. The pattern of the tapestry
changed and then they sang, *Nazareth* I may reasonably
suppose I have a good many years of life before me but I
do not think I shall ever be so stirred again. Five thousand
little beings singing with one beautiful great voice. A
voice now louder, now softer but thrilling to me across the
great crowd of people and filling me with desperate long-
ings to do something really great and really good. The

voice stopped. There was a great burst of applause and a
fluttering of handkerchiefs from mothers in the audience
to their children in the choir. They sang other things, all
well, and finished with a most stirring rendering of *God
Save the King*. But I took *Nazareth* away in my heart and
it is in my heart now, never to be forgotten. After that
there were some children doing musical drill, more side-
shows, bath buns and lemonade, lucky tubs; a scrambling
run to the station and a long wait for a train. And so home,
Lily dangling a toy out of the window all the way, to the
great amusement of the people at the railway stations and
of herself and companions. I said good-night and went up
to the Cabin in the Strand and had a disgracefully good
meal which was, I believe, the direct result of William's
snobbishness, which at times is quite overpowering. And
this meal served to bring to a close a most memorable day.

Sunday, May 17th, 1903.

It has just been raining with almost tropical violence
and the two may trees, red and pink, that face my window
look very beautiful; like two gargantuan bouquets. The
road is full of puddles, so the people are not promenading
in their Sunday clothes; but nature holds up her head all
the better for the grateful downpour.

I have been thinking that it is rather sad that all my
literary ambitions should end with this. With the writing
of a journal which can never be read by anyone but myself
owing to the perfectly damnable handwriting. But it
almost seems as though this will be the case. For since I
started this three weeks ago I have not written a syllable
of anything else with one exception which is happily torn
up. If I fail to make a mark in literature I do not think it
will be through a want of capacity. But everything I have
ever done in that line has been so aimless and I fear so

feeble that it is enough to make a stronger-willed man than I am despair. I have written a farce which Margaret slated unmercifully and justly; serious poetry, which my family damned with faint praise, a short comic poem which wasn't bad in its way; a story, of which the second half was good, and loads of other stuff of every description, but all mediocre. And yet I cannot say that I have given up all hope. For there are moments when I think I shall some day be able to make some sort of a book out of this, as I think I said the other day.

By the way, a curious mark of the weakness of my character might be deduced from my frequent use of such expressions as "I think," "I fear," "I suppose." It started with the Island story where of course it was quite natural in the writing of a man who could not be *sure* about anything. But I must try and break myself of the habit here.

The blossom fallen from the fruit trees owing to the rain has turned the lawn into a meadow full of daisies. To-day I saw a rough picture of a tabby-cat painted and cut out of tin, put up to frighten away the birds from some newly-planted seeds.

Monday, May 18th, 1903.

I have not got much to say to-day but I have been thinking that there are several little things I have left out about Saturday's business of which I should like to have a good impression. During the concert I was sitting next to a bright little boy of about ten or eleven years of age who waited near me patiently enough the whole time in order to get my programme, which I should otherwise have liked to have kept. A curious thing about this youngster was his great fondness for babies, a rather unusual trait in boys. A number of these babies were practising their newly-acquired art of walking up and down the passage

D

that ran in front of our seats, and rolling indiarubber balls under ladies' skirts, who good-naturedly recovered them. And every now and then, this odd little chap got up and made a grab at one of these babies and kissed it. Both the babies and their mothers strongly approving of the proceeding: while a youth of equal age, who was with him, could hardly conceal his admiration for his Don Juan of a friend. And he had such a quaint, odd way of peering up into my face after one of these exploits, that but for the beauty of the children's singing I should probably have cultivated him further. In the interval between the sacred and ordinary parts of the concert the children made a most extraordinary effect by holding up their different coloured sheets of music under the direction of the conductor. A proceeding which my juvenile friend informed me was known as a book drill. The appearance of all those thousands of music books, now coloured and now white, according as they turned them, being moved first slowly and then gradually faster, was vastly fine. And when they all produced white handkerchiefs and waved them and then folded them diagonally so as to give the appearance of a fleet of little white-sailed ships all sailing in different directions the result was astonishing.   In the second part of the programme they sang a song beginning I think "Early Morn at Dairy Farm" and with a rousing chorus of the cries of animals ending with a triumphant cock-a-doodle-doo which was deservedly encored. But fancy encoring five thousand performers! I read in the paper that there were altogether ten thousand school-children at the Palace on Saturday and I can quite believe it. The place seemed literally bubbling with youth. And to-day I seem to be moving in a crowd of centenarians by comparison.

In one respect this book is already proving rather a failure. For try how I will I am quite unable really to put

down my sensations at any particular moment. And that
is what I should like to do. I wish to be able to write
such a photographic account of any pleasant experience
that I may always be able to taste its joys again by merely
reading what I have written about it. But the further I go
the more unreal it seems to become. It is not I, Richard
Middleton, who am writing this book. It is someone quite
different writing a book about R. Middleton. It is always
the same. I am one man at the office, another man with
the children, and yet another man at home. And now it
seems that there is a fourth gentleman to be reckoned with:
The Biographer. Is it surprising that every night I dreamily
wonder what sort of chap will get out of bed to-morrow?
Good-tempered and sensible or melancholy and a fool. I
am both on occasion: and so it is that I shall never be
generally popular. For the world is liable rather to judge
a man by his bad humours than by striking a happy mean
between those and his happier moments. I must be content to choose my friends amongst children, who always
see me at my best, and what better friends could I want?

Tuesday, May 19th, 1903.

It has been *such* a beautiful day and although both my
door and my window are open the candle is hardly flicker-
ing, so quiet and still is the evening.

Since writing the above I have been for a walk in an
attempt to dispel the indescribable blackness of my mind.
I walked up as far as Hampton and stopped there a little,
trying to photograph (mentally!) the scene. It was just
that brief time between the vanishing of the sun and the
fall of night when there is a kind of half light—Oh Lord,
I mean it was twilight. I was standing just by the river,
which was slipping down quietly and unruffled except by
the little fish and the falling insects. Just opposite me

across the stream was a large house-boat with gauzy yellow curtains which, with the red shades of the lamps within, gave every tint of orange from bright red to bright yellow. The whole being reflected just as brilliantly on the surface of the waters: behind this were two great black chimneys sending out clouds of black smoke which streaked across the cloudless sky and looked unspeakably picturesque. To the right was Hampton church with its tower standing out clear against the sky, while the village itself showed prettily as a cluster of varied lights. A little behind that, the electric trams showed now and again through the trees, lit up very brilliantly and producing a series of light blue sparks from the overhead wires. While their bells, never inharmonious, sounded strangely beautiful; the grating of the tram-wheels and a dog barking incessantly somewhere over in Hampton were the only other sounds to be heard. A couple of bats were making dreamy circles over the surface of the stream and once a water rat splashed noisily under the bank. The peace of the evening air, and the points of light interspersed with unfathomable shadows on the face of the waters pleased me greatly and the only discordant note was the never-to-be-forgotten presence behind me of the hideous black face of Hurst Park Racecourse.

A woman's voice made a strange effect on me to-night. I only heard her say one word, "What?" But there was a kind of hesitating prurient beastliness about her tone that gave me the horrors. There was a man with her and they were walking along the towing path away from Molesey. And—but "Honi soit qui mal y pense." I hope I was mistaken. But I fear not.

Sunday, May 24th, 1903.

Summer has been with us for four days and I have not written a word. I have been working late at the office and felt tired in consequence, but that was not the reason. The fact is at present I am in a very curious condition. Really in good spirits but weighed down with the dread of melancholy to come. But yesterday I had such a strenuous day that I feel nice and philosophical now in consequence. And the blue sky and the general enjoyment leave me as happy as they find me!

A pigeon is cooing out of window somewhere and tickles my memory pleasantly with thoughts of the wood-pigeons at Farnham and the sun peeping through the pines and making little golden circles on the ground; and the coolness of the trees and the whispering of their branches up above like the murmuring of the sea; and the squirrels and rabbits staring at me until I make that hasty movement which sends them scurrying off; and above all the tranquillity, the calmness of hushed nature. But the blacked road and the tepid asphalt outside are also good in their way. Oh! rare philosophy.

Monday, May 25th, 1903.

A rather featureless day owing to my wasting three good hours earning overtime. However it is becoming more and more necessary to me to have plenty of money so I must not grudge the lost hours. Last night I read a life of *Heine* which affected me greatly. To-day I have been trying to buy some translations of his books, but there seem to be no cheap editions. I must get them out of Mudie's. To-night I seem only able to chronicle the most diminutive of beer though mine is always pretty small. I have nothing better to say now, but coming down in the train my brain was flooded with wave after wave of brightly coloured ideas. Query where have they gone to? 'Nother query. Were they really brilliant or did they only seem so on an empty stomach? Oh Lord! Good-night!!!

Tuesday, May 26th, 1903.

Too full of a grand new story to be called *Kitty* to scribble much in this. Also of wild schemes for a solitary holiday at the seaside, of which more anon.

Sunday, June 7th, 1903.

Nearly a fortnight and not a word written. So much for overtime and a weary mind. And I do not feel inspired now. For the Bank Holiday (hateful name) I went down to Farnham by myself and enjoyed it in a queer sort of way. I went down on the Saturday afternoon and came up on the Tuesday morning and during Sunday and Monday I could not have spoken more than twenty words altogether. I told two people the way (one quite wrong!) and I asked the time from another and that was all. That was real solitude, but the woods were beautifully fresh and full of life, and I took more splendid walks over the wild commons out by Tilford and Frensham, so I was never dull. Nor did I feel lonely except at twilight. For when the sun had faded in a faint pink blush in the west, when the stars were beginning to show in the cloudless sky and the shadows beneath the trees were changing to an unfathomable blackness, then, and only then, I found myself wishing that I had someone to talk to, some congenial spirit, (if any spirit can be permanently congenial to such an egotist as myself), by whose side I might stand, and know, that in spite of her silence, she was feeling the same influences, she was filled with the same world-wonder, the same *joie de vivre* as myself.

That richly endowed country was designed by Nature for two things—a perfectly splendid place to be a child in, and a Garden of Love. And yet these woods are comparatively unfrequented, as though Nature was disappointed with the children and the lovers and so kept them away. It is true that at most seasons of the year you will find strange silent country children picking up fir cones and dead branches for firing, and in the autumn they gather the withered bracken for the same purpose. And they are certainly more fortunate than their cockney cousins who have to clean filthy doorsteps or sell papers until eleven or twelve at night in the mud of the London streets. But I wager that the news of a circus or a merry-go-round in Farnham would fetch all these children out of their lovely woods and send them hurrying, their hot little hands clutching tightly a few begged-for coppers, to the same sort of amusement that affords the London children also their rare moments of pleasure. However, I am going to bring Lily and Elsie down to Farnham one fine Saturday, and I hope they will enjoy it as much as the roundabout and swings at the Crystal Palace. *Nous verrons.* As for the lovers, I thank God they are not there, for they would not be the right sort. The ignorant foolish little general servant, the beer-swilling grocer's assistant who will marry her if he finds he cannot get what he wants in any other way, playing with cheap cunning a game which is not love or even intrigue, but which is as bestial and animal as the frolics of a dog and a bitch, these are of all things most abhorrent. And I am afraid that even with the men and girls of the country villages the courting is little more refined. But what a place it is! I could almost love an ugly woman in such surroundings. The sun on the fir trees, picking out a branch or a stem here and there and making them pre-eminent above their shaded neighbours; the paths through the woods, cool and restful, the baking hot clearings purple with heather and heavy with the hum of a million bees; the pine needles beneath the trees yielding, aromatic in scent, and soft to walk upon, broken here and there by a patch of moss or a little miniature forest of bracken. Further afield are precipitous hills topped with stately pines; the oak forests at Walmer making a pleasant change to our own fir woods but in my opinion by no means a preferable one.

At Tilford Mill the little river rushes along through a border of water plants; its spring bubbles eternally from the bottom of a little calm cold pool and thence overflows to join the river, while all around stand stately trees through which one catches glimpses of splendid meadows, or a country lane overhung with high green banks set with wild flowers, yellow and white, pink and blue. Now one leans on a gate to look across a field of bright red clover hedged with yellow gorse, to the stretches of common round the Devil's Jumps, green and purple and brown. Now one stops to admire some pretty cottage in its little garden—a fairy palace in a kingdom of flowers. Then there is the great pond at Frensham with the water-fowl skimming across it and a little girl in a red dress paddling on the soft white sands at the edge, and singing a song to a lovable little tune of her own. What a place to be in love in! But the lady was missing and I left Farnham ages ago,—last Tuesday. The world will not wait while Richard Middleton seeks for the right fair lady and makes love. And so I am back in London as before; watching and waiting for something to turn up.

Monday, June 8th, 1903.

That remorseless tyrant Avarice with its weapon of overtime has once more robbed me of such scribbling energy as I am wont to have. I have just finished Dobson's *Life of Goldsmith*, which is not striking and savours rather of one of those pieces of literary hack work that sapped poor Noll's powers. He writes half-heartedly, quotes,

quotes, quotes and rarely expresses an opinion of his own, on the mass of evidence for and against what he has found in Prior and Forster. Surely a life of Goldsmith should be interesting at all events. However, the book has made me think a little better of Johnson, and I prefer to think well of everyone when I can, so the time spent in reading it is not wasted, and I don't think Austin Dobson would be much troubled if he knew what Mr. Middleton thought of his work.

I think it probable that if I could see the future ahead of me I should break my pen and burn my book and permit my mind and soul to become absorbed into the routine of the office. If I am to fail, it will not be for the lack of working and I should be able to bear my failure with a proper show of philosophy, though God knows what sickening tremors of passion and disappointment will throb my heart. I should like to write a book in the character of such a failure. Represent him as looking back to an eager and ambitious youth and tracing his gradual absorption into the humdrum channels of ordinary everyday life. It would naturally be rather a sad little book but I should make him brave and resigned and there would of course be certain solaces, perhaps a wife and children; a keen sense of humour and the deadening power of middle age on the nervous sensitive side of a man. The whole book would be written as far as possible in a tender reminiscent vein as one who could laugh at the follies of his youth and at the same time in his inmost heart regret them—"And the thoughts of youth are long long thoughts." Long enough surely to influence the mind of a middle-aged man and make him thoughtful and kindly in dealing with eccentricities of the new generation of youth that has grown up round him even while he was still viewing the world with the eyes of one who learns. I could introduce a charming little love episode which would come to nothing but which would be started in the manner of Stevenson. They would wander into love like two children walking hand in hand into a dark room. And like Stevenson's children they would be in love before they realised what the all-important little word of four letters really meant. And the awakening and the subsequent parting! My finger aches to begin them. But the planning of all the damnable machinery; all the irksome scaffolding on which the book must be raised, that is what chokes me. And until my experience is considerably enlarged I think it would be the merest folly to attempt any such complicated piece of work as a long study of an exceedingly complex character.

Tuesday, June 9th, 1903.

What shall I write about? The dog gnawing a bone in the hall, or a youth: "in the hump," sprawling on a sofa, or of Shakespeare and the musical glasses. Let's turn over.

Thursday, June 18th, 1903.

It has taken some time to turn over. Ugh!

Tuesday, October 27th, 1903.

The eve of my twenty-first birthday. I am writing a book (yet another!) *The Adventures of a Gentleman Tramp.** More surprising, I have had the strength of mind to write some six chapters or twelve thousand words. Pray heaven I stick to it and finish something at last. Of course, when the first draft is done, it will all have to be revised so that there is a lot of work before me. Since I

* This MS., now in the possession of Richard Middleton's Literary Executor, is both too verbose and too incomplete to claim inclusion here. Middleton's similar fragment, *The Autobiography of a Poet,* has been rejected for the same reasons.—J. G.

last wrote in this I have made a lot of friends in the child line, of whom, one especially is noteworthy, but I have described her somewhere else. Here I shall rest content with saying that she has a dear delightful little nose which asks questions, and that her name is Dorothy Yendole, pronounced Yendell. She lives in Covent Garden.

In the summer I went for a week to the coast of Normandy, and have, I hope, stored useful impressions. I must try and keep this up to date, as it may be useful.

Wednesday, October 28th, 1903.

To-day I came of age. I went on with my story though I only wrote some five hundred words of padding. Glad to hear that Margaret liked the fiddler bit.

Children are rum and aggravating little brutes and yet I like them so! To-day I met one whom I have known now some months and with whom I spent the whole of last Saturday afternoon. And she did not know me even when I spoke to her. She thought I was a stranger. So instead of explaining I went away raging like a fool. And I suppose next time I see her I will be blackguard enough to pretend to be cross. The dog Dougal is sitting opposite me and wants another lump of sugar but he's not to have any more. His allowance is two.

Sunday, November 1st, 1903.

Read *Footnote to History*, which I like. Finished seventh chapter of my book, which Margaret is very nobly copying out. But lately the inspiration has run but slowly. Let it but last at all and I'll be grateful. Went up to town this afternoon and ran into *her!* I didn't pretend to be cross as *she* knew me this time. I wasn't a blackguard after all so all's well. Book has made me lazy. Good-night!

Sunday, November 8th, 1903.

The eighth chapter is just finished, so it has taken a week to write a chapter of under fifteen hundred words. How's that for laziness? And before now I have written three thousand in a night. Browsed in about twenty books this week. Read none. Sign of moral degradation.

Monday, November 9th, 1903.

Saw Lord Mayor's show from Strand. Great crush. Rather tired. Read Le Gallienne's *English Poems,* which are good. To-night whacking into the ninth chapter started last night, 17,000 (computed) words done. Hope I'll stick to it. Vale!

Sunday, November 15th, 1903.

Ninth chapter finished and two pages of tenth. Uninspired. Read Arnold's *Indian Idylls,* which I liked. I started writing the *Adventures* on the sixteenth of August so I have now been at it a month. Eighteen thousand in a month is good, even of a rough draft, but I started in a hot fever and did wonders where now in my lazier moments I do nothing. For the book itself, I have not learnt to hate it yet, but that no doubt will follow.

Thursday, April 13th, 1905.

Having happened on the first part of this journal after eighteen months forgetfulness, it has struck me that though in some ways deplorable, it is not entirely lacking in interest.

I may say that although I regret he was so *very* sentimental I can't help feeling sorry for the young man who started this diary. For his hopes and ambitions alas! have passed with the "neiges d'autan." That story that should have been such a wonder lies unfinished and unfinishable in a drawer. Its successor, a blank verse drama, no less, will reach doomsday as a fragment consisting of one act of wondrous length. And the writer? Well, in two years no doubt he will blush for the youth of to-day.

The pear and the cherry are once again in bloom and the apple trees in bud, the kingcups "triumphing" burn by the edge of the running brook and I hope the gardener has left a daisy or two to shine like stars amongst the grass of the lawn.

And I wonder whence come the roses they sell so cheaply in the streets.

I am reading Lang's *Aucassin and Nicolette* for the first time in my life and I find it splendid.

> Sweet the song, the story sweet,
> There is no man hearkens it,
> No man living 'neath the sun,
> So outwearied, so foredone,
> Sick and woful, worn and sad,
> But is healèd, but is glad
>   'Tis so sweet.

"Is it *not* sweet?" as Tommy might have said.

Tuesday, April 18th, 1905.

I have been to Farnham for the week-end while yesterday evening I was with Hugh playing that forgotten game ping-pong with the Fox girls.

A word here of my manner of life nowadays. I do sadly little work at the office all day and come home at night and sit in the drawing-room with Margaret where we form a literary côterie of two, with our aunt as an occasional and corresponding third. I buy lots of books from that worthy firm, Messrs. Jones & Evans of Cheapside, which for the most part Margaret reads and I intend to, though I certainly have devoured the first two volumes of Purchas lately and propose starting Coryat next week after the Easter holiday.

My usual evening pastime is to sit opposite a blank sheet of paper with a pen in my hand, while Margaret plays minuets and Schumann's *Kinderscenen* on the piano. Thus, I flatter myself I am forwarding the great cause.

The Athenæum is the Mecca of our pilgrimage ("Golly, what a paper!") and *The Academy* our relaxation, and at meal times I sit with a dark and scowling face as one who ponders great things though Lord knows my head is empty enough.

Margaret is a wingless angel, with a devotion that makes me heartily though secretly ashamed, and an enthusiasm that oppresses me with a terrible knowledge of my own imperfections. Sometimes, even, I find myself dreading the day when she will find me out! 'Tis only in my moody moments, however, that I deem myself so poor a stick. For, sometimes I have a proud conviction that one day I shall make my mark, somehow. Like Barrie I say to myself,

"What shall I do to be for ever known
And make the age to come my own?"

What indeed.

On Thursday evenings I go to Morpeth Street and cultivate my so-called "low" acquaintances, people I am glad and proud to know; after Margaret and my aunt, the most congenial companions I have.

Elsie's father is a man with a considerable sense of humour, an admirably dry wit, the true tact of a gentleman and a considerable fondness for literature. For instance, to take an illustration at random, he knows and likes *Daphnis et Chloë* in French, and Beaumont and Fletcher, Jonson, Chaucer and Burns in English.

For the last, I never knew a man who quoted his Burns with such wit and enjoyment.

Her mother, well, I wish I could do her justice, but my knowledge of the sex is so small that I feel her many qualities much better than I can describe them. I think, perhaps, "thorough good sort" describes her best with a passing notice of the terrific battle that daily takes place between her mother's love for her only little one and her desire to bring up her child in the way she should go. Is it a tribute to a dear weak feminine heart that the child is dreadfully spoilt? for alas! Elsie is.

But Elsie has saving graces in the shape of a love of books and a sense of humour that may bring her round when she comes to years of discretion. And in spite of a certain precocity she has many pretty baby's ways still.

Her cousin Una *ætat* twelve also comes to tea on these occasions and is the best and most admirable child I ever knew and no prig.

She is extremely clever as her rather high forehead suggests, extraordinarily well mannered and considerate, is gifted with a refreshing and unfearing candour and has a voice of little bells that I love to listen to. She is always ready for a game or a joke and with it all is, like Kim, something of a small imp. I believe her total lack of fear gets her into some pretty good scrapes in her small way, but I am sure that she has that about her to get her out of them again; and she talks of punishment as a man might talk of Fate, a thing to take as part of the day's work but never to be feared. Her mother's lightest word is her law.

So much for my "low companions."

I have just read the introduction to the Globe *Chaucer*, which has made my head ache and me marvel at the pains men will take for the sake of letters and their artistic souls. It gives me the scandalous notion that one-half the labour and intellect that has been given to the study of Chaucerian texts would have produced as good work as the original. But if their bent is thus, how right are they to follow it.

I wish I could lick my idle body into the same joyous energy but, for the nonce, bed.

April 25th, 1905.

I have been down to Farnham over Easter to the rendering peaceful of my mind and the recreation of my body.

Books re-read. *Inland Voyage. Admiral Guinea. The Scallywag. Monk of Cain. The One Before. Skirts of Happy Chance.* Small amount of *Chaucer.* Book read, *The Quest of the Golden Girl,* by Richard le Gallienne, he nearly ripping but somehow misses it.

I walked to Headley on the Saturday (about eighteen miles altogether) and had quite a Le Galliennish episode. Nearing Headley I passed a rather tall and pleasant-faced girl striding along with a baby on her shoulder. She might have been seventeen. I grinned first at the baby and then at the girl, and she no whit abashed grinned back at me. I reached Headley, had lunch at the inn and half a mile from the village met the girl once more, this time without the baby. We should have grinned again of course and gone about our business, but somehow without the chaperone our grins would not come off. So I sat down by the wayside while she walked on very slowly, turning every few yards to see if I was still looking. And so to the turn of the road where she stood a long time, while I fumbled desperately for the handkerchief that I could not find with which to wave farewell. Till suddenly with a little girlish run, she passed round the corner and out of the world, whilst I passed on feeling chilly. I narrated this to Margaret (with embellishments) and she said scathingly "minx," which gave me to laugh. But I wonder whether the girl treasures so trivial a recollection as much as I do. A breath of romance like this wafts us over a mile of dull road splendidly and my vanity will not permit me to count for nothing in that country girl's thoughts.

At Farnham, I find myself hanging round *le maison* Barrie like an autograph hunter, which is most loathly. But the admiring flesh will not let me keep away.

Yesterday Margaret and I saw the gorse alight at Frensham. The flames rose nearly twenty feet high and looked very curious amongst all the yellow blossom, but oh the blackness afterwards. They beat it out with great branches cut from the hedges and Margaret thought that I ought to help but I did not.

To-night I started overtime. Also Coryat's *Crudities*.

April 26th, 1905.

Continuing Coryat's *Crudities* I once more marvel at the scholarship that men could once boast. What chance would a book run now prefaced with hundreds of "panegyrick verses," in English, Irish, Welsh, Greek, Latin, French, Italian, Spanish and the Utopian tongue? Yet one gentleman was able to write verses in Greek, Latin, French, Italian and Spanish as well as the mother tongue. To-day I moved downstairs once more at the office and left the little room of youthful companions where I had spent so gay and easy a time. I shall have a difficult task to steer clear of quarrels in my new quarters for they are all at loggerheads already, and it seems as though one requires the qualities and defects of a skilled diplomatist to keep one's head above water down there. There is more in the life even of a clerk than an outside observer might think. Cheerfulness should be the right talisman as everywhere,

E

but 'tis a counsel of perfection. By the way, I have recently become a member of the Bibliographical Society, but it gives me shame to see what a lot the members know. *Que diable* . . . . but they can't kick me out now!

To-night I have a headache as usual after overtime and the 12/5 which a careful calculation shows me to have earned to-day is earned indeed. Yet at any time I would gladly get a headache writing verse if I thought I could get five shillings for it when done, which is one of the mysteries. Bed.

April 28th, 1905.

Mental or rather verbal note—I always like part of what I read to be incomprehensible to me, as thus I know that I am still climbing.

April 29th, 1905.

Another summery, showery day and a holiday. I tramped to Hammersmith, walked thence to Kensington and read my *Academy* and *Athenæum* in the gardens. Lots of children and brats at the Round Pond as usual, and in fact it was a very as-usual holiday and a very pleasant one. In the evening I continued *The Marsh Girl,* a little story of cowardice. It's thus that a holiday should be spent. By the way, in the morning a very old woman was helped into the tram by her elderly daughter and came as far as the Infirmary. Very old people always make me wonder. But the look on the daughter's face was nice.

There were a couple of ducks on the Round Pond each with a family, twelve and ten respectively, of little fluffy brown ducklings, tiny things. They all looked just alike but the mothers knew them apart, in fact administered the most severe chastisement to any unhappy little wretch who attached himself to the wrong brood.

April 30th, 1905.

I often think that if Margaret was not so nice to me, I should be much nicer to Margaret.

May 1st, 1905.

Worked overtime and came back tired but managed to write 1300 words of a new story, *The Courage of Fritz*.* I have been pretty amiable at the office to-day.

Two years later, in April 1907, Richard Middleton resigned his position in the Royal Exchange Assurance Corporation (which he had served since 1901) and began the adventure of living wholly by his pen.

"I never thought life could be so unredeemably good as it has been for the last six weeks . . . after the hell of the office." R. M. in a letter to Henry Savage (14. v. 1907).

---

* Published with its sequel stories in this volume. The reader's indulgence is craved; he should bear in mind Middleton's age at the time of their composition. The harsher the criticism brought to bear upon them the less charm these fantasies are likely to exercise.

TALES AND FANTASIES

FRITZ AND SWEET ANNETTE

(i) The Courage of Fritz

THE sun was shamefully high in the heavens when Fritz arose, tenderly bathed his aching head in cold water and prepared to pass into the street. "Wine," he said to himself, "is the one thing I do not fear; and yet, 'tis but a scurvy companion. My head might have been broken last night, and I should have felt no worse than I do. Heavens above! what a life!"

He made these very sage reflections from the shelter of the doorway, what time he looked carefully up and down the street, as a wise man should in time of siege before venturing out, for who can say what changes may have taken place while he has slept; but the women were gossiping tranquilly before their doors, and the children were playing their games in the dust of the street, so Fritz thought it safe to go forth.

"Where are the good citizens this morning, neighbour?" he cried to a stout but comely lady who distinguished herself above her companions in conversation, by the rigorous and masterly manner in which she drove home her points with the shaking of a bare and muscular arm.

"The *good* citizens are on the ramparts fighting," his neighbour said with a somewhat unnecessary amount of emphasis on the word good, and a wave of her elegant arm to point the direction of the assault.

"Ah!" cried Fritz thoughtfully, swinging round to gaze in that direction. "I hope they will win," and he coolly turned on his heel and walked down the street with his back to the conflict, totally disregarding the queer looks with which the women regarded him.

"They are so careless with their bullets," he said to himself with a smile. "I had much better go and visit sweet Annette."

Presently he came to the little white house with the roses. He stopped and looked up at the window on the first floor.

"Annette," he cried. "Sweet Annette."

Annette peeped out. "It is you!" she said.

"Yes, it is I. Good morrow, love!" cried Fritz gaily.

"I fear you are a big coward, Fritz," she said, shaking her head at him.

Fritz laughed cheerfully.

"What a foolish little dove it is! Just because I do not like shedding blood. I do not love killing people, Sweet Annette, but, oh! I love you!"

But Annette did not smile.

"You speak well, but folk say you are a coward, Fritz. And I, I will not love a coward!"

"Yet you love me. Therefore I am not a coward—is it not proved?"

"Nay, I tell you I *shall* not love you," said Annette, stamping her foot. "Unless you do something big and brave to give people the lie. I know you can!" she added, pleading. "You who are so good."

Fritz wagged his head pleasantly at the flattery and murmured, "I am too modest to do showy things."

"Nay, but to please me," said Annette. "I know how it is, Fritz. You fear that I shall be frightened when I know you are fighting bravely on the wall. I can show you what a soldier's wife I shall make one day." She lowered her voice and spoke quite passionately for Annette. "Fritz, I swear I shall not look at you again till you have done some vast prodigy of valour, such as is worthy of you. But when the citizens carry you here in honour on their shoulders, I shall come down and marry you." And before Fritz had time to reply Annette slammed the window and disappeared.

Fritz stood in the road, frowning dejectedly at his toes. "Heavens above! what a life," he said. "There are other women, and yet I think it is this one I want."

He began walking slowly, very slowly, towards the ramparts, where he could hear the muskets rapping like hammers on a board. At length after many pauses and much thought he arrived at a point on the town wall about half a mile from the fight, which was a great deal nearer than he had ever been before.

The sentinel offered him a musket and showed him the shortest way to the fray, but Fritz declined courteously.

"I have rather a headache"—he was beginning, when a spent cannon-ball came rolling along the top of the rampart for all the world like a bowl, and Fritz incontinently took a leap into the moat.

Fortunately for him the said moat was not broad, and he soon scrambled ashore, where he sat and disconsolately viewed the town wall, and wondered how he could get back, for all the gates would certainly be watched.

"Heavens above! what a life," he said. "See where my rash and impetuous nature, and my love for sweet Annette, have brought me. Now am I cut off from all hope."

But his melancholy musings were all of a sudden disturbed by a shout, and looking up he saw that a stray soldier of the enemy had seen him, and was running up to take him prisoner.

Fritz could run fast, and did, for setting off at random across the country, he soon left his pursuer and beheld the gleam of a white tent behind a group of trees, and had reason to suspect that he was running straight into the enemy's camp.

He hastily dropped down behind a thicket, and while regaining his breath, steadfastly watched the camp for any sign of danger; but movement there was none and he gradually crawled nearer and nearer, supposing that after the sporting custom of the time the enemy had left their camp to guard itself.

This indeed appeared to be the case, for the flaps of most of the tents were hanging idly in the wind, and there was no one within them; so that soon Fritz straightened himself up, and walked boldly into the camp to see if there was anything he could steal.

But the soldiers, fearing perhaps the predatory instincts of their comrades, seemed to have carried their valuables with them, and hope had almost died in his breast when he saw a rather finer tent in the centre of a bare space, that suggested the possibility of better results.

Fritz approached it and peeped through an airhole at the back to see what might be within.

Seated at a table was the general studying a plan! Fritz felt he was lost indeed, for his limbs quaked beneath him, and he was far too frightened to run away; it was to this fact that he owed the invention of a bold expedient, which should win him the sweet Annette and make him beloved of all the city.

He would cut the ropes of the tent, overwhelm the general, do him up in a parcel of tent cloth and drag him a helpless prisoner to the city.

It was sooner thought than done, for his hands shook so that it took him five minutes to extract his knife from his girdle. Then he ran quickly round the tent, cutting all the ropes as he passed.

All at first went well. The tent collapsed and Fritz gathered together the edges of the cloth so as to make an elongated packet of enraged and struggling general; and he was tying a rope round the neck of the bundle when a silver serpent hissed through the tight part of the sack and the general emerged through the slit with his sword in his hand.

Fritz's legs again failed him.

"I will not attack you at a disadvantage," he said handsomely, as the general arose.

The general looked at him in amazement.

"I think you are a very strange young man," he said, "for it seems that I have *you* at a disadvantage."

Fritz bowed with grace.

"In the meantime," continued the general, "you had better help me with this tent."

Fritz saw no chance of escape, so under the general's eye he knotted the ropes and repaired the damage he had done. When he had finished, the general waved to him to enter.

"After you, sir," said Fritz politely.

The general smiled.

"Strange," he said thoughtfully, "strange," and he raised his sword.

Fritz went into the tent rather hurriedly.

The general followed him and sat down at the table.

"You know, young man," he said, "as a deviser of plans you have my admiration. It is only in the performance of them that you fail."

Fritz favoured the general with another of his beautiful bows.

"But," went on the latter blandly, "I really do not see why I should not have you hanged."

Fritz started.

"Oh! General," he cried, "that were indeed a pity. You see me young, active, courageous, witty and of pleasant mien and you would change me to this!" and he stamped on the earth that was the tent's sole floor. "No! No! a thousand times No! General!"

The general regarded him with a *farrowing* eye.

"You speak with eloquence," he said, "and I suppose your other qualities are as you state. I do not know. Still, logically——"

But Fritz cut short his period.

"General, logic also is with me in this matter. Tell me, why are you laying siege to the town?—Is it our money, our trade, our cathedral or our priests that you covet?"

The general blushed.

"I have my weakness," he owned.

"And if such a man as yourself, General, with such talents, can put himself to so much trouble, because the ladies of our town are notably fair, is it to be wondered——"

"I apprehend your meaning," said the general. "'Tis a lass has brought you to this hap."

"Sweet Annette," murmured Fritz sentimentally.

"A pretty name," said the general kindly. "And a pretty lass I'll be bound."

"Sweet, sweet Annette!" cried Fritz with enthusiasm. "And I was to be the sacrifice on love's altar. A general, no less!"

"Now if a colonel would have been of any use to you——"

"General, you overwhelm me!"

"Nay, my boy. You may have him and welcome."

"But, General, are you sure that you can spare him, that you do not want him yourself?"

"No gratitude, young man," said the general graciously. "I am glad to give him to you. Would he were two; for indeed it seems to me there are too many colonels in this campaign!"

And while Fritz stood spellbound with joy, the general wrote a safe-conduct to help him on his way back to the town.

"The colonel is in chains inside that yellow tent on the right. As a gentleman he cannot but assist you in any story you may invent to account for the possession of him."

The general introduced Fritz to his prisoner, and they started soberly towards the town, but ere they went Fritz said farewell to his benefactor.

"Good-bye! General, and once more a thousand thanks for your munificent present."

The general's face clouded.

"Good-bye, young man," he said. "And may you marry your sweet Annette."

Fritz's heart was moved towards him.

"Ah! General, you too have loved!" he cried.

The general flung his arm across his eyes. "Good-bye," he said once more, and stood a melancholy but attractive figure in the opening of the tent till he was lost to their sight.

"What did you do?" said Fritz to his captive.

The colonel shrugged his shoulders with comical resignation.

"I threw double sixes," he said, and together they came to the town.

.   .   .   .

Night was dark over the little white house when the torches came and lit up the roses.

Sweet Annette looked forth from her window, and saw her Fritz borne as a hero on the shoulders of the citizens.

"Oh! did not I know!" she cried gladly, and ran downstairs to greet her lover at the door.

And there let us leave them.

(ii) How Fritz got his Medals

Fritz had married the sweet Annette, and they lived together very happily in the little white house with the roses, and only the neighbours grew tired of their love songs.

One bright morning, when Annette had gone to the market and Fritz was at home looking after the house, he heard a merry outcry in the street, and looking forth saw an elderly military gentleman of prepossessing appearance being dragged along at a trot by a half-dozen lively children.

Lovers have poor memories, and until the company halted at his door, Fritz failed to recognise in the gentleman, that general who had served his cause so well and who had helped him to win Annette. But when Fritz saw the general dismissing his youthful guides with money outside his gate, he knew his man, and the town being now at peace, hastened to greet him from the window.

"Good day, General! Good day, General! Hooray!"

The general looked up with a gratified smile.

"Ah! Fritz, so you know me again, do you?" he said, "and how is sweet Annette?"

It was Fritz's turn to be pleased.

"You remember her name!" he cried. "Oh! General, you are indeed good."

The general chuckled.

"Never yet," he said, "have I forgotten a lady's name."

Fritz hesitated a little before replying.

"If you would enter our poor dwelling——"

"It is for that purpose that I have come," said the general calmly. "I wish to speak with you in private," and he entered the house.

Fritz hastened to meet him on the stairs, and conducted him to their ample apartment, from the window of which of old, Annette had looked down so sweetly.

Before accepting Fritz's offer of a chair, the general insisted on examining the pictures and furnishings of the room;

every fresh object he seemed to view with increasing de-
light; and when at length he came to the hearth over which
Fritz had traced a verse suggesting his perpetual love for
Annette, the joy of the general knew no bounds.

"Ah, youth, youth!" he cried, "I am indeed well come
here."

"And welcome," said Fritz.

The general sat down.

"I have come," he said, "because I need a friend. And
somehow I hope to find two."

"You will, sir," said Fritz, "I can promise you that."

"And first," continued his guest, "I must tell you that I
have no longer any troops to command. I lost my general-
ship at the dice."

Fritz pressed his hand in silent sympathy. The general
blinked a little, cleared his throat, and then went on
imperturbably.

"To a young man that would be a serious reverse. It
finds me unmoved. In the course of a life crowded with
pleasant incident, I have had eight worse falls than this at
the hands of Fortune; and I have one worse before me."

In spite of his philosophy the general—for so let us continue to call him—really did seem a little melancholy, and
Fritz fetched a bottle of wine in the hope that it might
console him.

The general's eye lit up as if it were reflecting the star-
light in the wine itself, and he seized the flask, declined
Fritz's offer of a glass, bit the neck off clean with one snap
of his still hale teeth, tossed off the wine, and dropped the
battered vessel on the floor by his side before Fritz could
express his admiration at the feat.

"An old campaigner's trick," he murmured modestly.
"But to our business. Young man, I am not so young as I
was."

"Oh, don't say that!" cried Fritz. "Never say that!"

"Thank you very much," said the general. "But it is really kinder to recognise the truth. I am not——"

"Well," admitted Fritz grudgingly, "perhaps not *quite* so young. But still, very young."

"That is better," said the general. "And that is the reason I look for your assistance in regaining my regiment. Old head and young arm, you know."

Fritz shook his head dolefully.

"I am sorry, but I am sure my wife will never let me go."

"Oh, but she will when she hears your prospect of advancement. I will make you a major-general."

Fritz rose and paced the room excitedly.

"The dream of my life," he cried. "And thus to be thwarted!"

"But indeed I see no thwarting," said the general.

"My wife," cried Fritz.

The general smiled quietly to himself.

"We shall see," he said, "and that shortly. For surely the dainty step I hear on the stairs is hers."

He had hardly finished speaking, before sweet Annette danced into the room, and he was compelled, being a gentleman, to gaze through the window for twenty minutes, whilst the lovers exchanged greetings after her long absence at the market.

"They are very young," he thought, as he snuffed up the odour of the roses.

At length Fritz remembered the general and introduced him to Annette.

After the courtesies the general approached the subject in view with soldierly bluntness.

"I have come to borrow your husband from you, Mistress Annette," he said. "I purpose making a major-general of him." He paused a second time and added as it were an afterthought, "The uniform is very handsome."

At these words Fritz started and struck himself on the forehead with his clenched fist. Too late he saw the perfidy of the general, too late realised the weakness of his spouse.

"Oh! that will be nice," cried Annette. "And will he have some medals?"

"Dozens," said the general.

"But you cannot spare me, love," cried Fritz; "I know you cannot."

"I will not stand in the way of your fortunes, Fritz. And I think I should like to see you in a uniform—with medals."

"Nay, I cannot," said Fritz bravely. "Love is founded on sacrifice, and rather than blight your young affections, I will overcome my inclinations in this matter. General, I cannot, will not go."

"Oh, my brave Fritz," said Annette proudly. "And you think your wife is of so base a clay. See!"

She ran to the cupboard and brought forth his sword, clean and new as on the day when he first purchased it, and stooping down clasped the belt round his waist.

"Go forth and be my true knight," she said, and kissed him on the forehead.

For once the ingenious Fritz was taken aback, and he gave way with as much grace as he could summon; and when the general proceeded to speak of comrades in arms and the rashness of young blood, he could not but throw out his chest and twirl his moustachios, however dark might be his fears for the future.

"I will await you in the street while you say farewell," said the general, as he departed with a spritely bow to Annette; and there in truth Fritz found him when he followed three hours later.

"I have kept you," he said penitently.

F

"No," said the general, "no," and together they walked out of the city. As they went the general explained the situation.

"As a gentleman, I must not endeavour to regain that with which I have paid a debt of honour, by force."

"But by guile," cried Fritz.

"Exactly," replied the general. "Your finer sense has found the solution; and it is to your admirable eloquence and forensic distinction that I look for success. Let us view it in this light. There is a general who has also my men. Granted. Here am I, a general if you wish, but without any men. Also granted. Now if the men are taken from that general and given to this general, it seems to me the positions are reversed."

"Then what you propose is——"

"Wholesale desertion. Given but the men, myself, I grudge to none the rank of general. And it is your part, my dear boy, to win over the men."

"Yet if the other general objects, surely it will end in force that way also."

But to this natural criticism the general made no response, other than a pregnant twinkle of his humorous old eyes.

"It seems to me that all we want is a little money," said Fritz after a moment's thought.

The general showed him a fat purse.

"I found this before I left the camp," he said.

Fritz looked at him with admiration.

"I am proud to serve such a master," he cried.

The general's face was reddened with a blush of pleasure as they walked on towards the camp.

In two hours they reached the spot, and the soldiers crowded round good-humouredly to hear what their old chief might have to say. This was Fritz's chance. He leapt on to a barrel and cried—

"Soldiers, tell me how much wine you get!"

"A quart a day," came the answer on all sides.

"At the other end of the town you will find a stout old officer who gives his men two quarts a day."

Fritz jumped down, feeling that his mission was accomplished, for at his words the soldiers were hastily collecting their baggage, and deserting at the double to the place he had mentioned.

"Come on," he said to the general. "We must follow and drown the bargain," and they panted side by side after the army.

Presently the general once more found himself in command of a camp full of happy men, for each of them had two quarts of wine within him.

Towards nightfall came the other general, striding scornfully through alleys of drunk soldiers.

Fritz's general greeted him cheerfully.

"You have come to enlist, my good man."

The good man breathed hard for a few minutes, glaring at the general with indignation and sorrow in his every feature. Then he threw out his arms to heaven in a fine and tragic gesture.

"You think you have conquered," he hissed. "We shall see." And he stalked proudly away in the dusk.

Fritz and the general went to bed.

The elder man was wakened in the morning by Fritz rushing violently into the tent.

"They have gone!" he cried.

"Who?" said the general anxiously.

"The soldiers," said Fritz sadly; "he has promised them three quarts."

When they had finished weeping, they held a council of war.

"It's no good," said Fritz, "we shall only get a few very thirsty ones. The others couldn't drink it."

"It doesn't matter," said the general; "they'll want it. It's human nature."

So Fritz went off hastily to catch the soldiers while they could still walk; the general proved to be right, for by midday they were all back again.

"We must take some steps," cried the general thoughtfully to Fritz, "or he'll offer them five quarts in the night, and it will mean six quarts to get them back. Commanding will come too expensive at this rate. Are they all drunk now?"

"Quite, quite drunk," said Fritz. "They're safe for the time, anyhow."

The general meditated.

"I have it," he said at last. "We must get three hundred carts and move them out of his clutches. Now, while they're quiet."

"And when they come to?" said Fritz.

"We shall give them some more wine," said the general, and they both laughed.

So towards evening the general and Fritz rode out of the city behind an imposing vista of carts, each full of sleeping soldiers, and as they slept they smiled.

Presently, Fritz, who was a poor rider for an officer, fell off his horse, and the general dismounted courteously to help him up. When they both started off again the procession was out of sight; but as they expected soon to overtake it they were not much perturbed.

But as time went on, and they failed to see so much as a cart, they began to get anxious, and they reined up their horses before a farm-house.

"I think you had better inquire," said the general.

Fritz rode up to the door and rapped on it with his whip.

An old woman came in answer to his knock, and Fritz raised his hat politely.

"Could you tell me if you have seen three hundred carts full of drunken soldiers, please?" he said.

The old woman looked at him with an unwavering eye.

"I have not," she said and slammed the door.

Fritz joined the general mad with indignation.

"It is a plot," he cried, and shook his fist at the mocking stars.

"Nonsense, man," said the general with unwonted testiness. "They must be somewhere."

Fritz looked at him in surprise.

"Don't let us quarrel, sir," he said.

The general flung himself from his horse and seized Fritz's hand.

"Would to heaven," he panted between his sobs. "Would to heaven I had had a son like you."

"You had a son?" asked Fritz.

The general sighed lightly.

"They hanged him last November," he said. "A nice boy, but rather spirited, perhaps. They were always doing something or other to him. Still, a nice boy. I shall always hate November——"

"And I too," said Fritz heartily.

"Spoken like a friend," cried the old man, remounting his steed. "And now to find our soldiers."

It was dawn, and the birds were all a-pipe in the trees before they found the men. They had left the carts and encamped, and Fritz detected the white tents from the summit of a hill.

As he and the general drew near the camp, they had a terrible blow. Leaning in a melancholy manner on an empty wine-barrel was the other general, awaiting their approach. Fritz's general went up to him and shook his fist in 'his face!

"You are a thief!" he cried. "You have stolen my men."

"I had thought to have shaken you off," said the other sadly. "Wine is so expensive."

For a minute the two generals looked at each other kindly, and then with one accord the word "Halves" sprang from their lips, and they closed in a cordial embrace.

.   .   .   .

Sweet Annette was leaning from her window with the roses all around her when Fritz came back, bronzed and dusty, but liberally decked with medals.

"Oh, Fritz," she cried gladly.

"Sweet Annette," said Fritz.

(iii) THE VERSES OF FRITZ

One sunny morning (for the right people the mornings are always sunny), Fritz arose early and slipped a poem, the latest outpouring of his heart, into the dainty little shoe of sweet Annette.

Annette must certainly have been accustomed to such tributes, for never a day passed without her finding one amongst her hair, or between her cup and saucer at breakfast, or twisted round the stalk of one of the roses that tapped against the windows of the little white house; but never had she failed to clap her hands with delight at the discovery of one of them and fill the ears of Fritz with sweet, musical boastings of his cleverness.

So Fritz's surprise and dismay can be imagined when on that bright morning, on finding his little paper, in place of her accustomed joy, she clutched it to her lips and burst into tears. Yet was his dismay but increased when he had kissed the tears away and besought the pretty mouth to give a reason.

The famous poet had described Fritz's verses as nice but not original.

Fritz fell straightway into the deepest despondency.

"That I was born," he moaned.

"Still, nice," cried sweet Annette aghast.

"But not original," murmured Fritz.

"Yet nice," she urged.

"Oh," groaned Fritz.

Suddenly he started to his feet.

"I have a friend," he cried, "the general! He will advise me."

"I believe in you," cried Annette. "But, oh, be careful for my sake."

"Yours till death," he said, and kissing her thrice picked up his sword and marched from the house.

The general at the moment was engaged in the deliciously futile siege of a neighbouring town; and Fritz found him fussing happily about his little camp.

"You have come to fight," he cried cheerfully to Fritz as that one approached. "We make our eighty-third assault on the town in half an hour. See," he added, waving his hand towards the walls, "the citizens gather even now to repel us."

"Nay," said Fritz sadly, "'tis something of far more importance than fighting. It has to do with poetry."

The general took off his hat.

"'Tis a thing for which I have a vast respect," he said gravely.

In the privacy of the general's tent Fritz told his dire tale. When he heard the *dénouement* the general trembled with indignation, and the moment Fritz had finished took a horn from the table and sounded a piercing blast.

"What have you done?" asked Fritz.

"I have raised the siege," replied the general with dignity. "I hope I know the duties of a friend. My men shall help to overthrow this cankered critic."

"I do not mind criticism," said Fritz, "as long as it is fair."

"For my part," said the general, "things people criticise favourably I try to like; but things people criticise un-favourably I *do* like. No . . . I don't think I am fond of critics. But let us start." And soon Fritz and the general rode out of the camp at the head of eighteen hundred men.

"It is my four hundred and ninth campaign," said the general.

They found the poet in a garden playing with children. He was old and white-haired and happy.

They halted the army a hundred yards from his gate, and dismounting from their horses walked into the garden to meet him.

"Good day," said the poet.

"I write verses——" Fritz began.

"Poor young man," said the poet. "I used to do so, but now," he smiled at the children, "I live poetry. It is better."

Fritz paused. This was not quite what he had expected.

The general pushed him gently aside.

"I think I had better explain," he said. "Between two old heads——" and he bowed politely at the poet.

That one looked at him.

"Surely I have the honour of addressing a distinguished soldier," he said.

The general flushed with pleasure.

"I cannot deny it," he said with soldierly simplicity, "to so great a poet as yourself!"

In a minute the old men were embracing, and in five they were sharing a bottle of wine in the open air and two

of the children had taken possession of the general, for
his uniform was hung with numerous and desirable
medals.

Meanwhile Fritz, who was not distinguished and was
wearing no medals, stood somewhat in the cold; but at
length, weary of the spectacle of his deserted ally hob-
nobbing in friendly fashion with the poet, he broke forth
in a bitter cry of reproach.

"My verses!"

The general remembered.

"Oh," he said to the poet, "you have said of the verses
of this young man, who is a friend of mine, that they are
nice but unoriginal. And of course, being young, you
know, and ambitious, it hurt him a little. So we thought
that in a private chat you might see reason to reconsider
your judgment."

"Oh, General! And your eighteen hundred men wait
in the road." Fritz marvelled at the traitor.

"Nice but unoriginal," murmured the poet absently.
"Have you the verses here?" he said to Fritz.

Fritz thrust a large bundle into his lap.

"Here are some of them," he said.

The poet picked one or two from the lump and read
them through, muttering silently to himself. Fritz, the
general and even the children watched him anxiously,
feeling sure that something miraculous would issue from
his lips.

"Bless my soul," said the poet suddenly, and rising from
his chair passed into the house.

Not a word was spoken by Fritz or the general while he
was away, and both were relieved when he returned bearing
a little packet of worn and faded papers that breathed faint
odours of forgotten springs.

He removed the ribbon that fastened them, and a few

dead flowers fell to the ground as he handed the packet to Fritz.

"My wife," muttered the poet apologetically as he went down on his knees to pick the brown blossoms up.

But Fritz did not hear him, for he was reading the poems, and as he read his heart sank within him.

"They are mine," he cried, clutching the packet to him and looking defiantly at the poet.

The poet shook his head sadly. "Neither yours nor mine, young man," he said, "but all the world's. Never yet was there a true lover who has not thought these things, and, alas! the greater part of them have written them."

Fritz returned the paper with a sigh.

"It is true," he said, "I am unoriginal."

And looking neither to the right nor to the left he walked out of the garden.

The general looked after him thoughtfully.

"He is very young," he said after a little.

"And we are two old fools," cried the poet with spirit, and they fell to playing at hoodman blind with the children.

It was dark before the general remembered his soldiers.

.   .   .   .

Humbled and torn in spirit Fritz strode home to his sweet Annette.

"He spoke the truth," he said bitterly. "They were not original."

Annette looked at his troubled face.

"It is false," she cried, "I know they are new. No one has ever said such sweet things before."

"Often have they been said," said Fritz.

"But never this love," said Annette. "Do not I know?"

"Do you truly think so?" asked Fritz.

"Truly I do," said Annette, and her brave eyes did not falter beneath his eager glance.

"Upon my soul," cried Fritz, "I believe you are right. They seem, somehow, to be different. I don't say better, but more loving and passionate, you know, dear."

"That's what I think," said Annette.

And when the sun went down Fritz was writing another poem.

(iv) THE ROSEBUD

It was that heavy day in a husband's life when he may be neither sorry nor glad but only afraid, and Fritz waited outside the little white house, fearing to look up lest he should see the roses drooping on their stalks and know that sweet Annette was dead.

Anon came a friend and looked at Fritz's white face and grieved.

"It cannot be till to-night," he said. "Go down the river in your boat and try to forget it or you will go mad."

And many times Fritz refused until sweet Annette sent out word that he was to be brave and go.

Under a sky of heartless blue Fritz sought his boat, cast it loose and lay back in it in misery, letting it drift down the stream as it willed.

And surely there was something of Lethe in the waters that washed the sides of the boat, for presently Fritz forgot his anxiety in a gentle slumber and was only wakened by the prow of the boat striking gently against the shore and the trailing of sweet-scented blossoms across his face.

Fritz sat up, and looking up the bank saw through the flowers a beautiful child standing on the shore.

"Come and play," it said pleadingly.

Fritz tied up his boat, and climbing up the bank found himself in a pleasant garden filled with flowers of many colours, but his eyes were on the child and he could not withdraw them.

It had the lithe and graceful form of a young boy with the gentler beauty and golden hair of a little girl.

Was it the sunshine that made this hair shine so brightly?

"What do you play?" he cried.

The child laughed sweetly and surely the laughter was human.

"I play with the flowers," it said, and flung a little bunch towards Fritz, so that they scattered over his coat and hung there as if skilfully embroidered.

"Pick some," said the child, and together they went round the garden picking great handfuls and forming them in garlands and posies. And the flowers Fritz plucked faded after a little, but those picked by the child threw out new buds and quickened in fresher life.

Presently they left the flowers and came to a fountain, where a little stone boy was throwing handfuls of bubbles to a basin of gold-fish.

"Look in," said the child, and Fritz gazed into the waters and seemed to see the face of Annette, not suffering but sweet and joyous. The child stood and watched him gravely.

"Who are you?" cried Fritz.

"I was a child," it said.

"But whose child?" he asked eagerly.

"I do not know," said the child.

An awful idea came to Fritz.

"Not mine! Not mine! Say you are not mine!"

"Nay, I am not yours," the child replied. "But see, there is a butterfly." And it began chasing the insect to and fro, while Fritz watched it gladly.

And for all its beauty he was thanking God that it was not his.

The sun drooped in the heavens and soon the child turned to Fritz.

"It is time to go back," it said.

Fritz stooped down and picked up a bunch of the flowers.

"Can I take these with me?" he asked.

"Nay, not one," said the child, shaking its head.

Fritz dropped them sadly, but when he was in the boat he felt a soft touch and it was the child that had thrown a white rosebud into his lap.

"You will lose it and find it," cried the child, waving good-bye, and Fritz clutched the flower to his heart.

As the boat glided away he once more fell asleep, and when he woke he was back in the town.

He leapt gladly out of the boat, but the flower was gone and he searched for it in vain.

So he passed up through the streets to the little white house, and he stopped without and his friend murmured in his ear that his wife was well.

And Fritz looked up and lo! beneath her window there was a new bud on the tree and the bud was white though the roses on the tree were red as blood.

"It is a girl," said his friend.

THE ROMANCE OF THE WORLD

In past days there dwelt in a wood with her mother a maiden of youth and great beauty, by name Ysolde. The birds and the squirrels that leap in the trees were her playmates, and happiness was with her from day to day. But at length the fair lady her mother went on a journey to a far country and came back no more, and sadly in this manner was Ysolde left alone.

She did not yield lightly to misfortune, but rather sought to make the woods merry with song and dance and passing from place to place as heretofore. But it happened that when the forest was stilled and the little birds were no longer singing, the spirit of solitude would trouble her, and her ancient joys be lost in bitter tears. And thence would come relief.

Now it chanced on one bright day that she heard the sound of a horse's feet speeding along the path towards her. And presently a most noble and courteous voice saying:

"Wherefore, sweet damsel, weepest thou so sadly?"

Ysolde plucked her hands from her face and then rose to her feet amazed, for she beheld the most beautiful youth that there has been, arrayed in silk and velvet, his mantle embroidered with the golden crown of a Prince, and dominion shining in his face like a glowing light. But truly, if Ysolde was astonished at the noble countenance and magnificent apparel of the Prince, no less delighted was that one with the tender beauty of Ysolde. Her hair lay drooping to her shoulders in gleaming masses of brown, while beneath, her eyes, yet moist with tears, were like two dark flowers wet with the dew of the dawn, now ruffled with gentle winds of surprise and delight.

"Oh, Prince!" she cried, and, her sorrows put off, gazed on his handsome raiment, for in that is ever a woman's joy.

But the Prince answered: "Greeting, O most fair." For he was a man, and the simple white garments of the maiden, neat and comely though they were, were nought to him beside the beauty of her face, or even the whiteness of her feet like silver.

When Ysolde heard these words, the red blood was in her face, and she gazed steadfastly at the ground, for none had told her this before, and though her modesty bade her not believe it, yet in her heart she was glad.

Now did the Prince utter sweet words unto Ysolde, and since it was in the time of spring her heart flew out to his, and when he asked her to come with him to be his true Princess, she cried "Yes" softly but joyously. And she mounted his horse and he bore her before him out of the woods and into the glad countryside with the sun shining hotly overhead; but the birds and the little squirrels that leap about in the trees were sorry to see her go because she had played with them so often.

So rode they together through the fair fields, what time, he told her of the wide dominions she would help him rule, but ever as they went he grew more sad until at last he reined up his horse and said:

"Now must we part for a while, beloved. But surely await me here, till I return."

Then Ysolde, perceiving by his sadness and the grievousness of his sighing that somewhat was amiss, said in a sorrowful voice:

"Art thou weary of me so soon, my lord?"

To this the Prince replied:

"Nay, even unto the grave shalt thou not weary me, O heart of mine; but I ride this way to slay a most fierce and monstrous dragon that has sorely ravaged my father's kingdom. So I pray thee wait here till I return."

At these sayings Ysolde was in no wise afraid, but replied softly:

"Where thou goest I go, O my Prince," and though the love of the Prince caused him to plead against this resolve, yet in his heart he was glad that his lady should be as brave as she was lovely.

And so they rode on, until the sun drooped in the heavens like a red blossom, and the words of love on their lips sank hushed in the quiet of evening.

And the wearied steed trod sorely up the side of a great hill, whose top touched almost the sky itself, and there stopped; for his work was done, and now was the time for the Prince to fight for his honour and his lady. And when they had dismounted they saw before them a great valley whose sides were dark with shadows of grey and purple and green. But lo! the bottom of the valley was a sea of leaping flame, red and yellow and aching white, for there lay the dragon in all his fearful greatness.

At the sight of this fearsome thing the maiden's heart fluttered in her breast, for he was an hundred times the length of a man and dreadful to gaze upon. So that she prayed the Prince not to approach him.

But he, no whit dismayed, smoothed her hair with his hand and kissed her brow, and drawing his sword from its sheath, began to descend the side of the pit to approach the dragon.

At first the maid did sit as one stunned, with her face lost in her hands and great fear in her heart lest she should hear Death crying from the lips of her Prince.

But anon she thought that if he perished she too could leap into the pit, and go with him to those Isles of the Blest of which poets of old did sing so sweetly. So finding courage in this thing, she stood upright by the horse, and gazed down the valley to see how her lord might fare. That one passed around the monster, seeking on every side for a point at which to attack him, but so thick were the monster's scales, and in such orderly manner were they placed, that in no wise could he descry a point of vantage. And so he came to the head of the beast, all clouded with fumes and horrid smoke, and lo! in the midst there shone his two great red eyes, wide open and watchful. And the Prince saw that there only could his sword strike home, but so great was the monster's head that he could not contrive to pierce him from where he stood.

So trusting that the thick armour of the monster would save him from betrayal, and breathing the name of his beloved right fondly, he set himself to climb the head of the beast.

The sun was now set, and the valley would have been black indeed but for the flame of the dragon himself, and perchance that same was weary with the great ravage he had made that day; for truly the Prince, with but one slipping, reached the summit in safety, so that he was scorched with the flame that came from the beast's nostrils below, while on either hand lay his eyes like two deep red waters.

Then did the Prince, with one word to his God, lean forth from where he stood and plunge his good sword deep into the monster's eye; but there came forth from the wound such a rush of flame and boiling foam that he needs must leave his sword and cling to the scales of the beast's head.

Now the dragon beat his head desperately from side to side and from rock to rock owing to the biting anguish of the

G

wound, and the Prince was in deadly peril of his life either from being thrown to the ground or crushed against the sides of the pit. And wishing to perish like a true knight with his lady's name on his lips he called aloud "Ysolde," and again "Ysolde." And lo! he looked up and there he saw his lady standing at the edge of the pit no whit afraid of the smoke and the flame, and in her hand she held his lance, that he had left with the horse, and though it was of great weight she flung it far and true, and it fell to his feet.

Now did the Prince raise himself up and seizing the weapon thrust it down through the dragon's unscathed eye, and through his very brain, so that he cried with a terrible sound of agony through the valley, and dropped his head to the earth in bitter death. Thus was the monstrous dragon slain that had ravaged all the Prince's father's country.

But the Prince and his fair Ysolde rode blithely from the land of shadows to the lightening sky, and it was indeed wondrous to behold how deep wounds love could make in those unharmed by a dragon.

And anon the dawn came over the mountains, and all was laughter and joy in the waking world.

WHAT IS LOVE?

I

THE boy discovered love in the spring of his sixteenth year. The apple-blossom still hung red and white on the trees when the steward's daughter (the minx was a year younger than he was) led him into the orchard and taught him that kisses were not mere childish folly as he had deemed them before. He learnt, too, that there were other kisses beside the lip-kisses of babies and the maternal kiss on the brow. The steward's daughter kissed him on the ear till he was fain to die of laughing; she kissed him on the eyes till he wept he knew not why; she kissed him on the nape of the neck till the earth danced round him like a ring of children at play. Already the boy had formed the habit of considering the environment of his emotional impressions. The red and white fruit-blossom and the birds that fought on the trees were quite as clear to him as the girl with her bold eyes and her eager cherry lips. But he had yet to learn that women will allow of no such rivalry to their charms. When she saw his eyes wandering the girl bit him in the arm. He promptly boxed her ears and she went away weeping, while he was left in the orchard to reflect on these things. The birds were still fighting among the fruit-blossom, but, now the girl had gone, he no longer found them interesting. He thought this was strange. There were so many fine things to like in the world. Why should this one business of kissing seem so desirable? He held up his golden arm, and watched the bright blood trickling from the little tooth-mark she had set there. After all it did not hurt.

He found her sobbing softly to herself, crouched down amongst the currant bushes. With a quick gesture he thrust his uninjured arm before her face. She gave it a little short kiss and covered her face with her hands. It seemed to him as though the birds were fighting in his heart. He felt that his face was red and white by turns. He noticed her neck and the short curls that hung there, and the line of her stooping back and the points of her elbows. He flung himself panting by her side. "You are so pretty," he cried, "so pretty!" She smiled at him in spite of her tears.

II

When he was eighteen, as he was a good oarsman, and had showed no special aptitude for anything else, they set him to mind the ford. It was pleasant, easy work, with now and again a passenger to be rowed across the river or perhaps a body of horsemen to be adroitly piloted between the dangerous pools. The rest of the time he was free to dream and make songs, which suited his indolent nature very well. He had a little house by the side of the river, and at night when he lay in his bed the river would make songs for him. It would sing to him of fish and waterfalls and even of the sea as a man might sing of heaven; but his own songs were mostly of women, because he was young and lived a solitary life. Sometimes he saw fair faces among the companies that crossed the ford, but they rode away into the world and he saw them no more. In fact, few of those who went by ever returned, though once after a great battle he was busy all night leading the spirits of dead knights across the river. They told him that they were going home, and he saw no reason to be afraid; there was nothing unnatural in that.

Then, one day a girl rode down to the ford whose beauty seemed to him to surpass that of his dream. And, while her servants swam the horses over, he rowed her across in his boat, and his eyes grew weary with straining to her face. When they had reached the other side she asked him what he wanted for his pains.

"The rose at your breast," he said boldly, but she raised her riding-whip and cut him across the face, and rode away. There was a mark on his face redder than a rose for more than a week, but the wound in his heart lasted even longer. And now his songs were all of her. One night when he was going to bed he heard a voice calling from the other side of the ford, and when he had crossed over he found it was his princess. But she had no horses or men any longer, and her clothes were torn and travel-stained. When she saw him she lifted the hood from her face. "Do you want me?" she said.

The youth dropped his eyes abashed. "Am I grown so ugly?" she asked, fiercely.

"Sorrow has made your face like a saint's," said the youth.

"No," said the woman simply; "it was love."

When the youth had rowed her across the river he took her to his house. "You can have my bed gladly," he said. "I can sleep in another room."

The woman looked straight at him, and he saw that even then her pride was not broken.

"I have always paid for what I took," she said.

"Then give me the rose at your breast."

The woman wrung her torn hands. "You are young and handsome," she said, "and you have a fair voice; but I do not love you."

"Then you have nothing to give me," said the youth, and he went into another room. When he rose in the morning she had gone.

He made no more songs of her after that.

III

The years passed, and he grew so comely that the maidens used to come down to the river at dusk, because it was cooler there, and when they saw him they would look over their shoulders and smile. This pleased his vanity, but when he found that they expected him to make sacrifices in exchange for their kisses he avoided them. No doubt they were pretty and kissing is an agreeable pastime, but why should they object to his writing songs? And when the girls discovered that he would not take the trouble to love them in their way they came down to the river no more, so that he had to content himself, as he did readily enough, with his dreams. "I know what love is," he would say to himself, "and that seems to be the end of it." He was only twenty-three.

But one day the spring winds gave him the itch for travelling, so he packed a knapsack, and, leaving the ford to take care of itself, set out to see the world. He had not then achieved the discovery that stars and women are pretty much the same wherever one goes, so that on the whole his travels were a success. He had learnt no trade, but he had a good voice and a knack for making songs that served him very well with the barbarians among whom his road lay. The men thought his songs quite worth a supper and a flask of wine, and his only trouble was with the women, who sometimes liked his songs too much. But by grace of his youth he did his best to please everybody, with such success that, after he had risen from street-singer to tavern-singer and from tavern-singer to minstrel at noblemen's houses, his travels terminated abruptly, a maid of honour aiding, with his appointment as minstrel-extraordinary to the king. The king was an old man and a bad sleeper, so that his position was far from being a sinecure, for every night he had to sing his weary majesty to sleep. But he enjoyed himself nevertheless, for, setting aside the maids of honour who pelted him with rosebuds from dawn to sunset, there was the queen—— She was young and dark of hair, and her face, that might have been carved from a frozen lily, was set with two passionate pools for eyes, and wherever she went the minstrel's eyes followed her like faithful mutes. And when on hot summer nights the king would lie on the white roof of the palace with the queen by his side and her ladies all around, the young man would sing to her, while the king snored to the stars, until the sun dawned on the distant mountains, and woke the tired roses that the short night had hardly healed of the languor of day. Sometimes the queen's face grew wild and wet with tears; sometimes she slept.

So one day a file of soldiers came to the minstrel's lodgings and hauled him off to prison. "What have I done?" he asked, innocently.

"We do not know; we are soldiers," they said; "but you seem to have irritated the king. Anyhow, you are to die to-morrow."

"Really it's too bad," thought the youth to himself in his cell; "just as I'm beginning to find out what love really is I've got to die and leave it all." However, it was no use worrying, so he wrote an epitaph for himself in admirable verse, made an excellent supper, pledged the queen in a cup of red wine and went to bed.

In the morning they flung open the door of his cell, and he rose from his bed to die; but in place of his executioner he found the queen.

"The king died last night in his sleep," she said, "so you are free. But you must leave the kingdom at once."

"Desire of my heart!" cried the minstrel, joyfully.

The queen smiled at him not unkindly. "You forget I

have a kingdom now. I like you and I like your songs, but the queen disapproves, and there's an end of it."

"But I don't understand——"

"You needn't as long as you are so good-looking," said the queen, and left the minstrel sitting in his cell. He was beginning to find women a little perplexing.

IV

The years followed the swift years, and the man met many women and lived many lives. Till at last lying in his bed one morning, it came to him to bind these many stories into the life of a man by means of one thread. And love, he considered, was the thread. He thought of the steward's daughter with her cherry lips, the mark of whose little tooth had long faded from his arm. He thought of the princess of the ford, but his face and his heart had alike forgotten her lash. He thought of the queen, and was glad that he had not spent the years at Court. He thought of others, many others, who had come and gone, and the sum of these thoughts was a certain self-satisfaction. "Really" he said to himself complacently, "I believe I am coming to know a little about love." So he dressed and went out into the street.

And presently he met a young maid, at the sight of whose face his heart sang the ultimate song. But now he hesitated no longer.

"I love you," he said, simply.

"Why," said the girl in astonishment, "you are an old man!" and she went on her way to meet a fool.

The man felt bitter at this rebuff. "If love and the knowledge of love cannot make me lovely, it seems to me that I know nothing about it." So, remembering a word of his mother's, he sought the advice of a priest. The priest heard his case, and said: "You are too old for girls and the smiles of girls. You should think of more serious things."

To which the man replied: "Love is the motive power of life for old and young alike. You are an ass."

There remained the poets and the philosophers, and as he had been a poet himself in his youth he went first to a philosopher.

"What is love?" he asked.

"Love is ambition, desire, hope, fear, joy, sorrow, courage, contentment. . . . In a word, it is ignorance."

The man looked at the philosopher doubtfully, and fled to the poet as if the devil were behind him.

"What is love?" he gasped.

"Love?" cried the poet, with an ecstatic gurgle. "Love is Christine!"

DEVONA'S CAT

A Romance of the New Childhood

The passages of a mind that we propose to traverse might have remained undiscovered and unsuspected but for the hasty action of papa in kicking Devona's cat, because Devona had put him right in a small point connected with French history.

This was of course wrong, and also, which he did not know, illogical, because Devona's cat was not thinking of French history at all at the moment. There was a suspicion of a mouse in the newspaper-cupboard, you see. But the neutral observer cannot stifle the suggestion that Devona herself was the cause of some of the subsequent trouble. She was not, had not been, nor ever could have been very fond of that particular cat, in whom detachment of soul was developed in a quite unusual degree; and yet her father's foot had hardly reached the ground after its regrettable "gambade" about the flanks of Devona's puss, when she ran across the room, caught the surprised and plaintive animal to her pinafored bosom, and turning imperiously to her father cried, "You are a very bad old man indeed! I am very, very angry with you." Having said these regrettable words she withdrew, leaving her father elated but secretly fearful of what the future might hold, and her more timid mother in tears.

Now we are aware that some children who mistake severity for firmness, and the explosions of temper for proper expressions of dignity, we say we know there are some who will hold that Devona was justified in speaking thus to a man, guilty of ill-treating a poor animal, mentally greatly inferior to himself but unfortunately debarred by Nature from a general expression of her views. And our grim and heroic ancestors would have agreed with this minority, thinking that gentler methods founded on logic rather than brute force only tended to make men and women intractable.

But happily in this enlightened age, under a better re-gime, the majority strive rather to check the little outbreaks of spite or petty displays of folly that age induces in their parents, by expressions of sorrow than of anger.

And there can be no doubt that if Devona had done so in this instance, her father would have tearfully owned him-self in the wrong, and with a clean pocket-handkerchief for father and a saucer of milk for the cat, the whole business would have been brought to a pleasant conclusion, and a recurrence of the trouble rendered unlikely.

But alas! What was the consequence of Devona's harsh words? Tears? Contrition? No.

When tea-time came, papa said that the tea, which was really very nice, had not been made with boiling water and pushed his cup away with a suggestion of disgust about his nose, while mama, who was burdened at all times by a kind of timorous loyalty to her husband, followed suit.

Devona would not give way, and so a meal which should have been the most pleasant of the day, only served to widen the rift between the naughty parents and their unwise child.

Nothing is more painful than to see a relationship which should be sacred, belittled and destroyed by folly on the one hand and the natural sin of age on the other. After this wretched meal was ended, Devona, continuing to act in her light-headed manner, sent her parents to bed un-kissed and went for a walk in Hyde Park.

She felt very miserable and it would perhaps be unfair to judge her too hardly.

You see, she was already ten years old, and there is no doubt one wants to be younger than that to rule two elderly and troublesome parents on the best lines. And Devona realised this. She knew that it was too late; that she ought to have strained every nerve to correct her parents when she was two, and so have secured them a pleasant and well-conducted old age. Why had she wasted her time on Woman's Suffrage and similar problems, when the chief duty of her babyhood had obviously been to secure the affections of her parents, while firmly insisting on her prestige in her home? And now it was too late.

She looked sadly at the babies borne past her in their perambulators, and wondered once more that Nature should have placed the strange ban of speechlessness, if not silence, on the human microcosm when the brain was at its prime. Two years of valuable thought practically wasted! But their cold, wise eyes gave her no comfort, and she feared their silent criticisms.

It was the first time in her life that she had treated her parents with so much severity; of course, it was for their own good, but supposing she was wrong, if she had been too harsh and they were crying their hearts out at home because their child was so cruel!

She sat down on a seat and sighed.

At the other end sat a baby of under three years old, who hearing her sigh turned a pair of sympathetic eyes on the unhappy child.

"Are you in trouble, my dear?" she asked.

Devona looked at her gratefully, there was such a depth of comfort in her voice.

"Oh, madam," she cried, "it is so hard to do one's duty by one's parents."

The baby knew at once what was the matter. "Come here," she said, "and tell me all about it."

And Devona told her all about the naughtiness of her parents.

When she had finished the baby nodded her head sagely.

"Don't you think, my dear," she said, "that you have been a little hasty perhaps? No, don't be cross, I have no doubt your parents are very troublesome, but still—I think if you were to try showing them how it pains you when they are naughty, and what a very real pleasure it is to you when they are well-behaved, I think then perhaps you might find them improving."

"Parents are so troublesome," sighed Devona, "especially at a certain age."

"It is quite true, my dear," agreed the baby, "but if you will take the advice of a younger child than you, the advice of one whose faculties are as yet hardly impaired by the dreadful puzzles of this world, I think you will find the gentler way is best."

"I will try, madam," said Devona bravely, "and may I thank you for your advice?"

"I am always so pleased to be of service, my dear," said the baby. "But you try. I'm sure you'll find it come easier after a bit. Especially as I see there is a young head on your old shoulders. Good-bye, my dear."

"Good-bye, madam," said Devona, and hurried home.

You can imagine how she ran upstairs to the night-nursery and what a shock it was to find that her parents were not there.

But from the play-room next door she could hear the sound of a gentle sobbing mingled with a curious vibration that she failed to recognise.

She opened the door gently and discovered her parents sitting in the dusk crying softly and stroking the cat.

The cat was purring.

"Oh, what pretty thoughts parents have," she thought. It was their atonement.

A minute later they hung round their daughter's neck weeping and promising to be good.

And we should be sorry to say that Devona's eyes were not moist at this touching moment.

For she had found the secret of her parents' hearts.

FAITH

SHE came downstairs while he was taking off his coat in the little dingy hall, and when he saw the sorrow in her face he blinked his eyes in fear.

"Is she dead?" he asked quickly.

She dropped her head on his breast, sobbing.

"The doctor says . . . no hope."

The man drew a deep breath, and then he stooped and kissed her.

"God—God knows best," he said with an effort, "but it's damned hard. Our only one, and some with so many."

He stood there puckering his brow, while the gas whistled drearily over his head, and his wife cried softly at his heart. Then he led her upstairs.

In her room the child was playing with her dreams, and from her small bed they could hear her talking, and hardest of all to bear, laughing to the comrades whom they could not see. The firelight seemed to have a share in her game, for it danced about the room as cheerfully as the child had in the past. The man and his wife walked into the room on tiptoe as if they feared to spoil her enjoyment. "So very little to die," he muttered, leaning over the bed, "so very little."

At the words the child opened her eyes, as if his hushed voice had penetrated to the dim garden in which she played. For a while she saw only the deep blue of the night sky, but then he realised with a thrill of unreasoning hope that she had recognised him.

"Dear!" he cried softly.

"Father," she said with a voice at once shrill and hoarse, "I want a necklace, a necklace of stars." The woman wrung her hands by the bed.

"We have no necklaces here now, darling," she said, "Father will bring it for you in the morning."

"I want a necklace of stars," the child repeated.

The woman looked hopelessly at the man across the bed.

"What can we do?" she said bitterly.

"A necklace, a necklace of stars!" the child cried.

The man looked round the room helplessly, at the grapes, the medicine, and the neglected toys. Then, with a strange light in his face, he caught up a piece of string from the table and turned towards the door.

"I will go and fetch it for you, dear," he said quietly, and he bore her cry of joy with him up the dark stairs and through the little door on to the sooty roof.

The air was very cold after that of the sick-room, and for a while he stood there in uncertainty, with the string hanging from his fingers and all the world of smoky light rolling like the sea below him. Then, with a quick, nervous movement, he tore the largest star from its place in heaven, and threaded it like a blazing jewel upon his string. After that it was easy, and when his string had become a glowing chain of stars, he tied the ends and set the moon there as a pendant. Then he retraced his steps to the child's room, but the staircase was dark no longer.

"See! see what I have brought you!" he cried, and he threw the necklace on to the bed. The child laughed out in an ecstasy of delight.

"The necklace of stars," she whispered, and she clutched the dazzling thing with eager fingers.

All night the great jewels glowed on the bed and filled the room with their lovely light, and though dawn, when it came, would have it that the necklace was no more than a loop of common string, the child knew better.

ONE SUMMER'S DAY

THE wet sponge fell on my face, and for a moment I experienced the extreme discomforts of suffocation; then I opened my eyes and saw Longden standing fully-dressed by my bed. I felt a thin thread of icy water winding round my neck, and shuddered in the bed-clothes. "Get up, you fool!" he whispered, fiercely; and as he raised the sponge I sat up hurriedly.

While I was slipping on my clothes I reflected, sleepily, on the folly of overnight plots. It was well enough to talk of rising at four in the morning to steal cherries, but it was idiotic to do it. I had been wrong to confide my dream to Longden, a man of stern stuff, who had probably slept with all his clothes on to make sure of waking at the right time. "Bring your towel," he whispered, as I nodded over my boots.

As we tip-toed through the dormitory I saw Bradford curled up like a cat between the clothes, an exquisite figure of sleep. The golden light of dawn glowed through the curtainless windows, and the air was full of murmurous snorings. The dormitory appeared to me then a pleasant, restful place, and I was loth to follow Longden's unintelligent back into the world of early morning. My mind played languorously with the idea of revolt; it would be so simple to throw off one's clothes and dive back into bed, but even while I caressed the notion, I knew that the ensuing shame could not be borne. So I followed him meekly along the passages till we reached the quad. It certainly was a lovely morning, but the freshness of the air and the purity of the sky only served to remind me that I had dressed without washing, and was, therefore, for the time being, a member of the criminal classes. Longden was engaged with other considerations. "This gravel makes a beastly noise," he said. "I hope old Henderson doesn't look out of the window." But we reached the headmaster's garden undetected.

We had thought to be the first upon the scene, but from the cherry-tree there came a noise of fighting birds, and Longden pulled out a catapult and sent a shot into the tree. "I want some new 'lastic," he said ruefully, as the birds rose scathless into the air. We walked across the lawn, and the dew made our boots shine as if they had been cleaned. I felt that beneath my heavy eyelids my tired eyes were taking an unusually precise view of the world. I saw an acid-stain on Longden's coat, and certain curious abrasions on his straw-hat that bore tribute to the accurate shooting of the fourth form. On the lawn there were worm-casts, and half-eaten cherries that the birds had dropped. They were chattering now in the neighbouring trees, and their resentment of our presence had my complete sympathy. At half-past four in the morning we had no right to be out of our beds; the earth might be safely left to the birds at that foolish hour.

But Longden had climbed nimbly into the tree, and the cherries were raining down. At the moment they had no more interest for me than shining pebbles, but as they fell I dutifully gathered them into a heap. While I stooped I was careful to keep my eyes wide open, for I knew that if I closed them I would fall on the lawn in delicious sleep. After a while, Longden slipped down from the tree, and we divided the cherries roughly into halves and stowed them away in our towels.

Longden threw his bundle briskly over his shoulder, and led the way to the open-air swimming-bath, while I

followed behind, marvelling dully at his tenacity of purpose. As we went down the streets their shuttered silence
made them strangely unfamiliar. Even the tuck-shops—
Dungey's and Smith's and the Noah's Ark—struck a note
of unsympathetic reticence, and it was hard to believe that
we were walking though our own noisy little town.
When we reached the swimming-bath the water looked
dark and cold, and the sun shining on the bank threw
strange shadows across it. "I expect it will be pretty cold,"
said Longden, undressing rapidly. I was privately of his
opinion, and I did not undress quite so quickly. I could not
understand a man who could regard the prospect of that
icy dip with apparent cheerfulness.

Presently he dived with a splash, and rose to the surface
gasping. It was impossible to misinterpret his aspect, and
I was lingering on the bank, seeking vainly for a valid
excuse for remaining warm, when he called to me to come
on, and I yielded to the inevitable, and dived.

For a moment it seemed that an icy hand had clutched
my windpipe, and that its owner was stropping a sabre
on my spine. Then I came back to the sunlight, and began
swimming fiercely to restore my circulation. Really, after
the first shock, there was something exhilarating about it.

It was too cold to stay in long, and after ten minutes or
so we both climbed out. The sun seemed to have become
much hotter while we had been bathing, and as we lay
basking on the bank, wrapped in our towels, the charm of
the morning conquered my remaining discontents. The
sky was very blue, and the birds were singing joyously in
the trees, and we lay eating cherries and flipping the stones
idly to the four corners of the earth. I threw a cherry to
a fat thrush who hopped in a hedge near by, but he looked
at it suspiciously and would have none of it, as though he
knew that I had not won it honestly. I was tingling de-

liciously from head to foot, and I felt as fit as a king perhaps may never feel. "We ought to do this every morning,"
I said blithely to Longden. "I don't see why we shouldn't,"
he grunted. He was trying to play knuckle-bones with the
stones of cherries.

And then, gradually, this divine mood passed, and a sinking within me told me that I had not had my breakfast, and
that cherries were a poor substitute. The fresh air of the
morning became oppressive, and, try as I might, I could not
speak above an undertone. Even Longden seemed to feel
the burden of the moment. "We can't hang about till
breakfast-time," he said. "We'd better get back to bed."

We dressed in silence, and walked back through the
town. The world had progressed a little in our absence.
The baker at the corner was taking in his shutters and a
labourer's boy whistled down the street to his work. I felt
like a rake before his cheerful healthiness. Everyone
seemed to be pulling up their bedroom blinds as we passed.

The dormitory was close after the open-air, but I was in
no mood to criticise it unfavourably. I undressed as quickly
as I could, but my fingers seemed sluggish and clumsy.
Round about me the air was charged with the music of sleep,
and as I slipped into bed my spirit gave a little sob of gratitude. I had hardly time to reflect on the bragging which my
exploits would allow in the morning before I lost that and
all other illusions.

THE BOY ERRANT

THERE are many ways of getting from Brighton to London, and doubtless the philosophical temperament can find merits in all of them, even in what I would venture to assert is the least pleasant method of all of accomplishing that famous journey. For to walk fifty miles at the close of a disastrous expedition in search of the unexpected, in failing boots and without money is a severe test for amateur pedestrianism, and, when ceaseless rain is added to the normal trials of the road, it needs an extreme optimism to accomplish such a task with an unquenched spirit. Yet physical discomfort is one of those experiences that we soonest forget, and I retain little of that aspect of the journey beyond a sense of monotonous greyness, and the discovery that the weariness of compulsory walking is sufficient to overcome such minor torments as hunger and lack of sleep. When I left Brighton I had not slept or eaten for two days; my feet were blistered; the unexpected had kept unseasonably aloof. When I reached London some twenty-six hours later the condition of my feet was tragic; but hunger and the will to sleep had left me. I only wanted to stop walking.

Nor, I thought at the time, had the accidents of the road justified the whole fond adventure; but, writing now, I am not quite so sure. For from the dimness that is blotting out the mud and weariness of those hopeful, unfortunate days there emerges a very definite impression, and I realise that chance is apt to exact a bigger price for impressions than this. I have eaten and slept since then, and my feet have long recovered from the anger of the Sussex roads; but the image of Willie—little comrade and fellow Bohemian for a night and half a day—lingers with me pleasantly; and as the details of my fantastic journey grow vaguer and more dream-like, this image becomes, in contrast, more vivid. It will remind me that once I tasted the more bitter wine of vagabond life when all else is forgotten.

It was on a grey hill not far from Brighton that he slipped out from a hedge, and started walking gravely by my side; and, so little accustomed was I to the frank, kindly comradeship of the roads, that instinctively I felt inclined to resent his intrusion on my graceless solitude. But there was something so fragile and, indeed, tender in his little wizened face and wasted body that it hardly needed a glance to make me ashamed of my too-English reticence. When, moreover, in answer to a few questions he blurted out his brief history, I discovered that he was the willing slave of one of those primitive passions that dreamers of the unexpected are bound to admire. His father, he told me, was a foreman in an engineering works, earning six pounds a week, and he had a comfortable home, but . . . the whole helpless spirit of vagabondage lay in his appealing glance. I caught, as it were, a glimpse of that comfortable home—its parlour, its ordered respectability, its unconscious but desolating dullness—and nodded sympathy. Seven times had young Ulysses run away from home; four times he had been taken back by the police, who had been very kind to him; and now, once more, he was limping back of his own accord. His boots were even more pitiful than mine, and he had the loose shambling gait of the genuine tramp; but, with the generosity of a true artist, he consented to overlook the gap that separates the professional from the amateur. He produced bread and cheese from his pocket, and I made pretence to eat as we walked along together.

He had the body of a child of eleven or twelve and the kind, tired eyes of an old man of eighty; but, at a venture, I should say he was about fourteen, and he was one of the vainest and most lovable creatures I have ever met. He would display the artless cleverness that is the common coin of sharp children, and peer at me from the corners of his eyes to detect my admiration; and then, in a breath, he would reveal unconsciously such wisdom as grown men buy with tears. His speech was fragrant with the romance of the road, but it was romance in detail, and not the large, vague romance that deals with dust and stars and the great, restful hills. He had sold newspapers in London and race-cards on Epsom Downs. He had lived with those dark folk, the gipsies; he had wandered about the country with fairs and pedlars. He had been bitten by dogs and bullied by righteous country lads; he had been thrashed by farmers for stealing apples and thrashed by the gipsies for failing to steal fowls. Doubtless, often enough, he had been cold and wet and hungry. And yet there it was, running away now from his home, now from some temporary master, he succeeded—dearly enough one would think—in satisfying the rebel in his blood, and even now, with his face set towards his home, he was planning a new venture. Hitherto, his expeditions had been confined to the southern half of England; but he had heard that there were plenty of kind people in the North, and, perhaps, in a few weeks' time—— "Yet they don't hit me much at home, either," he reflected, wondering a little, perhaps, at his own restlessness.

Possibly, to the inexpert Bohemian, his most suggestive confession was his own utter weariness of bread and cheese. Anywhere, he told me, he could get more bread and cheese than he could possibly eat; but he greatly preferred bread and butter, which was comparatively scarce. Sometimes a woman would give him a good meal because he was so small, and one or two had wanted to adopt him. "But that's no use to me," he said, boastfully; "I can look after myself, I can."

Indeed, it was hard to say whether he was to be envied or pitied as he shuffled along by my side, bragging of his adventurous existence, that was, in truth, barely to be measured in terms of human hardship, and yet, at the same time, endured with a spirit, a fierce independence, torn as it were from Nature herself, that made me feel that my tame reliance on civilisation was a dwarfing form of cowardice. Yet as night fell he revealed a weakness, childish and touching, but at the same time difficult to reconcile with his manner of living. He, who had slept in a hundred ditches, and divided food with a hundred savage comrades, was afraid of walking in the dark! It was raining steadily, and I had the wild, illogical desire to get back to London that he professed to share, so stopping was out of the question. And so, as I trudged wearily across the night holding his arm in mine, I felt it tremble, and now and again he whispered hoarsely in my ear: "Tighter! hold it tighter!" It was as if night had made him forget all his street-boy tricks and cynicisms, and he had become a child once more.

By the time we reached Crawley he could walk no farther, and so we turned into a field to rest. With the simplicity of habit he flung himself on his back on the wet ground and fell asleep, with the rain beating on his face, as easily and lightly as if his mother had tucked him into bed. I separated my boots from my bursting feet and stayed miserably wakeful. Everyone I had met that day had taken me for a tramp, and I had almost come to believe myself in my mission. But now I realised that I was a fraud; that there were many things I had to forget and even more I had to learn before I could win the friendship of the wide earth and sky. I envied the boy his easy philosophy. We had ragged together about Crawley in search of water and had failed to find it; but the driver of the night mail to Brighton had given the boy some jam sandwiches, and he had immediately forgotten his other need, while I was still thirsty. It is a strange truth that even the profession of tramp demands an apprenticeship.

Day came at last, weeping and miserably grey, and after a while the boy woke up, and pronounced himself willing to continue our journey; but we had not gone far before it was apparent that he had over-estimated his powers. Again and again I had to stop while he rested by the roadside. Presently we came to a grocer's shop, and he produced a secret store of pennies and bought half a loaf of bread and some butter. But I could not eat, even for comradeship; and, while he was taking his breakfast, he admitted that he could walk no farther. The desire to get back to London had taken complete possession of me, and I felt that, if I did not go on, I should never get there at all. So I shook hands with him and left him eating his bread and butter. Some ten minutes later I heard a faint shout, and, turning round, found him limping along the road behind me. But, when he came up with me, it was only to confess that he was "done." We shook hands again, and presently I lost sight of him, a faint black speck sitting by the wayside.

Since I found a comrade so generous and friendly, I feel I did not venture on the southern roads in vain. I have not seen the boy since. Perhaps he is threading the Yorkshire Wolds, where the chalk is white and there are wild pansies;

or, perhaps, he lingers still in his "comfortable home." But I have only to shut my eyes to feel his thin arm trembling in mine, and to hear his voice in my ear: "Tighter! hold it tighter!" And to this clear-cut impression the whole story of those grey wet days has dwindled with the years.

THE CLERK

He was a paper-cuffed clerk, old and weary and forty-five years of age, and he left his office at quarter past four like a man who has been too long in prison and cares not whether he goes or stays.

But he passed down along Cheapside and Fleet Street and the Strand and on and on till he came to the purple mountains stained by a mad sun of crushed whortleberries.

There he stopped and wrung his hands a little and cried to the sun.

"Oh, sun, if you could speak you would join me in my song to my beloved, you would say to me, 'Oh, most miserable, how quiet she is and how cool, there is the soft-ness of new snow on her cheeks!' And I should say, 'Truly there is a magic of old stars wandering in her hair!' Now though you are dumb you are more fortunate than I, for you can smile on her and touch her, but I, I, woe is me, can only pass by trembling——"

And he went on to the garden of dull red walls and peach trees and roses and there was a moon there very lovely.

And he cried to the moon in his bitter sorrow:

"My beautiful is very young as you know, having kissed her in the night, oh fortunate moon, and her lips are like a new bud. But you are as old as the hills and I, I am forty-five. Weep with me a little."

And he passed on to the field of stars, but to these he said nothing, because they were part of her.

Now he was mad, and things happening, it fell that he was at home in his own bedroom, and she whom he loved lay in his bed, wakeful and wondering, but he sat apart in the room.

And outside the window the moon smiled and the sun lightened the east in his joy, but the stars trembled because they were part of her.

In the house a clock ticked off the seconds in the darkness and sung the hours on a little bell, and the hours were very short; yet the clerk sat there marvelling that he had done this thing—that he had stolen her whom he might not speak to, and that she should rest in his bed.

And his blood that had grown weary of longing for the hills and the song of the glistening sea, and his mind that had known too long the yellow desk and electric fires and faces of unloved companions, was stirred by the bitter old desire, not as of old in sorrow to break her, but now in joy to kiss her and make her his.

And he heard her breathing and stirring in her sleep with a rustle of wings, and the tears of fire wove in his eyes and wandered down his cheeks.

For he knew how long it had been and how lonely ere yet he had taken the sun and moon for his friends and won her too; for all the old and bitter longing now that she was his, she was no more than a dream. Even her breath that sweetened all the room was only a thing thought of long ago. Even her hair that gleamed wonderfully on the white pillow was only a memory of the sunshine of a boy's spring.

Surely if he touched her she would vanish as had all the others.

She was all he had longed for, all he had desired. His lost ideal. He would not have her perish with the rest, so he sat apart in his chair and watched her with filial wakeful eyes.

And the sun came up over the houses and through the

window and, kissing her, made her very sweet. And the birds sang at the panes, and her lips moving a little seemed to echo the song, and when her lips parted they were like the breaking of all the rosebuds.

The clerk drew his chair nearer to the bed and leant forward to listen.

Surely there was a singing not of birds. A voice that was not new singing an old song of the spring.

And then bending forward he felt her cool breath beating on his cheek and wrapping round his face. Roses and thyme and lilies.

And the song swelled in his ears and he knew it for his own. The song he had never been able to sing.

And he saw her lips parting——

It was better to lose her, better to take the risk. If it might be, one kiss——

He stood up with a great cry and fell forward on to the bed, dead.

SUMMER TIME

Well, we are married and 'tis summer here,
   We are those lovers who
   Heard the birds sing.
This is the place where all the violets were;
   Surely the sky is still as warm and blue—
   Where is the spring?"

THEIR pulses beat a little faster as they neared the little wood.

"After all these years," he said, with a trace of sentiment.

"Yes," she said simply; and then they came to the stile, and he gravely helped her over.

"This is the wood!" He laughed, but it sounded false. "It has not altered anyhow."

"No, it has not altered." She spoke solemnly.

"It might have been yesterday."

"A thousand years ago—perhaps. Or not at all. I wonder——" There was no bitterness in her voice. She spoke as one who states a fact.

"Dorothy. Not to-day. I swear not to-day. Dear——"

"To-day and to-morrow and for ever. It is no good to pretend. We didn't pretend then, Willy."

He frowned thoughtfully.

"I wonder whether it was all our fault. Perhaps it was the trees, and the flowers, and the blue sky, all in one conspiracy against us."

"Oh, it is Fate," she said. "Fate has just made fools of us, that's all. We thought it would last for ever; that's folly. Nothing lasts for ever. And now we make the best of it; that's brave."

He said, "I wish to God we didn't," and they walked on

down the grassy path in silence. They each knew what they were seeking, though nothing had been said about it —the tree, the great oak, on which in rustic fashion, with many a loving jest, he had carved their linked initials.

"They do it in books," he said. "We shall do it in real life."

And after ten years they had come back.

"Anyhow, I'm glad we came," said he.

"I'm sorry," she replied.

"Why?"

"Because it proves it," she said. "That year, that year must be dead indeed, when we come like tourists to view its remains. Had there been any hope we should have stopped away. If anything, any little thing were left it would have hurt us too much to raise this spectre from the ten years' dust. But it doesn't matter, now we have only common sense, which was the one thing we lacked then."

"How silly we were, and yet how wise!"

"We were people of sentiment then, we are sentimentalists now. False coin. Our raptures don't ring true."

"Raptures," he smiled at her painfully. "This is worse than I expected, Dorothy."

"Oh, I knew it would be pretty bad," she replied calmly. "It was bound to be. But it's good for us; makes us honest, you know, teaches us our place—if we have one."

They reached the clearing, and after all it was a trifling shock to find their oak tree gone.

A peeled stump stood graceless in the centre, and that was all. Dorothy looked at it silently for a while and then burst into laughter.

"It's about the height of a tombstone," she said. Then, after a pause, solemnly, "I suppose it is a tombstone." And she walked up to it and seated herself comfortably on the top. "Perhaps that's why the lightning struck it."

"To blot out our boast?" he said.

"No, so that I can sit on the stump."

He was pained.

"Dorothy," he cried. "It may be—no, I suppose it is bad, but it isn't as bad as that. Why can't we look at the pleasant things that are behind us without tearing them so to pieces?"

"Ghosts! ghosts!" she chuckled. "That sounds like Ibsen. I don't tear them to pieces, Willy. But when I find myself possessed of an unwholesome memory, I try to crush it; when I find a comfortable stump, I sit on it. That's common-sense."

"That memory isn't unwholesome. It is we that are unwholesome now, Dorothy. And it is because you know that, that you are ashamed of the past."

Dorothy looked at him steadily for a minute.

"Do you really think so, Willy?" she said quietly. "Yes, I suppose you're right. I'm trying to make the best of it. Trying to make a laughing-stock of Fate. Trying to forget. And what would you have me do? Pretend? Speak with lies? Live with lies? Love with lies?"

"No, but—— Oh, I think there must be a better way than this," he cried passionately. "There must be on an earth that is not hell. Your tears are not less true because you think I do not see you weeping. I am not less sorry because you prefer not to notice it. Dorothy, I have been thinking, will we not meet again in regret, as we met once before, here, in this very place, in joy? Can't we start again in a different way? A more lasting way. Then we loved because the gods were kind. Can't we love now because they are cruel?"

Dorothy shook her head. "Look at me," she said abruptly. "What do you see?"

He looked at her and hesitated.

I

"Precisely," she cried, "and now when I look at you, what do you think I see?"

"You are cruel," he murmured.

"Not too cruel," she said. "Because you still love the girl of ten years ago—because I still love that boy if you will—that is why there can be nothing now. Willy, I never look at you without the ghost of that boy stepping in between us. Thin and dark, and with a face like a poet."

He swore softly.

"Yes, and when you look at me," she went on inflexibly, "don't I know, don't I see your eyes looking everywhere for something? You are looking for a hat with pink ribbons. You are wondering where that girl can have hidden herself. You are wondering why she does not come running to you with outstretched hands—'Love, it has been so long!'"

"Don't, don't. Not here. It seems like blasphemy."

"It doesn't matter. The gods are dead. Youth, Love, Romance; Common-sense has slain them every one. We sit on top of a mountain, old and wise and ugly, and deal in facts. The gods are dead."

"Oh, let's walk on," he said. "This day has been wretched."

"It was bound to be," and she slipped down from her seat. They walked away from it quietly.

There was one more place to visit, the little hollow where he had waited for her, and where they had been wont to build their castles.

"Cupid's Cup," he said softly.

She laughed. "I expect they've sunk a well in it or something," she said.

"No, oh no!" he said seriously.

They had not. The Cup was as they had left it some ten years before, a valley in miniature, floored with grass and flowers, and with silver birches climbing up the sides, and at the bottom in *their* place stood a young man, a young man who was thin and dark, and had a face like a poet.

He had not marked their approach, being too intent on listening to the footsteps of someone who was drawing near on the other side of the Cup to his arms.

Husband and wife turned away forthwith, and walked back to the stile in silence.

He broke it.

"She ought not to have sung that," he cried.

Dorothy turned to him with a little pathetic smile.

"Don't you see now?" she said. "Don't you understand? We are moved on. That's all. We had our turn, now it is for those other glad ones. We are too old now. We shall be very civil to each other, no doubt. And happy. But glad never. I like you and you like me, I think. We are quite friends, you know. If I had known, I would not have had things go differently. It was worth a lifetime, that."

"Dorothy, if I did not think it was a lie——"

"Oh, well, never mind. It doesn't matter. But that girl: she was pretty, don't you think?"

"Pretty. Yes, I suppose she was. But she ought not to have sung *that*."

Dorothy looked at him nonplussed for a few seconds.

"Well, well," she said.

And they walked back to the station.

THE WRONG TURNING *

It was a dark night, and the traveller shuddered as he strode along the white road. On each side of that sorely-made way lay the marshes, waiting for a chance slip to catch the blunderer by the heel and slowly suck him under, when nought but the will-o'-the-wisps would know the manner of his passing.

Had it been light he could have seen the dry land shake and tremble and melt into greasy waters, or muddy banks rise like the heads of great reptiles through the surface of pools, but the darkness hid these horrors, and he could only hear the choking of the falling mud, and the harsh cries of sea-birds far away.

He clutched his bag closer to him and hurried on, keeping carefully to the middle of the road, and looking anxiously ahead at the surface of the way, for fear that a land-slip might have turned the path of safety to a death-trap. So it was he noticed far ahead amongst the dim stars and marsh flames a light, that burned with a steady glow, and neither flickered nor danced.

The traveller paused in some surprise at the sight. He had been told of no house to be passed on the way, while if it should be the light of a fellow-traveller, that one might well be a thief or worse; and where would lie his safety in so forsaken a spot?

But the light burned quite steadily, and the traveller continued on his way reassured. It was, without doubt, a house. As he drew near, and the light proved to come from an un-curtained window in a squat and miserable dwelling, his

* The prize-winning story in *The (London) Morning Leader*. Wednesday, 27 December, 1905.—J. G.

doubts recurred. What honest man could endure to live in such a place; and its ill-appearance was hardly redeemed by the sign that hung creaking across the sky—"The House of Woe." Who had ever heard of such a name for an inn as that? He had come to a standstill while he scanned the place, but the name decided him; and with his heart like a lump in his throat he began to steal past the place on tiptoe, praying that they might not keep a dog within.

Thus he crept along by the black wall, and had just come to the end when he pulled himself up with a terrible shock.

The road went no farther, and the black waters lay muttering at his feet.

After the first sensation of panic, he found himself thinking with a curious calmness. Of course, the explanation was simple. He had mistaken the path to the inn for the road he should have followed; and all he had to do was to retrace his steps, and all would be well.

So he set himself again to his tiptoeing, and once more passed the house without disturbing its inmates.

But now a new difficulty presented itself; round the inn the ground was dead white, so that it was hard to tell where the road might be. He struck out at a venture, hesitated, took a step, and felt his leg sink to the knee in a soft mass that closed on it like steel. With a frantic effort he flung his body backwards on to the firm ground, and fought silently with the mud in the darkness. At last he rolled back free, but exhausted, with the air striking his panting lungs with the force of a blow.

After a while he pulled himself up and gazed fearfully around him. Behind lay "The House of Woe," dark and forbidding, while before lay the deadly marshes chuckling at the victim they had failed to keep. He felt he durst not venture towards them again while his leg was yet numb with the force of their grip.

He stepped slowly towards the house with the mud oozing in his torn boot, and as he went he comforted himself, as timid men do in lonely places, with the thought of great cities and their carefully regulated police. He could have stayed where he was all night, but he felt himself wrought on by a petulant desire for action, being, in truth, too fearful to remain passively between the known dangers of the marsh and that dark and repellent monster with the luminous eye.

The sound of his knuckles on the door set his heart fluttering again, and he would have given kingdoms for the moment, if only the sound might not have been made. Yet his knock was not answered, and so contradictory is the nature of man that after a few minutes he was banging lustily and impatiently on the door, and swearing to himself at the dilatoriness of those within.

The door opened at last, and a man appeared in the dim passage, who, without listening to the traveller's explanations, stood aside silently to let him pass.

That one hesitated, felt that he had gone too far to retreat, stepped trembling past the man, and heard with a heart of lead the door banged and fastened behind him.

At the end of the passage a slit of light showed the presence of a doorway, and with the man treading closely behind the traveller pushed this open, still with the same dread of something terrible within. But his fear seemed misplaced, the room might indeed have been the living-room of an old inn, with its oak panels, wide fireplace, sides of bacon, and strings of onions pendant from the high ceiling, and a bright enough fire burning on the hearth, with the additional light of the lamp in the window, which he had seen from without.

Seated by the fire was an elderly man engaged in stirring the contents of a pot, while in the further corner, with her back turned to the door, was a woman bending over the bed of a little child. Neither the man nor the woman looked up to see who had entered, and when his conductor, still without a word, motioned him to a chair by the table, the wanderer began to think the whole household was deaf and dumb. To walk into a room in the dead of night drenched with mud and water, and to escape practically unnoticed, was disconcerting, and it hardly reassured him to suspect that he was the object of secret scrutiny on the part of the two men.

But when he looked up sharply he only saw the old man stirring his pot, and the other gazing stolidly at the fire.

Suddenly the girl got up and swung round to the room, and as he saw her face the traveller knew why his feet had wandered to that place, and why he was afraid.

"You, Lucy!" he cried.

"Me, Hubert," she said quietly. And deep silence fell on the room.

He sat like one already dead, white and speechless. Lucy and the men and the sides of bacon danced madly in his vision, and he was afraid they would know he was a coward by the loudness of his breathing, but there was such a weight on his chest that when he sought to close his lips he was nearly choked.

It was the silence that he hated—the silence and the suspense. Why did not something happen? Anything rather than those mute and incurious figures.

"For God's sake," he cried, and the tears welled in his eyes at the sound of his voice, so sad and appealing.

There was a pause, and then suddenly the elder man, Lucy's father it would be, threw back his swart and bearded face in a hoarse cackle of laughter. Again and again he renewed it, his dried lips pulled back from the yellow teeth and the cruel red gums; even so might the Prince of Darkness mock a lost soul.

Lucy had turned back to the child.

Anon the man grew tired of his laughing and fell once more to stirring his broth, tasting it from time to time with his spoon and pursing his lips at the heat.

The cruelty of it. The traveller could endure it no longer. He staggered to his feet and clutched his hat to his head, his bag lying forgotten on the floor.

"I—I think I will go out," he said with an effort, and moved to the door.

The man by the fire spoke at last.

"Put the gentleman on the right way, Lucy," he said, and there was a glint of malice in his voice.

Lucy left the bed and walked to the door. She had not always had that iron face. The wanderer followed her quietly and hopelessly down the passage and out into the night. He had only needed one glance at that grim face to know what was his fate.

As he trod behind her through the greying marshes he heard the waters laughing cruelly each side, and the sound reminded him of the man he had left behind in "The House of Woe." And as he thought of that name he knew many things.

"You liked me once, Lucy," he said, but his words ended in a gasp. With a rapid leap or two the woman had passed to a spot about twenty feet off and he knew not which way to tread.

"Your child. I am its father. You cannot kill me."

Lucy did not seem to hear the words, but she began singing very softly, and with a thrill of horror Hubert recognised the words. It was a love song.

She sang without a tremor, but for the rest it was the same sweet voice that had charmed him so much before, and he had prided himself on his taste in such matters.

He heard her fascinated to the end of her song; and as he

listened a wave of something like remorse broke on his self-centred mind.

"You know I meant to come back, Lucy," he cried when she had finished. "It was all a mistake."

She looked at him with hard and steady contempt. "I saw you go that morning," she said.

He bowed his head, for there are some things that even the worst man cannot think about without shame. There was no romance about that flight at dawn, that creeping down the stairs with his boots in his hand, that painful straining to hear if Lucy had wakened, all this had been sordid enough. And she had known all the time and let him go.

There was none of the fierce spirit distracted and led astray in this; he merely felt like a mean man, found out, and for the moment he was genuinely penitent, and so lost to externals that he did not even notice that the reason his feet were of lead was because he was slowly sinking, that the mud had risen above his boots.

"I'm sorry, Lucy," he said humbly.

This was a better way.

"Why did you say you loved me, Hubert?" she said sadly.

"I was a brute."

He was watching Lucy's face when he said this, and a sudden change, suggestive of fear, made him look down. The mud reached nearly to his knees.

For a minute he struggled, trying desperately to withdraw one leg, but he only sank the deeper. At last he desisted, and looked wistfully across at Lucy.

"I'm gone," he said.

Lucy stood irresolute, with her face half-turned away, and her fingers plucking at the front of her gown.

"I can't!" she cried suddenly, and came running to his

side, her trained eye choosing the spots which she knew to be comparatively safe.

He held out his arms to her, and she took his hands one in each of hers as if she would embrace him, but she made no effort to help him out.

"I'm sinking, Lucy," he said plaintively.

"Yes, Hubert," she said simply.

The mud had passed his waist, and she knew no effort of hers could release him.

"You are cruel," he cried, struggling feebly in the scarcely liquid mass.

Lucy dropped his hands, and placing hers on his shoulders thrust his body back with all her might. His arms flailed desperately in all directions, but the mud was sliding over his chest and over his chin and over his face.

When the surface had ceased to quiver and the bubbles had passed, Lucy drew forth her hands and straightened herself against the dawning sky.

"It was better," she said.

And she turned back to her child.

THE WELCOME HOME

HE stood in Charing Cross Station, wrack cast up from the sea, looking idly at the strange faces and wondering what home meant to him. In all the years that he had spent, blown hither and thither like spindrift by the sea, he had thought of England, of London, as home. But now that he had come back from his haphazard wanderings, he realised that the thing in truth was only a name. While he had been seeking his singing rose in the weary wastes of the sea, his princess with the bright eyes and the lamp-lit hair had changed, and it seemed in the moment's bitterness as though singing roses were of no more worth. All the faces were strange. . . .

And yet he had to make the best of it. Doubtless in time he would find another princess, not so merry with love as the old, perhaps, but with a deeper knowledge in her sad eyes. He had money, and this was a city of shops, shops of pleasure and love and sea-worn memories; and if a night or two might not restore the old wine to his lips, there was always the patient sea. He shrugged his shoulders and passed out of the station with the crowd, the crowd of strangers.

For a while, used as he was to the great sea-spaces, he could hardly breathe in the genial turbulence of the Strand. The people drove him from side to side, and though their faces were friendly he longed to stretch his loose limbs that seemed cramped by the crowd. And so he wandered off into the quieter streets, where the stars were like those which had balanced above the tropic masts, and where he might

fling about the pavements as he wished. And presently he
came to the theatre.

Although the front was brilliantly lit there was not a
great crowd before it, and he thought with satisfaction
that he could probably get a seat, even though the bills announced that this was the first performance of a new play.
And he felt that the name of the play was a good omen.
"The Welcome Home." Perhaps after all he would find
the princess somewhere, the princess who pined for the
singing rose. He went into the theatre gladly.

At the box office they gave him a seat at the back of the
dress circle, where his unorthodox attire might be con-
doned. To him the lights and the glow of the theatre
represented a dream fulfilled. Often he had thought of
these things at sea. The orchestra, the well-dressed men,
the beautiful women, they had filled his mind when the
sea had lashed at his face like a whip, and the wind had
buffeted him like an angry crowd. It was pleasant to be
home.

And the play, he realised that it might not be a great
work of art, yet it danced with his mood as a child might
dance with a doll. How long, how weary long, he had
been away at sea. It was very good to be home.

When he came out of the theatre he realised that the
princess had not really changed. There was an end of the
foam, and the rain, and the swift-scudding clouds. The
great seas would sing for him no more. He had come back
to a place of laughter, and dreams, and languorous delights. He fell asleep with a smile upon his lips, a smile that
his mother would have recognised. It is good to be home.

.   .   .   .

In the morning it seemed natural to him to turn his steps
towards the place which had given him back his dead.

As he passed down the street it broke upon him in the grey morning light, a place with broken windows and unpainted woodwork, the shattered wreck of a theatre.

"Oh, the Old Frivolity!" said the policeman, "it's been shut these twenty years!"

FATE'S SOLUTION

MORRIS'S BUILDINGS, Southwark, were decrepit and ramshackle in the last degree, and nothing but a continuous and expensive course of repairs saved their owner from an order for their destruction. That one was wont to swear when the builder's accounts came in, but tenements are highly profitable, so Morris's Buildings continued to exist, when a better-class house in the same condition would long ago have been pulled down.

The Authorities saw that they were safe, if not sightly, and the inhabitants held their peace because they were poor.

This adjective certainly applied to Charles Anderson and Mary Wade, who each had a room near the stars in that gloomy building. They also had another feature in common—they were both highly unpopular with the other inhabitants of the tenements. Charles, because he spoke like a gentleman, and no one has a right to give himself airs in such a place—Mary because she lived alone without a "husband," and for a young woman that was not considered "respectable."

Perhaps it was their mutual aloofness from the society of the Buildings that had made them to some extent acquainted; when they met on the stairs they talked for a minute or two, and once she had mended his coat sleeve. And that was all.

It was New Year's Eve, and Charles was making his way upstairs with a bottle but ill-concealed under his coat. On the topmost landing but one he overtook Mary. They each said good evening and paused in their upward course. And there was a momentary silence.

Somewhere down below Stevens and a select party of exiled compatriots were keeping it up, and the gusts of shouting and laughter made the upper part of the house seem very silent by contrast.

This struck Charles and he spoke to Mary with a faint bitterness in his voice.

"It's as quiet as heaven up here to-night, and as cold."

"It is very cold," she said, and added sadly, "It is always cold."

They mounted the last flight of stairs together. "I have a fire in my room," he said as they reached the landing. "Come in and make good resolutions."

She looked at him doubtfully.

"Unless you are afraid?" he continued.

"I'll come in," she said quietly. "I'm not afraid. Why should I be?"

"With all the stars in heaven for chaperons," he said as he opened the door of his room. "It is a fine night. 'A wonderful fine night of stars.' Good Lord! That's Stevenson. You don't know him I suppose."

She had never seen the interior of his room before, though there was little in it to surprise her, with the exception, perhaps, of the small heap of books in the corner. The bed covered with newspapers for blankets, the broken window-pane stuffed with the same useful material, the crazy wooden table, the packing-cases, the bare and rotten boards—these she had in her room; but hers was cleaner because she was a woman.

The fire, however, was unusual enough, and their first thoughts were centred on that. Charles placed the bottle on the table, and going down on his knees by the fire, blew the ashes tenderly from the bars; then, with a small piece of wood, and a couple of diminutive nuggets of coal, he stirred the wretched embers into something like a blaze.

"There!" he said proudly, and getting up from the floor he drew a couple of the packing-cases to the front of the fire. "Now we can talk."

Mary sat down and looked gratefully at the flames. "It was cold," she said.

"Yes," said Charles. "I'm glad I have a fire. I was lucky to-day. Till I was poor I never had blue blood in my veins as far as I know, but now it shows quite plainly in my nose."

"I'm never lucky," said Mary, smiling a little. "And I have always been poor. I suppose you like the sunshine more than the others though—it makes some difference."

"Properly considered we are the salt of the earth. We rise daily and overcome all the tyrants that make the well-to-do miserable. Heat and cold. Rain and fog. Hunger and thirst." His eye wandered to the bottle on the table. "Some of us have not quite overcome that last tyrant, by the way, but I, for one, never have indigestion, and I shall not die of the gout!"

"How can you talk like that," she said gently, "when you feel it so? I like to hear you joke, and yet—I suppose it is all a lie. You know what poverty really is. You know it is below laughter——"

"No, it is above it," he answered quietly. "Above laughter, above love, and above life, for it slays them all. Dear life! what a thing this poverty is. It makes crime a virtue, virtue a crime, fools wise men, Poets Anarchists. It makes me a sot, and you a brave woman—but I daresay you would have been that anyhow. Oh! how great a thing it is to be poor. We are part of our Mother Earth, because they cannot help it, and nothing more. But, if ever I were rich, phew!"—he spread his arms round the garret, "I should be Nero. And you, you should be my Empress. How we should crush them! Not the poor smallest who are so easy to crush. But those others, landlords, publicans, sub-editors if you wish! Oh, I didn't mean to say that about my Empress. It was rude. I beg your pardon."

Mary had blushed at his words, but now she drew nearer the fire, and stretched out her hands to warm them. "It is cold, to-night," she said.

Charles laughed at the bottle on the table.

"I know what will warm you," he said, "Whisky. Hot whisky and water. Punch without lemons."

Mary smiled and shook her head.

"I don't like it. I'm afraid," she said.

"Nor do I," cried Charles. "I hate it. But the effect. The exhilaration. I'm a poor bad literary hack, a bad one, mind you, sober. I am Czar of all the Russias in my cups. Not that I get drunk," he added quietly, as he thought he saw her frown. "Oh! I know it's weak. D—d weak. But I just tipple when I have the money."

"I am sorry," she said, looking steadily at the fire. "I did not know you, yet I always thought you were so brave. I saw you were a gentleman, and as poor as—as one of us, and I always found you with a smile on your face, and a joke on your tongue, and it did me good. I said to myself, See how much harder it is for him than for you. And I felt more brave myself."

"I am sorry," said Charles humbly. "I did not know it mattered to anyone but me. I did not know anyone cared."

He looked at Mary interrogatively, as if to ask whether it was the fire that made her cheeks so red.

"I care," said Mary softly, and Charles saw that it was not the fire. The room was very quiet.

"I suppose—" said Charles at last—"I suppose you never guessed I was thinking a little, no! a great deal of you too. Well, I thought you were plucky. I think you are plucky to come in here to-night. And you came because you are good. 'My strength is as the strength of ten be-

K

cause my heart is pure!' It is so with you. Well, I have a certain amount of strength in me in spite of the whisky. I don't know what it is. I think that is what idiots call the problem of life. To find out where one is strong, so that one may avoid the places where one is weak. But however that is, I know this. Here are two of us, side by side in a manner, each finding life difficult, and each trying to fly our flag nevertheless. Mary! Can't we fly the same flag? Share the same difficulties? Can't we marry? Oh! I know there is the whisky. That shall go overboard, never fear. Don't you see? I know we have had no love-making, no pleasant foolery. That's because we are not players but realities, not living but fighting for our lives. Your strength for my weakness. My weakness for my strength, Mary?"

Mary was crying a little, crying and shaking her head. "I'm very sorry," she said at length—"I am sorry. I can't marry anyone because—I am married already."

"Married already," Charles repeated quietly. "Married already. What a pity."

"He left me and the baby died," she went on. "Four years ago."

"The beast," said Charles. "The beast."

"I married him," she said.

"Oh, I'm sorry," he said. "Of course there must have been some mistake. He could not have left you on purpose."

"Oh, but he did. He was very cruel before he went. Yet I liked him once."

"And now—" said Charles—"and now his ghost spoils all. And I don't know whether I am sorry or glad that you are so good."

"Please," she said. "Please. It is so nice to be here by the fire."

Charles got up and heaped coals in a profligate manner on the little grate.

"We may as well have a good one," he said. "It is New Year's Eve, and it will be well if I have no more troubles in the New Year than a trivial dearth of fuel!"

She looked at him sadly.

"You are so good to me, and so sorry."

"Mary," he said, "I feel like the devil. Why and why and why not? That's the song in my brain. You are good, and I want to be good. But we can't. Poor people can't be good. We have got to fight and we want help. What does it matter what they say?

> It matters not how strait the gate,
> How charged with punishments the scroll,
> I am the master of my fate:
> I am the captain of my soul.

Mary, that is the thing. Captain of my soul. I know this thing isn't wrong. It is only fate would have it so. Mary, can't we master fate? You and I. Against the world. Knowing that nothing we can do is wrong, because we are ourselves the only judges. Knowing that God knows how hard it is!"

Mary shook her head again.

" It is no use," she said. "Can't you see that we should lose the one thing that we have kept? The one thing that has been given us to keep. You say I am good. That is to-night. What would you call me to-morrow? How should I judge myself to-morrow? I have only this one little thing. I have tried to be good."

"Oh, I suppose you are right," he said. "I said I was the devil. And yet I have tried to be good sometimes, and it all ends in whisky and—the devil. I remember words in the play, 'If love were all!' I suppose if Love were all we should be King and Queen to-night, Mary. As it is—I know you love me."

"I—I am married, and my husband is alive," she said, looking at him startled.

"I know! I know! Why are you afraid? It is not me you fear—it is yourself," he cried, and he strode towards her and seized her by the hands.

"If I were a brute. No, I am a brute. If—if—I am the captain of my soul. Mary, Mary, you love me. Are you the captain of yours?"

She stood there looking into his face.

"Ah," she cried. "And you said I was strong. I, who am so weak."

"You love me! You love me!" he cried; and the world swam before him because she trembled so beneath his strength.

Mary was crying.

"What shall I do?" she sobbed. "Oh, why is it so hard?"

"Why! Why!" he echoed. "But there must be a way. We are not meant to be slaves. We are not meant to suffer so."

He had let go one of her hands, and they stood hand in hand in the firelight like children, and like a child she cried.

Suddenly the quiet of the stairs and passages was turned to horror by the shrieks of women, and panic-stricken cries of men. Dully through the door there came "Fire! Fire!" in senseless iteration, and the street below was filled as by magic with an excited crowd.

"The house is on fire," he said to her, and with the words a film of smoke came curling under the door.

Charles clutched her arm closer to him, and went to the door. The landing was filled with bitter smoke, and there was a spit and crackle of flame below.

"It is the stairs," he said, stepping back into the room,

and shutting out the smoke. He led her gently to the window.

"Dear, I think this is the answer. You are not afraid?"

"I'm not afraid. Why should I be?" she said, smiling.

"I am so glad," he said, and he flung open the window. Below them in the street he could see a mass of white faces upturned. All about lay the lights of houses and streets, with the stars over all.

"Good God! how rich we are!" he cried. "We are letting in the New Year. And I think it should be happier than the last. I see that you were right. Quite right. Still there is no harm now."

And he bent down and kissed her.

"It will not hurt much," he said.

"No, it will be very sweet, dear," she said, and she smiled into his face.

And so they waited.

THE LAST ADVENTURE

GEORGE AUSTIN FANINGFORD was a young man with a temperament and a handsome income. The former served to make him attractive to all save the very sedate, the latter, which the foresight of a shrewd father had caused to be paid quarterly, enabled him to allow his joyous nature full play, so that he took life as young poets take opium, in a series of magnificent quarterly carouses. The length of these periodical expressions of his youth was determined by fortune; sometimes when he was unlucky his money would last for a weary two months; once a gorgeous thirty-six hours sufficed to land him in a Brighton lodging-house, penniless and with no more clothes than those on his back. One feature, however, of these temperamental effervescences was common to them all. Always at their termination he would wake up like a man who had been dreaming a pleasant dream and could not quite remember what it was, and this romantic vagueness was only dispelled on the rare occasions when the troublesome curiosity of the police served to expose some part of his lurid adventures. In one sense, of course, his awakenings differed from those of a man who merely wakes from his sleep; for he often found himself involved in problems of no little complexity, and in the difficult situation of having to supply an answer without any knowledge of what the conundrum might be.

On a night of November, three weeks after his quarterly cheque had been paid into the bankers, George stepped back suddenly, but without shock, as was his wont, into the material world. He was a man of nice taste, but he could find little to criticise in the decorative scheme of the charming room in which he found himself seated. The carpets were silky as the back of a Persian kitten, the curtains and tapestries were of subtly undecided colours, the furniture had that air of fragile discomfort which modern designers appear to have derived from a study of modern morals; in a word, it was a room that no one could live in— a delightful example of the attractively useless. Nor was it displeasing to George, who did not extend his defiance of convention to his clothes, to find that he was wearing evening dress; and though the clothes were not his own, it was reassuring to trace in their delicate lines the cunning hand of Dawson, that dreamer of sartorial masterpieces. And George was regarding the situation with expectant complacency, when the door opened and a woman, beautifully dressed and with a face that was more than worthy of the creation she wore, walked blithely into the room.

"Now, George, dear," she said, "are you ready for supper?"

To a man of his varied experiences there was nothing extraordinary in being addressed in terms of affection by a woman he had never seen before in his normal life. But that he should be invited to sup at an hour usually devoted to dinner, by one who was beyond doubt a member of the world which he himself adorned, appeared to George in the light of a miracle. And it did not escape his notice that beneath her pleasantly frivolous manner the lady was regarding him with a certain keenness as if she too had cause to wonder.

The true art of diplomacy is to proceed, and George hardly allowed himself a pause in which to register his surprise before he rose and assented with the grace that had cost his parents four thousand pounds.

"I don't know what the servants will think," his companion said, prettily, as they passed along the ferny corridor. "I never do know what they think; possibly about sun-spots or the blind Celtic fish."

"My man is the eighteenth European authority on the chemistry of the ancients," said George. "He writes monographs about it and sells my things to pay for having them printed."

"Of course that isn't true."

They laughed together as they entered the supper-room, a vast chamber of the dimensions of a banqueting hall.

"No, I'm afraid it's only conversation," George admitted, while secretly admiring the curves of her throat. "But all the true things have been said so often."

She looked at him oddly. "I wonder whether they have. Some things are true enough, but——" She screwed her lips into a grotesque smile and they sat down at the table in such an offhand way that George felt that he must have supped with her before in his dreams. The meal, though cold, was admirable, and the wines fit for an undergraduate in the first flush of his credit, but there was no sign of the servants who might wonder—what?

"This is an adventure," George said to himself, cheerfully; and then aloud: "I don't know about that, I'm sure" —he wished that he knew her Christian name. "I myself am to some extent a student of the extraordinary, and, if I may say so, I have seen some unusual things and been in some out-of-the-way places. But, really, the possible is soon exhausted and miracles are rare. Ninety-nine out of every hundred of my adventures are mere perversions of the obvious. In tabulating them I have divided them into ten groups——"

"And how many of the Commandments have you broken?" she asked, smiling queerly.

"All but one, I'm afraid," said George, wondering a little at her quickness.

She laughed aloud.

"Why, that's what you told my husband," she said. "You are not up to date."

Here was something to puzzle about, thought George. This pretty problem had a husband and he had told him—and what in thunder did she mean by her last remark?

"By the way, where is your husband now?" he said, casually.

In itself this does not appear a very humorous question, but it certainly had a remarkable effect on the lady.

"Some people would call you grim," she murmured, between her shrill ripples of laughter. "Perhaps you'd like to have him down to sup with us; he's upstairs, you know."

"Well, I don't mind, you know," said George, feeling his way towards an explanation, "so long as I do not lose the pleasure of supping with you."

The lady looked at him with bright lights of excitement in her eyes.

"It would be a thrill, wouldn't it?" she said, rising, "if you'll help me to carry him."

So her husband was an invalid, a madman, or a picture. "I hope it isn't leprosy," George thought to himself. "There's something about this woman——" But he dutifully followed her upstairs.

She stopped outside a door on the first floor, with her hand on the handle.

"Shall I knock?" she said, flippantly.

George nodded, and her little knuckles set a playful echo trotting lightly down the passage like a child released from lessons. Then she opened the door and beckoned him in.

Thirty seconds later he reeled out of the room into the corridor with a white face and his body shaking.

"Good God! What have you done?" he cried.

The woman, who had followed him, was hardly less disturbed.

"Don't say you've got a conscience! Don't say you've repented! You've been splendid up to now."

He glared at her fiercely.

"What do you mean?" he stammered.

She stood looking at him in obvious amazement.

"It's not possible," she muttered to herself, frowning. Then she caught him by the arm and led him up to a mirror which was set upright in the wall. "Look!" she said, watching him.

On the white front of his shirt, just below his tie, George saw the imprint of four red fingers, and as he looked he wavered and sickened, and thought of the dead thing in the room behind him.

"I thought it so bizarre of you to change everything but that," said the woman, in the tone of one who is disappointed.

George pulled himself up and turned his eyes on her pitifully. "What am I to do?" he cried.

"I should think we had better finish our supper."

He followed her down to the supper-room like a child, and like a child he marvelled that the bitterness of his regret should leave the fact unaltered. The woman seated herself and proceeded to eat with a good appetite, blinking at him over the flowers, while he sat miserably fingering his glass.

"You want about a magnum and a bottle," she said, critically. "It's no use wasting any regrets on him. He was really of very little use to me."

"What are you?" he said, suddenly, gulping a glass of wine.

"That's much better," she replied, with a nod of approval. "I? Well, I'm a widow, I suppose."

He looked at her speechlessly.

"You see," she went on, calmly, "melodrama isn't life, nor is it rational for people of education to fall back on crudities when they do have an excuse for self-expression. Now, what is the situation? I wanted my freedom without a bother, and I have got it. You have spent your life in a search for adventures, and here you are. He—no, I'm not as bad as that. I won't say anything about him. But you can go away after supper and call it a dream if you like."

George drank another glass of wine.

"The body!" he said.

"Polymelus!" said the woman, thoughtfully. "I never thought of that. What *does* one do with bodies? I suppose I've got a trunk somewhere, but I never was good at packing, and my maid is one of the new sort, you know, and objects to everything out of the beaten track. I shouldn't be surprised to hear that she was a novelist."

"Oh, I can't! I can't!" cried George. "Say it's a joke! Say it isn't true!"

She shook her head at him reproachfully.

"More of your Lyceum imaginings, George," she said, sadly. "It wouldn't go down at the Court Theatre, you know. As for this business of a murder, if I must use your sentimental terms, I can easily burn down the house, or something. Thompson, my late husband's valet, now, is a very sensible man, and a thousand pounds, or perhaps two——"

George cut short her remarks, and surprised her by uttering a laugh like the bark of a startled collie.

"Do you know what I ought to do?" he queried.

"Nothing," she said, promptly.

"No, it isn't that. I ought to take that pretty neck of yours and choke you. What difference would it make to anyone, to anyone on earth?"

"Well, you're not going to do it or you wouldn't have mentioned it," she said, calmly. "Besides, it would be bathos. Now, if you'll be a good boy and go home and forget all about it, it will save a lot of bother. And I will give you a very sound piece of advice."

"Well?"

"Don't come out adventuring any more. You haven't got the temperament for it. You allow yourself to be turned from the pursuit of your ideals by trivialities. It is so silly."

George looked at her for a few seconds with leaden eyes.

"I think I shall go home," he said. "I suppose you can manage the body; for all I know you may have done this sort of thing a dozen times."

"No, it's the first time," she said. "But there's really no reason to make a fuss. You've only completed your set."

He walked out into the entrance hall, and the woman followed him. When he reached the door he turned round and looked her in the face.

"If I gave myself up for this——" he said.

"I'm afraid I should laugh dreadfully; it would seem so noble of you."

He bit his lip and opened the door.

"This is my last adventure," he said, with a faint note of tragedy in his voice. "Good-night!"

"At any rate, I think I should wear a hat if I were you," the lady remarked, sweetly.

And so at last he went.

"The servants will be back to-morrow, and it is ten o'clock," thought the woman. "I'm going to be pretty busy, it seems; but anyhow, I spoilt his exit." And she went back to finish her supper.

LITTLE MISTRESS MINE

We have loved the quiet sky
With its tender arch of blue,
Little mistress mine—Good-bye!

LONDON BRIDGE on a golden day in early March. It was eleven o'clock in the morning, when the pavement is chiefly given up to loafers, and the passing of business men and women is temporarily checked. A few errand-boys were there and a painter of cheap water-colours and there was a steady flow of heavy wagons and empty 'buses across the bridge. Finally, at the City end of the bridge, leaning over the parapet towards the Pool, there stood a man, or rather a youth, and a woman.

"So you see, Herbert," she said, "this is the end of the story."

A few belated gulls, forgetful of the sea, floated by, their keen black eyes searching eagerly for sprats. The maker of cheap water-colours threw them a piece of bread and they flashed down to the water with a flicker of quick wings; but the youth was looking at the woman's face.

"Only six months," he said hoarsely. "Six months, and you said it would last for ever!"

"Remember I am thirty-three, Herbert," she said, watching him. "Six months is an eternity for a woman of that age. Besides——"

The youth looked at her gloomily.

"There is someone else, I suppose," he said.

"I happen to like you rather," she went on without heeding his interruption, "and I might almost have been your mother. It makes a difference, you know."

She smiled on him; one of the charming, ingenuous smiles that made her face look boyish.

"You did not say that at first," he cried, "and I—I am very old for my age. Everybody says so."

The woman looked quietly at his large broad head, his rough neglected hair and the queer features that never seemed to match.

"You have nice eyes," she remarked inconsequently. "I believe I've noticed it before—the night I met you down at Greenwich perhaps. Stars, you remember, and the park of pale shadows and the children in their white pinafores gliding between the trees like moths. There must have been a blue moon that night, I think."

"What does it all mean, Kitty?" he said. "I can't do without you. I really can't. All my good times have been with you——"

"You have been a good boy, a very good boy indeed, and we have enjoyed ourselves very much. And now you must go back to school and do some work. That's because I'm fonder of you than I expected, I suppose."

"I don't understand."

"You never will understand. At least not until you have a boy of your own and he's eighteen years old."

"But the office is all right. You haven't interfered with my work. You haven't really, Kitty. I never did care for it much."

"I don't know what I have done. I wish I did. Perhaps it's too late. Herbert, I wish we were on that barge with the white dog going down to Greenwich. Yes. Together."

"Kitty, you don't want to leave me. You don't!".

She went on talking with half-shut eyes as if she had not heard him.

"Even down to the sea, and the dog would bark up

and down the boat this sunny March morning, and the smooth, green lands would slip away and the sea would come up, the sea of pure hearts, and you would look into my face and call me——" She opened her eyes suddenly, and her cheeks reddened. "I'm talking nonsense," she said.

"I wish I knew what had happened," said Herbert.

"London Bridge is broken down and you shall build it up; with walls of paper and printer's ink for cement. And I shall look on and say, 'I did it.' Unless it's too late."

"I don't understand."

"It is the duty of prophets not to be understood till after the event. It prevents the individual from upsetting his destiny."

"I think you're jolly unkind to-day, Kitty. You say you don't want to see me again for years, and you don't tell me why, or anything."

The woman turned to him thoughtfully. "I suppose," she began. "No! wait a minute."

The minute was a long one. The artist folded his easel and went his way to paint "Dawn over the Tower Bridge." Two children stopped for a minute on the bridge to turn a skipping-rope for a child while they chanted strange shibboleths:

> Fie, Cissie Fisher, I'll tell your mother,
> I saw a black man kiss you in the parlour.
> How many kisses did he give you?
> 1, 2, 3, 4. Salt, mustard, vinegar, pepper!

The skipping child broke down and they moved on. Even the expert cannot long survive a "pepper."

"Understand," she said, "that I do this because I am fond of you. Too fond of you. I did not know things

could happen like this. I have met men who have started
like you, very young. And—they were not nice men. And
they were not men who had done their work. Men must
do their work—yes, and women too. I have learned this
and I am doing mine now."

"Go on," said Herbert.

"I believe that I have been wrong all this time. Not
ordinarily wrong, but really wrong, you know. I mean in
the way I liked you."

"I *loved* you, Kitty."

"In the way I loved you, Herbert. I think—if I had been
you—I mean that I not only wish you to be a man, but I
wish you to be a man for all you are worth. That way—
you understand."

"Well——"

"And I am stopping you, so I am going away."

"You will help me, Kitty."

"That's what I hoped. No, it's what I wanted. But it
isn't true. It never is true. As far as a man's work goes,
woman is only another obstacle to overcome. I can't help
you, Herbert, except by keeping out of your path. I can
only watch you!"

A small boy with impudent, bright eyes stopped and
touched Herbert's sleeve.

"Tell me the time please, guv'nor."

When the boy had gone, she continued:

"You see, it is not as though we were alone. There are
all these other people. Girls perhaps. They are bound to
come in sooner or later. That's why I preach to you
so; because I'm jealous of someone you have not met
yet."

"I shall never love anyone as I have loved you."

"Of course, there won't be the same freshness, but there
will be something else quite good in its way. I think she

will be young and she will have dark hair. She will speak with her lips shut and teach in a Sunday School. If you had crossed my hand with a silver piece I might have given you a better fate."

"You are very unkind."

"At least I have never called you Bert. You asked me to when I met you first."

Herbert winced. "You have taught me so many things," he said humbly. "Why must you go?"

"In five years' time you will put that more neatly, I expect. Why is it that when one meets the perfect woman she always develops a conscience? Yours is only calf love you know, Herbert."

"Is his love better then?"

"I wonder whether any woman is perfect. It pleases me to see you jealous even though I mean—yes! I do mean to let you go."

"I know you are in the wrong, Kitty. You are doing all the talking."

She laughed aloud.

"Who told you that, I wonder, or is it your own discovery? It doesn't matter; nothing matters save the avoidance of the ridiculous. Good-bye."

She held out her hand, but he looked away.

"I shan't take it, Kitty! It isn't fair."

"I shall come back when you want me."

"I want you now——"

"No, you don't. You've had all the best of me and I must keep the rest. One of these days perhaps——"

He looked at her with dull, incredulous eyes and she smiled back with a tremulous mouth.

"Very well, then," he said suddenly and touched her hand.

"Good-bye!" she said again and turned away over the

L

bridge, leaving him to walk back to the office with a slow step and an air of stifled misery.

She stopped a four-wheeler half-way across the bridge and told the man to drive her home; a woman can cry in a four-wheeler without being perceived.

THE INHERITOR

ARTHUR BRADFORD pushed away his plate of tepid bacon and eggs and looked at the letter with swimming eyes. His aunt Geraldine, whom he had only seen as a stern vision that disapproved of his mother, had died intestate, leaving property to the value of over twelve thousand pounds.

And he was the only heir, he, Arthur Bradford, clerk in the employment of the Commonwealth Insurance Co., on a salary of £115 a year.

Over twelve thousand pounds—at four per cent. that would be nearly five hundred a year, perhaps he would get five per cent., he knew people in the City who were wise in such matters, six hundred pounds a year—the bed-sitting-room with the faded, silly furniture grew dim and uncertain to his sight; the white table-cloth seemed to move beneath his fingers; it was all so strange.

Once, three years before, when he had first met Molly, he had applied ambitiously for a vacant post, and had narrowly missed getting it. The salary would have been £150 a year, and it was pleasant to recall the old bitterness, now that he need work no more, now that he was rich.

He walked to the window and opened it with fumbling fingers. The sky was grey and threatened rain, and at any other time the outlook would have depressed him; but to-day he felt that he had at last inherited London, its streets and shops and horses were in a manner his; he could ride in its carriages if he wished.

He thought of Molly in the little dull shop across the water, the shop that sold penny packets of notepaper and gorgeous penholders and ill-printed classics bound in cloth for eightpence halfpenny, and at the thought he smiled. For they could marry now, they for whom marriage had always been an impracticable ideal, they for whom love had been perforce little but a series of Sunday afternoon walks in the park; they could marry and live where they pleased, even in the green country of which folk wrote in books.

Other men, he reflected, in the face of so great an inheritance would make haste to forget the little shop assistant whom they had loved when they were poor. But that was not his way. No! She should share his fortune and serve at a counter no more. He felt that he was not a mean man.

He looked at his watch and saw that he was too late to be in time at his office; and he did not care. He would send them a cheque for a month's salary in lieu of notice, and he found a certain pleasure in the thought that his sudden resignation at balancing time would inconvenience them. Perhaps they would see that his services were worth more than the paltry sum they had been paying him, perhaps even they would offer him an increase in order to tempt him back. He pictured himself declining with a certain courteous dignity; after all, they were a decent enough lot of fellows, he bore them no ill-will.

The rain still held off, and he found the room close and too small for his new aspirations and put on his hat and coat to go into the streets; he would walk across to the shop in Lambeth and tell Molly of his good luck, of their good luck, rather; that would be the graceful way to put it, and then how glad she would be! Of course he was only doing the decent thing, yet he could not help feeling that there were a good many men who would fail to do it in similar circumstances, for although Molly was a quite exceptional girl, she was not, of course, of the same social rank as——

He checked himself with a certain shame and glanced in

the faces of the people who were passing to see if they had detected a thought that seemed to him treacherous; then he laughed aloud at his fear and the thing that had caused it.

Why, he was on his way now to tell her of his good fortune. Over twelve thousand pounds, say, if he invested it carefully, some six hundred and fifty a year; how happy she would be! He was going to tell her immediately, the very hour he had heard of it himself. Surely that was what a good man would do.

Now he would be able to buy her new dresses in place of the old drab blouses and skirts and the soiled aprons. And they would forget that she had ever worn such things and served in a cheap stationer's shop, or if they did recall them it would be with pleasure, because they belonged to a grey past and would come again no more.

How mean the shop was, he thought, as he approached it, and how grey and soiled the street in which it stood. Dirty babes too young for school scrambled in the gutters while their mothers, unkempt and ragged, breathed gin and profanity from the doors of the decaying houses. The few shops with their muddy fronts and unclean windows appeared to be on the verge of failure; the one in which Molly worked might well be, he thought, for who in such a neighbourhood would want notepaper or gaudy penholders or cheap ill-printed copies of Ainsworth's novels?

He stopped before the shop and looked through the window past the sheets of verses by the talented author of "The Fireman's Wedding," and saw that Molly was standing inside behind the counter; so he slipped quietly through the open door to take her by surprise.

She was fixing picture post-cards of the most fatuously vulgar character in melancholy rows by means of paper fasteners, and hanging these rows as they were completed from the long gas bracket that was suspended from the ceiling. The dust from the swinging bracket had made her face dirty, there were smudges on her blouse and on her apron, she did not look so pretty as she did on Sunday afternoon in the park. When she looked up and saw him there was mingled with her surprise that he should come to visit her during office hours, obvious annoyance that he should find her in such an untidy condition; but he had news, wonderful news for her.

"Over twelve thousand pounds, Molly, over twelve thousand pounds!"

When he had finished his story and displayed the letter she burst into tears.

So this was the end of his fine thinking and of his generosity, this was the manner in which she received the news of his good fortune, of their good fortune. Arthur Bradford tapped his fingers on the counter in his annoyance. He did not know that she was crying because her face was dirty and she was drab and old—because the shop was dark and the post-cards vulgar and the boxes on the upper shelves so covered with dust that to move them was torment—because the little boys of the street were wont to run into the shop and mock her across the counter.

Still she cried; Arthur could see two women looking curiously through the window and a third approaching to see what they were looking at, and he saw, as if he were a neutral observer, himself the rich man standing in the dark, low shop pleading desperately with a dirty, ill-dressed girl who received his entreaties with sobs and chokings; he felt a wild anger rise in him that anything should have happened to mar his happiness on such a day of good fortune.

Then the horror overcame him; he saw himself and his business laid before a scornful, grinning crowd, he felt that he had allowed himself to be bound to a world of muss and vulgarity and grimy tears at the moment when fortune had given him wings to rise; he saw love as a thing that choked and sniffled.

The crowd had lapped across the door when he burst out of the shop.

Still the rain held off. Folk passed along the twilit streets with their lips parted as if they were thirsty. There would be no peace until the yellow clouds broke and washed the heavy air.

So this was the end and he was a bad man after all. And yet he felt that he had tried to do the decent thing. Why had she cried and made him look ridiculous? Why had everything been so dusty and grey? It was true that it was not too late to go back, but he knew he would never do it. He was free; and even the thought of the untidy little figure crying as though its heart would break in the dark empty shop would not make him retrace his steps to a grey street and a grey business. Was he not rich? And after all, she— she would forget him and marry someone of her own class. Oh, he was a hound and a blackguard, but still he had meant well. A good many men would have dropped her without telling her of their good luck, but he had told her at once, and now he was free and would forget all about it.

Over twelve thousand pounds. What might he not do?

On his table at home he found another letter from the lawyers. Perhaps they were sending a cheque on account.

As he opened it, the storm burst and the rain dashed against the window-panes with a muffled roar, like the tapping of many fingers on a counter. So the old woman who had disliked his mother had made a will; there was a matter of twelve thousand pounds for three charities, and he, Arthur Bradford, who had lost Molly, would be a clerk for evermore. He dropped his face in his hands and cried like a child.

A HUNGERFORD INTERLUDE

BRADFORD stood on Charing Cross foot-bridge and gazed steadfastly into the water, a pleasant enough occupation, and infinitely preferable to the odour of the onions which were being cooked for his supper at his lodgings.

While he was thus engaged he became aware of a man who was pacing nervously up and down the wooden planking, as a timid passenger might pace the deck of a ship. Now those who use this deplorable bridge do so in a steady business-like fashion, covering the ground rapidly, with minds intent on catching trains or, if incorrigibly lazy, stopping frankly like Bradford to look, after a common human weakness, over the edge.

But this one did neither, and Bradford turned round to look at this unconventional monster, who neither was honestly idle nor went about his business.

The stranger was not one of those men of strongly-marked features whom novelists love to describe; just an ordinary-looking member of the caste of pointed beards. And now you know him very well.

After a few more turns up and down he approached Bradford and asked, "How long do you propose to remain here?"

"Why?" said Bradford, naturally enough.

The man hesitated a little before replying. "You see," he said timidly, "the fact is I wish to jump over the edge."

"Oh!" said Bradford, and after a pause, "What for?"

The timidity of the stranger increased until Bradford found it quite painful to see. He stuttered and mouthed a long harangue without Bradford being able to catch anything except the two words "My wife." Then he stopped.

"Your wife," said Bradford encouragingly, but the stranger read another meaning in his voice.

"Oh no," he cried with passion. "It is not that. Heaven forbid. She—she—my wife says, in fact, well." He wandered in a confused tangle of words.

"Well?" said Bradford patiently.

"My wife says I have broken her heart and so"—with a pain-pitiful reminiscence of the Surrey Theatre—"and so I must die!"

Bradford suppressed a primitive desire to laugh and tried to grapple with the unreality of the scene. "Your wife says that," he said feebly.

The man shook with impatience. "She says that I have broken her heart, and so I say I must die."

Bradford meditated. The man was so timid and in a way so matter-of-fact. He talked of suicide as one talks of duty, half-heartedly, but nevertheless as a thing to be done. Still, he might be joking. "Are you serious?" he asked.

The man shook his head. "I know," he said with the sigh of an unsuccessful artist. "I know that my manner is sadly lacking in conviction. But really you know it does sound so silly to talk of death and that sort of thing even when one has quite made up one's mind."

That was just how Bradford was feeling himself. "It does indeed," he said frankly. "But will not your wife relent?"

"My wife is a queen of women," said the other proudly. "It is I who have repented. I have broken her heart. I must die."

Bradford thought vaguely of the police, but how could he betray this timid trust? Then he had an idea.

"You know," he cried, "the worst of it is I can swim!"

"Well?" said the man.

"I should have to rescue you for the sake of my own respect, and in the effort I might be drowned. That," he said, finding the stranger's style infectious, "that would be unjust."

The would-be suicide looked melancholy.

"What a nuisance," he said at last. "Still," more hopefully, "you might turn your back for a minute, you know."

"No," said Bradford firmly. "It won't do. If you do it at all now you will ruin my whole life. I will think I might have stopped you."

The stranger sighed, "I suppose you are right."

"Yes," said Bradford, warming to his part. "I am very sorry to hinder you in any way, but you see you shouldn't have told me."

"What a nuisance," repeated the man.

"You can go back and no one will be any the wiser," Bradford suggested.

"I—I wrote a letter," said the other, troubled, "to my wife you know. Penitence. Brute. Set her free. Watery grave." He relapsed into vague mutterings.

Bradford whistled his perplexity. "By Jove," he murmured, "you have put your foot in it."

"Yes," said the stranger, pleased with Bradford's sympathy and the complete blackness of his own outlook, "I think I have."

Then ensued a silence which lasted until Bradford's brow ached with the ornamental frown which he thought betrayed the proper amount of sympathetic interest in the other's worries. Then arrived Fate in the shape of a large and excited woman, who gave expression to unrestrained relief when she beheld the stranger.

"Kate!" cried the latter, with nothing now of the melodramatic in his voice.

And then and there before Bradford's eyes they embraced heartily.

The woman remembered first.

"Come away," she cried. "And don't be silly."

And the man followed her humbly enough without saying anything to Bradford in farewell. That one watched them go and wondered if he was really awake.

"How absurd!" he murmured, and tried to laugh.

But somehow he couldn't.

A LOST ARTIST

I DON'T profess to know what the moral of this story may be; or rather, to put it more honestly, I am afraid of the obvious moral. I ask Caxton, and Caxton throws out his hands and shrugs his shoulders and speaks of other matters, which are signs that Caxton is annoyed. I speak about it to the fellows at the office, and they laugh, which might be taken as a symbol of comprehension, if they did not invariably laugh when they don't understand anything, to prove that it is a matter unworthy of consideration, an outside thing, *ergo* folly.

I cannot but admire their consistency, for they laughed right through the whole affair.

Williams, who is my hero, was a clerk in our office some ten years ago. He had been there some ten more and had managed to acquire the correct clerkly expression; the blinking eyes, the thick fussy moustache and the bald spot on the top of his head where the tall hat covered it, all the qualities, in fact, which constitute a good clerk. From his appearance one would have prophesied him a steady four-teen years' service of the firm, marred by neither serious errors nor brilliancy, and terminated with a pleasant potter-ing suburban existence. For the rest he did not have much to talk about outside "shop," and we always called him "*old* Williams." Now the one thing certain about a clerk of the Williams type is their certainty; it is possible to judge years beforehand where they will get to—what jobs will be given them, what salary they will obtain. Their career knows neither leaps nor checks. Williams had been there ten years and was getting two hundred. In another ten years he would be getting three hundred, and so on. The rest might achieve sudden distinction or the sack, but Williams we thought was safe.

And one day Williams walked in his unambitious way into the chief's office and resigned, in order, as he put it, to take up an important musical post.

All these years he had had a secret vice, though we had never suspected it. He played the violin.

Of course he stayed out his month's notice. He was far too good a clerk to dream of upsetting his office by a sudden departure. But though he heard his future discussed freely round him, though he was closely questioned by the most wily of our men, he would say nothing more. He had studied music for some years. He liked it better than clerking. He was going on the twelfth of next month. And that was all.

The days passed quickly enough, the twelfth came and Williams drew the salary due to him, said a staid good-bye to those of us whom he knew and passed out; I, for one, never expecting to see or hear of him any more.

One felt instinctively that he would not set the Thames on fire with anything he touched. He was a moderate little man. A new junior was drafted in, some of us got a move up one, and our world revolved as before. As I have said, he was not the man to make much difference anywhere.

It was about two years after this that I learnt dominoes as played in the City, the scientific game. At first sight the fact does not seem of primary importance, but it was the cause of my renewing my acquaintance with Williams, for it drew me to the Persian café.

The Persian café is a large underground room in the City where the elect drink coffee and play dominoes or chess. The tables are marble-topped, and on a field night the clicking of the dominoes all over the room resembles the sound of castanets.

It is a not unpleasant place when the air is full of tobacco-smoke, and the coffee is always extremely good.

It was here that my instructors brought me, as a matter of course, and it was on those marble-topped tables that I was initiated into the mysteries of the game—or rather games, for there are variants. On the wall I saw a notice to the effect that twice a week a Hungarian string orchestra ministered to the pleasures of the frequenters of the café.

The next night was one of these red-letter occasions, the orchestra consisting of two violins, a violoncello and a piano, and the first violin, as you may have guessed, was Williams, formerly of ours.

I must confess that at first sight he appeared to have altered. His moustache was trained somewhat differently, his hair was appreciably longer, his raiment was a weird caricature of a uniform, and above all there seemed to be a sort of dignity about the man that was lacking in the old Williams. But I had not the smallest doubt as to his identity. His important musical post was that of leader of this little orchestra. It was for this that he had thrown up his two hundred a year and prospects. Our certain Williams.

I did not shine as a domino aspirant that night. I was too much engaged in watching the first violin. He was magnificent.

Understand that I do not refer to his playing. I do not know much about music, but I could not help realising that Williams was no Paganini. No, he was something infinitely greater, Paganini and Don Quixote together if you like, or Tartarin and Kubelik—that was the way he struck me. I felt myself overcome with that sense of awe

that secretly fills every Philistine when he knows that he is
looking at an artist. Perhaps you do not admire the results,
but you are stricken with the seriousness of purpose that
has produced them. In fact, the less you understand, the
more you are afraid. It was so with me when I heard
Williams play the violin. Of course it was no solo, there
were others; the humorous man with the long, sandy hair
who reminded one of photographs of Mark Twain; the
'cellist who had the jaw of a prize-fighter, and the pianist
who looked like nobody in particular, but for me, only old
Williams counted. And he was quite splendid, only to be
described lyrically. His face shone like the summer sun and
he rocked to and fro like a rose-bush in a squally wind, his
whole body vibrating with the music. And Lord! when
the end of each piece came, and a few of the audience would
tap feebly with their dominoes by way of applause, what
could be more dignified than the proud bending of his
body, signifying as it did that while taking no credit to
himself, he, as an unworthy representative of the Art of
Music, thanked them? That was how I read it, and how
could one criticise the music where the musician was so
overpowering? My only regret was that the old boy did
not have a more appreciative audience, especially when I
saw his eyes scanning the inattentive room between the
pieces, as if their owner were searching for roses.

I waited till it was all over and then went up and spoke
to him. He was very shy, but he spoke quietly and with
dignity of small beginnings, and there was no bitterness in
his voice when he deplored the character of his audience.
They did not understand, it was a pity—that was all.

I must confess that it was with some hesitation that I
mentioned my discovery to the men at the office. We were
all such Philistines, you see. But in spite of that I knew I
could trust them to do the decent thing by Williams, and I

saw that a judicious claque could do much to cheer his lot in the Persian café.

At all events I let it out, and the next time Williams was due to play there were some twenty of us scattered up and down the room amongst the domino men. I think we worried them a good deal that night. The applause that followed the playing of each piece annoyed them, as a thing unwonted, and when towards the close of the evening we forced an encore there were murmurings.

But Williams' face was a sight for the gods, and we all left the café in a healthy glow of virtue. I say I had trusted our men to do the right thing, but as events proved I had hardly calculated on the effect our claque would have on the other frequenters of the place. But the fact is they were all Philistines too, and when they found the orchestra so much appreciated, they began to think there must be something in it, and that their attitude of aloofness would, if sustained, mark them as men ignorant in artistic matters.

So by degrees they all joined in, until at the end of two months the thing had blossomed to a craze, and band nights found the café crowded, and dominoes banished from the tables. Every item in the programme met with hurricanes of applause, and Williams was forced, by popular mandate, to render solos.

He told me that the management had doubled his salary unasked, but the place always was run on decent lines.

All this was well enough, and yet I must own that I was afraid when I saw to what lengths the business had gone. It had done Williams no end of good for the time being, but the craze could not last, and when it reached the length of pelting him with roses nightly I knew that it was time to act.

So then I did what I ought to have done in the first place. I went to Caxton.

Caxton is the great musical critic and no end of a swell in places where these things matter, and he has a theory that it is good for his mind to converse with fools outside business hours, so to speak; or at least that is the way he explains his encouragement of my barbaric City conversation. When I find his attitude of superiority annoying, I merely have to picture him as a clerk in an office and all is well.

So I went to Caxton and told him the tale of Williams. He was interested, though he pooh-poohed my observations concerning the nobility of Williams' attitude before the public. But he promised to come and expose the charlatan if that was what I wanted, and I had to be contented.

By this time the first freshness of the thing had worn off for me, and I was consequently at full liberty to watch Caxton, when I got him to the Persian café. But his is a quiet unexpressive sort of visage, and I could not obtain much information, while from his lips there came forth nothing but appreciation of the coffee. He did not know there was anything so civilised in the City, he said. Nor did he convey much light on his views in the cab on our way back.

Omitting oaths, the only connected remark I heard was, "He ought to have written verses when he was a boy, like the rest of us," and this appeared somewhat cryptic at the time.

I think he also said I was a d——d fool to meddle with other people's affairs; but I was not sure of this, and he would not heed my questions.

But the next time I went to the café Williams was not there, and a stranger was performing in his place to a dis-

M

contented audience. I left the place hastily and took an omnibus up to Caxton's flat. He was dressing for dinner, but I ignored his oak and burst in upon him.

"What have you done with Williams?" I cried.

"Williams," he repeated absently.

"My Williams."

Caxton hesitated visibly, which is unusual with him, but I suppose he saw I was desperate.

"Mr. Williams takes up an appointment in the Wonderland Insurance Company on the eighteenth," he said, struggling with his white tie.

I looked at him in amazement.

"Good Lord! what did you do?" I said.

Caxton tried to continue dressing unmoved, but he made a fine mess of his tie. "D——n you," he said. "Get away!"

"What did you do?" I repeated.

Caxton almost lost his temper. "I told him that he was a fool," he said. "And he did the melodramatic, broke his violin and so forth. And presently he became sensible and I got him a job. That's all. Now go! for the Lord's sake."

I went away, and as I went, I forgave Caxton for his amazing lie, because he is a modest man at heart and is ashamed, like the rest of us, of being discovered doing good. Also I saw that he was sorry for Williams, and angry because things had gone wrong with him somewhere.

Of one thing I am sure. Caxton did not tell him he was a fool, and for my part I do not think he was. There was something admirable—but what the devil does a Philistine know about such matters?

I have seen Williams once since.

It was at a City smoker, and oddly enough Caxton had come with me to get materials for a humorous article on music in the City.

In the middle of the evening Williams turned up, and did funny things with a violin, played it like a banjo, imitated a cat, and such fooleries, and he didn't do it badly either.

But I felt annoyed for some reason or other, and Caxton looked furious.

His turn went very well, and there were enthusiastic demands for an encore at the conclusion. And he stood there smiling, and bowing away, in something of the old manner, and I felt very sick. Till all of a sudden he turned white as a sheet and slunk sheepishly off the platform.

"Stage fright," said Caxton brutally.

But we both knew that he had remembered.

A POET'S HOLIDAY

THE PHILOSOPHY OF TRAVEL

IT may be said that a man is bound to the agreeable illusion of youth until he no longer expects to find something rather wonderful round the next corner. It is this youthful capacity for wonder that sends grown men laden with tinned meats to the North Pole; it is this that nerves the seafaring trip-per to make forlorn excursions to Boulogne; it is this that induces small boys to thrust their heads into rabbit-holes. When we are disillusioned and realise that wherever we go on the round world we take our limitations with us, that it is only in our own hearts that wonder can be born, the desire to visit other countries becomes little more than the desire to escape from an environment of which we are weary. We cannot travel away from our passions—our thirst for song, our hunger for expression, our theory of joy that is one long pain. The man who is hard ridden by his desires will find peace no easier to win in the midst of the desert than by his own fireside. His body may travel ceaselessly between the two Poles; his mind and his heart are imprisoned still in their lifelong cells.

I think that there must be a spirit of childishness in most people that enables them to take pleasure in seeing new things without asking whether their novelty has any signi-ficance. It is this naïve curiosity that accounts for the extra-ordinary tediousness of the letters that we receive from friends and relatives travelling abroad. They describe churches and museums and picture-galleries, or it may be lakes and mountains; it would be more interesting if they would tell us how these marvels really impressed them apart from the tyrannous approbation of guide-books. As a matter of fact we know very well that it takes a great man to appreciate great works of art, and our tourists would be far more sincere, and therefore far more amusing, if they would write about the things that excite them, though it be only the queer little gooseberry tartlets they have for lunch. But there is a kind of emotional snobbishness that will not confess to the pleasure that is to be derived from trifles, though it is only the very exceptional man who derives pleasure from anything else. Those who possess this especial vanity had better stop at home, for wherever they go they will learn nothing of men and women, and, more important still, nothing new of themselves. For, when all is said, there is this one advantage in moving from one place to another: we shall never discover Arcadia or escape the anguish of existence, but in a fresh environment we may succeed in exploring some untrodden byway of our own natures. Whether a man goes to Margate or the Himalayas, he may not hope to discover more than that.

And yet there is the illusion of the marvellous which makes it difficult for any human being to pack a portmanteau without sharing in some degree the feelings of a merchant-adventurer fitting out an expedition to the islands of rubies and gold. It may be doubted whether anyone ever wholly conquers this illusion, and for my part I confess that at such a time I find even a prosaic thing like a roll of collars or a cake of soap agreeably romantic. I feel compassion for the man whose soul is so dead that he can write labels for his luggage without a thrill of excitement. I remember how glad we were to do this at school when we were going home for the holidays, and even when it was a question of going back to school again. We were at pains, by aid of capitals and exclamation-marks, to impress the importance of our "tuck-boxes" on the railway mind. We lose something in later life by intrusting the carrying out of these trifling tasks to others; but repetition stales the adventure.

Well, our boxes are packed, either by ourselves or by someone else—our tickets are taken, and with a faint quickening of the pulse we prepare to set forth on our sentimental journey. Let us forget for once the philosophic truth that, after all the pains and discomforts of travel, we shall find ourselves exactly where we were before we started. Let us make-believe—any child can do it—that we are going to a place where the men are more kind and the women more beautiful than any we have known before— a place of young laughter and old song; above all, a place where we shall be masters of our own natures, and have peace at last from the wild unreason of our days.

The apples and flagons are in the rack overhead, and I have an agreeable companion, whose baggage chiefly consists of books of verse. There are people on the platform to see us off—Christine, still mindful of the wiles of Chloe, and a wise, sad little man who has made a great reputation as a wit by continually laughing at himself. For a painful twenty minutes we talk banalities, and I am reminded of a famous essay of Mr. Max Beerbohm's without being freed from the spell. Then the train starts, and relief gives us a fleet happiness.

It is three years since I last went to Brussels, and then I went on a cargo-steamer without any luggage at all. When we were within an hour of Antwerp I saw something which was a good example of the fact that the extraordinary is not always the wonderful. Within a hundred yards of our little vessel, in broad daylight on a calm sea, a great passenger-boat, the *Montezuma*, ran into a steamer fully laden with cargo and cut her nearly in two. There was no loss of life. The crew of the cargo-steamer had plenty of time to scramble up the sides of the *Montezuma* before the smaller

boat sank. The whole business was oddly unimpressive.
Somehow or other the calmness of the sea and the bright-
ness of the sunshine gave the calamity an air of artificiality,
and I have seen a far more convincing wreck on the stage of
Drury Lane Theatre. There was only one strange moment in all those pregnant minutes. The deck of the cargo-
boat was laden with agricultural implements, and just as
she sank I had a brief vision of green and red ploughs standing among the salty meadows of the sea. After that we
went down to breakfast.

This time I crossed in a fog, and the air was full of the
bleating of nervous ships. I walked up and down on the
deck, and looked in the faces of my fellow-travellers,
wondering why they, too, were at pains to journey from
one place to another when everywhere on earth joy has a
briefer hour than sorrow. I was going to visit Brussels and
Amsterdam and Paris, and afterwards other places, perhaps;
but wherever I went I should find men and women laughing, crying, hoping still. It is not necessary to travel in
order to behold such miracles, but there is a distemper of
the blood that finds tranquillity in wandering. Perhaps we
were all suffering from the same complaint, and the vessel
was in truth a hospital-ship. I recalled a poem of Ernest
Dowson's, and murmured it to the fog between the lamentations of the myopic ship, "For I go where the wind goes,
Chloe, and am not sorry at all." I doubt whether anyone on the boat had a better reason than that for their
pilgrimage.

LITTLE PARIS

WHEN children are pulled through picture-galleries by enthusiastic adults they have a pleasant way of turning their backs on the pictures and looking with an absorbed interest at the other students of art in their neighbourhood. It is possible that the children are right; indeed a not very thorough study of the question leaves me convinced that the people one meets in picture-galleries are more interesting than any pictures. But that is beside my point, which is that it is not the fault of the individual if he is impressed by the wrong things. Thus at Brussels there are some very good pictures and some very good architecture. A Belgian friend assured me that there are three things that Englishmen always go to see—the Palais de Justice, the Wiertz pictures, and a certain little Rabelaisian fountain that would, my friend said, have been pulled down years ago if it did not please the tourists to find the Belgians "shocking." To my eyes the Palais de Justice lacks dignity, and Wiertz was an artist with a touch of that madness that is not akin to genius; but I doubt whether my principal impression of Brussels is at all more dignified than that of the average tourist. Brussels, having wide streets and being moreover hilly, is a windy city, and if I had to make an allegorical drawing of the city and its inhabitants I think I should draw a picture of a cynic running after his hat. Everybody one meets here who is at all intelligent is proportionately cynical; but their splendid phrases of disillusionment are always spoilt by the malevolent genius of the place, which sends them running after their hats like children after butterflies. It is only indoors that they can bring their witty condemnation of life to a joyous conclusion.

This Belgian cynicism seems to me to cut far deeper than the delicate phrases with which many Frenchmen express a scepticism that they do not feel. It seems as if they had been endowed with a gift of destructive introspection that is fortunately rare among nations: "Geographically and racially, Belgium does not exist; we are a mixture of two races, speaking the language of a third. Brussels is a suburb of Paris, a kind of ambitious music-hall. We have a King by grace of England and France and Germany. He is like the Wiertz Collection—good to amuse the tourists. All our principal artists and men of letters live in Paris, for we are content to do everything a little less well than they do it there. At one time we hoped something from the Socialists, for they had some clever men at their head. But these men, who had once been rich, had only turned to Socialism in order to become rich again, and now that they have succeeded, the Socialists are as stupid as any one else. The inhabitants of Brussels are all monkeys—when they are not mimicking Paris they are copying some other place; but more Englishmen come here every year, so that we have a future. Meanwhile we are pulling down all the old houses to make room for them. They are very nice, and they spend a great deal of money, but the place will be too dear for us to live in it soon. Of course they call us names because we provide them with the kinds of amusement that they expect to find in wicked foreign countries; but we know that they always do that and don't really mean any harm." That is the sort of thing that I have heard twenty times during the last few days, and it is not less suggestive because the cynics take an obvious delight in coining their cynicisms.

In reality this kind of good-humoured bitterness is no new thing in Belgium. The attitude of the Belgians towards the late King Leopold was a case in point. The King disliked his subjects intensely because they were unambitious, and thwarted his very genuine desire to increase the importance of his kingdom. In revenge they laughed at him to their heart's content. I was in Brussels some years ago when a very scurrilous pamphlet was published attacking the King's too notorious private life. The pamphlet was bound in red, and for a week the whole city blushed joyously. The pamphlets were sold openly from one end of the place to the other; everybody bought them, and everybody laughed. Now the Belgians laugh no more at the late King Leopold, because they think that in his death he has robbed them of the millions they paid, very unwillingly be it said, for the Congo. Money is the one thing this very thrifty nation takes seriously. In some subtle way it is an additional offence that the King should have entrusted the defence of his will to a Socialist advocate. On the other hand, the new King is rather popular, and has, it is said, a smile for everyone; but at heart the country is lazily democratic.

As for the people who do not think, I should say they were quite as happy in Belgium as anywhere else. They eat well and drink well, and Brussels at all events is materially prosperous. One sees very few men and women whose poverty is below the level of self-respect. One sees no drunken people at all, though the facilities for drinking are extraordinary and beer is very cheap. Yet for all their economic welfare I do not detect that growth of intelligence that English Socialists would have us believe is the necessary consequence of cleanliness and good food. The London street-arab, with his dirt and his empty stomach, is far more alert than the relatively prosperous *gamin* of Brussels. In the poorer class cafés, where the men drink beer with heavy tranquillity, or play solemn games of cards, there is very little talk. The Belgians have, it seems to me, very little to talk about, so far have they narrowed their interests down to the immediate satisfaction of their senses. To eat well and drink well and smoke well, to have a good wife, *une femme pot-au-feu*, as someone defined it to me, and, above all, to have a stocking full of money for the bad days satisfies them wholly. They have no pride in their country or even in their city. Their local patriotism confines itself to grumbling at little details in the management of the trams or railways that interfere with their after-dinner comfort. At best they achieve an unenlightened materialism, at worst an unenlightened individualism.

This, of course, is a general impression rather than a reasoned study. But it is at least more generous than that formed by many intellectual Belgians. It is as pleasant as it is unexpected to hear those who have visited England praising the general popular intelligence at the expense of that of their own country. The best Belgians, they say, are Frenchmen, and this is true enough if we can conceive a France without illusions and without patriotism. Brussels is contented, and even proud, to call itself Little Paris; it intends to be a great deal more like Paris before it has done, modern Paris, the Paris of *café-chantants*, and music-halls, and other week-end delights being understood. But I would qualify my impression with the observation that intellectual Brussels does not extend its cynicism to matters of art. On such matters it is charmingly enthusiastic and agreeably catholic. It reads Kipling and Wells, Frank Harris and Chesterton, and discusses them with real interest and intelligence. The city is flooded with English books, and it is pleasant to reflect that they are not only read by English visitors.

IMPRESSIONS

IT is perhaps convenient to divide the impressions formed
by an individual into two groups or degrees: these are
emotional impressions and intellectual impressions. Our
first impressions are all emotional; our intellectual impressions come afterwards, when our reason has had time to
correct the superlative lyrics our senses love to scrawl on
the surface of our consciousness. Thus a few weeks ago,
in the window of a flower-shop in Bond-street, I found
among the noisy brilliance of lilies and orchids a little pot
of blue forget-me-nots. I tasted immediately the full joys
of the Wordsworthian simplicity—I felt like a little lamb
a-prancing on the hilltops, or like a child living in the heart
of the country, that teeming slaughter-house of Nature,
and yet innocent of all knowledge of death. That was the
emotional impression. Then it occurred to me that, for
all their modest simplicity, my little forget-me-nots were
as exotic as any of the other flowers. We do not find them
in England in the month of January, so they must have
come frozen from the Canaries, or pickled from the South
of France. Their simplicity was a pose, and only proved
them more perverse than their neighbours who flaunted
their gay foreign dresses without thought of deceit. That
was the intellectual impression. It will be seen that, though
they are contradictory, both my impressions were justifiable
as far as they went.

Most of my impressions of Brussels have reached
the second degree, and the enthusiasms that have sur-
vived the chastening process are not perhaps of a very
important character. I have eaten the best Roquefort

cheese I have ever tasted during the last few days, and I have drunk some home-made Chartreuse that was delicious. The reader may smile, but these are pleasures that are not illusory, and such pleasures are rare. I have discovered a waitress in a café who has read all the works of Anatole France, and who told me that she thought his style, though admirable, belonged to the eighteenth century rather than to the present day. I have drunk cherry beer, an historic and fortunately moribund beverage. I have been to three balls, two carnivals, and a fire. The balls were dull, the fire was amusing, the carnivals call for fuller treatment. But none of these things impressed me so much as the fact that the sensible Belgians had put a flower-shop down in the middle of a long arcade devoted otherwise solely to bookshops. I bought the "Memoirs of Casanova" for 4s. 6d., and a great bunch of violets for 5d., and felt that I had done a good day's shopping. I wonder whether sometimes they get the books of verse mixed up with the nosegays.

The first carnival led me to coin the aphorism that there is no sadder spectacle for the individual than the efforts of other people to amuse themselves. After the second carnival, in which I no longer filled the rôle of philosophic spectator, I discovered that the joy of crowds is a protest against the sorrow of individuals. Both these aphorisms are true, and it follows that in carnival time the wise man will make haste to don the fool's cap in order to spare himself the pain of observing the folly of others. Theoretically, if we admit that every man has a secret desire to lay aside his dignity from time to time, a carnival is rather a fine thing. To wear a fantastic costume is like trying on another person's character—a wholesome pastime for any man; while the huddling of houses together to form a city becomes almost reasonable if the citizens come out now

and again to dance and sing out of tune on the pavements.
In practice the carnivals at Brussels have fallen on ill days,
partly owing to the prohibition of confetti and partly because masking is now almost confined to children and
students, Apaches, and the general cosmopolitan riff-raff
of the place. It would be better, perhaps, if the game were
left to the children, who may be trusted to play all games
gracefully, and dance up and down the streets with extraordinary spirit and energy. The poorer children, who could
not afford to hire costumes, settled the problem simply
enough, the little girls donning their brothers' knicker-
bockers and the little boys their sisters' petticoats, and the
result was quaint and innocent and pretty. It may be my
prejudice against the Flemish character that caused me to
find the high spirits of the adults a little forced, though I
can understand and sympathise with the natural eagerness
of the Flemish women to wear masks. But, in spite of the
dubious character of many of the participants, the fun
seemed harmless enough; and, again, I noticed a surprising
absence of drunkenness, above all surprising to anyone who
has studied the bearing of British crowds on bank holidays.

It will be seen that the carnival did not impress me par-
ticularly, but it helped me to understand Brussels. Like
most cities, it really consists of a number of cities imper-
fectly mingled, but on Shrove Tuesday it seemed for a while
to have blended into a recognisable whole. The bourgeois
Brussels was joined for an hour or two with the Brussels of
the tourist; the Brussels of the Apache touched the Brussels
of the middle-class Englishman, who lives here because he
can be rich on a moderate income. For a moment I seemed
to see a great unshapen beast, heartless, and with only a
small brain, but with strong instincts and a subtle tongue;
gourmand rather than *gourmet*, keenly avaricious, but for
the rest torpid, heavy, sluggish. Then—really, we can't
N

help our impressions—I saw instead a little cat who washed her face drowsily in front of the fire, with one eye on the mouse-hole in the corner by the coal-scuttle. I stretched out my hand and the cat purred. I don't know that I believe in the permanent truth of either of these impressions myself; but perhaps I shall never see Brussels as one city again.

A poet, as M. Abel Torcy remarked to me the other night, is an *animal de luxe*, and, personally, I find this a good country for such animals. It is pleasant to be able to claim the profession of poet without arousing either mirth or sympathy. In Brussels there are a great many poets and very few volumes of Belgian verse. In England there are a great many volumes of verse and very few poets. Whether this is due to the efficiency of the one country or to the thrift of the other, I do not know. But at all events the Belgian poets are more satisfying to the eye than the majority of their English *confrères*. They look fat and well-nourished, and the luxuriance of their hair and beards is astonishing and delightful. I have always thought that a poet gains by being unconventional in his appearance; in no other way can he so easily secure the solitude that is necessary for the development of his art. In Brussels, however, the musicians are quite as wild as the poets, and even more numerous; so that the most rebellious of poets runs the risk of being mistaken for a member of an orchestra, a man who draws his salary regularly every week. It is this, perhaps, that makes the Belgian poets seem a little bitter.

The fire which it was my good fortune to witness on the night of my arrival had its curious aspect. The upper half of an hotel in the principal quarter of the city was burnt out, and by the time we reached the place the roof had already fallen in, though the firemen were still playing on the building. We passed quite easily through the crowd into the café on the ground-floor, and found it brilliantly lit with electric-light, though water was pouring through the ceiling all over the room. We sat down at a little table that almost escaped the torrent, and immediately a waiter appeared with a napkin over his arm and asked us for our orders. No one seemed in the least excited, though these were the firemen who, we were told, wept tears of rage during the fatal seven-minutes' fire at the Exhibition because they found there was an utterly inadequate pressure of water. Everyone I meet in Brussels is anxious to say how sorry they were that all the beautiful English exhibits should have been burnt. After seeing them at work the other night I do not think the firemen can have been to blame.

THE PHILOSOPHY OF TRANQUILLITY

WHEN my holiday is over—though the holidays of a poet should have no end—I think I should like to settle down to the serious business of life in a canal-boat. It will be remembered that Stevenson expresses a similar desire at the end of the *Inland Voyage*, and Stevenson had a pretty taste in life. He was wise enough to bracket the onion with the nectarine as Nature's noblest confections, and many people must have echoed his longing for a yacht and a string quartette of his own. It would be a pleasant task to fit out a canal-boat for an aimless, delightful voyage. The bottles of old wine, the books of verse, a crew out of one of Mr. Jacobs's stories, a rack of muskets for make-believe—all these necessaries would have to be chosen with loving care. It would be well perhaps to take Southey's advice, and add a "kitten rising six months and a child rising three years," so that youth should not be forgotten. Chloe, with all deference to Fitzgerald, we should leave behind, lest she should take it into her little head to make a wilderness of our sufficient paradise. There is nothing, as the Water Rat remarks in the *Wind in the Willows*, half so pleasant in life as messing about in boats, and if we made up our mind never to get anywhere, and never to accomplish anything, life in a canal-boat could not fail to be delightful.

I came to this conclusion a year ago at Rickmansworth, and the canal-boats of Belgium have strengthened my opinion. It will always be a matter of regret to me that when I once journeyed from Antwerp to Brussels by canal I slept all the way, and so failed to keep any log of the voyage. It is the shape of canal-boats that attracts me, and the pace at which they go. They are clearly built for comfort rather than for speed. Here in Brussels every canal-boat has a cheerful dog with a curly tail, a cage or two of birds, and a number of small children, whose ages can be estimated from the washing drying overhead. The stern of the boat, where the domesticities triumph, is painted bright green and yellow, and here a section of the family is always having tea or some equivalent meal, watched over by a woman of astonishing breadth, stolen out of one of Rubens' pictures. Of course there is a serious side to the business. I happened to stop near a depôt where these salty mariners get their drinking-water, and with a real thrill I watched two small boys row up in a boat with the ship's cask aboard. That was how the Elizabethans watered their ships, and I could not blame the boys for emphasising the importance of their mission. While I was looking on at this, an old gentleman in green carpet-slippers came up and told me something very interesting at great length. Unfortunately he spoke in Flemish, so that I only understood every third word, and had to content myself with smiling amiably in reply. This double-language question must be rather troublesome sometimes. It is strange to hear children addressing their parents in Flemish, and the parents answering in French. I am told that there are some Belgians who know neither language, but express themselves in a mixture of both, though fate has spared me their acquaintance.

English novelists who sigh over their diminishing royalties may at least be glad that they were not born in Belgium. I was talking the other evening to a novelist whose first novel won the prize given by the Belgian Government every year to the author of the best novel in French written by a Belgian. In spite of this he only sold a little over a hundred copies, and made a net loss of thirty pounds on his book. It seems that there are no real publishers in Brussels, and

that while Belgian writers have to face the powerful com-
petition of French authors, the French publishers will not
look at a book by a Belgian unless he has forced his way
into one of the literary cliques of Paris. It was a sad story,
and to comfort him I told him of an English novelist who
said to me that if he took more than six weeks to write a
novel he made a loss on it. But the commercial side of
literature is an unpleasing business that no longer concerns
poets—they, at least, are free from any harassing doubts
as to the pecuniary consequences of their work; and this is
as it should be, for love is the only wage that can command
the noblest labour. That it will not pay hotel bills is the
fault of society and not of the publishers.

I learn from the calendar that I have been here three
weeks, but they have passed like a peaceful summer afternoon. Yet tranquillity, though we woo it so ardently, is at
best a negative boon, and, being English, I shall soon have
to seek another country. Brussels, with its cobbles and its
admirable but noisy service of trams, is not really a quiet
city, but the wit of man has not yet invented anything so
nerve-destroying as the motor-'buses of London. Yet it is
clear that the true causes of tranquillity lie deeper than this.
Probably few readers remember the poem, though it has
won the approbation of Mr. Andrew Lang, in which that
inconsiderable versifier, Thomas Haines Bailey, expressed
a passionate wish to see new faces. There is a good deal of
human nature in the thing, but it is a cry for peace and not
for adventure, for new faces do not really astonish us so
much as changes in the old. As a matter of fact, things seen
for the first time hardly ever surprise us, and a man paying
his first visit to Niagara may be more impressed, but
certainly is not so astonished, as the Member of Parliament who finds a water-main burst in Westminster. When
we leave our normal environment we expect the unexpected

and rob wonder of its fire. A dragon-fly in my suburban garden would thrill me more than forty aeroplanes at Nice.

It is idle to seek tranquillity in places or among people that have shared the especial hours of joy or sorrow. We shall find old echoes ringing in the "porches" of our ears, we shall find old emotions moving wistfully in our hearts. For me London is scrawled over with a kind of emotional shorthand of past days and nights, that rouses a deep unrest in my heart and gives my mind no peace. There are streets that haunt me, and faces, even faces of people whom I do not know. That is why I find Brussels restful, where the houses do not know my histories, and the faces I see in the streets have no significance for me. If it were not for the string-bands in the cafés that will play old songs they ought to have forgotten long ago, Chloe by now would be dead and buried with the millions of Chloes that were before her, waiting for the millions of Chloes that shall follow after. As it is she lingers, dimly sweet, like an old tune that we heard Pan play on his pipes when we were boys.

THE HOPE OF THE ARTISTS

IN this age of terminological exactitudes it is a luxury to own that one has made a mistake. In writing of the King of the Belgians in *Little Paris* I ventured to say that he was amiable, popular, and on the whole not very important. Now, I would say that the King is the most important man in Belgium; for in a country where native art has hitherto been uniformly ignored he has already proved himself, in the best sense of the word, a patron of art and artists. How far this may be due to the influence of the Queen—herself passionately interested in art—I do not know; but in any case it must not be forgotten that it takes a wise man to be influenced by a wise woman. Belgium to-day is a nation of extremely efficient shopkeepers; but the King has said publicly that to be great it is not enough for a nation to keep shop with success—it must also have some concern for literature and art in general; and by his own friendly attitude towards artists he has already succeeded in creating something like a revolution in the bourgeois mind. He has held a reception of Belgian artists, he has had a Belgian poet to lunch, and, in fine, he has gone far to convince the Belgians that it may not be necessary to go to Paris for their art.

The extent to which this lesson was needed may hardly be realised in England, where the majority that ignores English artists ignores the artists of other countries with equal fervour. But an amusing instance of the dependence of Brussels on Paris opinion comes to hand. Some time ago a new play by two Belgian authors, *Le Mariage de Mlle. Beulemans*, was produced in Brussels, and ran for only

thirty performances. It was then produced in Paris, where
it was a great success and ran for three hundred nights.
Paris having approved of it, it has now been revived in
Brussels, and will run for ever. The play has no particular artistic merit, but the incident is worthy of the
country that waited for a Frenchman to discover Maeterlinck. Similarly I was told of a picture that was hardly
noticed by the critics when it was first exhibited in Brussels,
but which won columns in the Belgian Press after it had
been awarded a gold medal in France and purchased by
a number of amateurs for the Art Collection at Dundee.
The Belgian critics are still afraid to praise their country-
men until Paris has given them a lead, and naturally Paris
is not eager to send many laurels over the frontier.

But now it seems likely that the interest displayed by the
King and Queen in the work of Belgian artists will check
this unpatriotic parasitism on the part of Belgian critics.
And it must be noted that this Royal encouragement is not
directed solely or even mainly to those painters and writers
whose discrete revolutions and reactionary audacities already delight and flatter the bourgeois mind. For here, as
in London, the artist with some technical accomplishment
and a tradesman's soul can always achieve success; it is a
mistake to think that it is only England that produces
Royal Academicians. I went to a one-man show here the
other day, where I saw fifty pictures, any one of which
would have been hung by our Royal Academy; and I was
told that the artist had sold the greater part of them. Portraits of women holding pocket-handkerchiefs and letters,
portraits of pretty children, nudes that were not naked, all
painted cleverly enough, but without a note of individuality or vision from one end of the exhibition to the other. It
is artists of this type on whom most nations hasten to
lavish official encouragement, though it is manifest that it

is they who want it least. For the vulgar mind is always intelligent enough to recognise and delight in the vulgar in art, without any official recommendation to assist it in forming a judgment.

It seems to me that the King and Queen of the Belgians are not only spiritually but also politically wise in seeking to foster the art of their country. The late King Leopold treated artists with the scant consideration that he displayed to everyone who did not minister to his laborious pleasures; towards the end of his reign he had the whole of his collection of pictures by contemporary artists put up for sale by public auction in Brussels. It is difficult to exaggerate the damage such an action may do to a monarchy. In estimating the power of the artist the Philistine imprisoned in his little moment forgets that the censure of great artists is as permanent as the flattery of politicians is evanescent, and this power makes itself felt through a hundred subtle channels. To-day, under the increasing influence of that spirit of democracy which for my part I distrust and detest, the kings of the world, as it were, stand ever on their trial. They are judged, absurdly enough, on their possession of the ordinary social qualities, as if it were any part of a ruler's mission to imitate the conduct of his subjects. Though they were probably hardly a contributing factor, the comparatively harmless peccadilloes of the King of Portugal were cited as eloquent arguments for the revolution. Yet there is always a risk that after he has achieved all the bourgeois virtues, his subjects may refuse to serve a King who differs in no wise from themselves, though his overcoat is trimmed with ermine and his bowler hat is made of gold. A democratic ruler is a paradox that can never appeal to the unsophisticated mind of the majority. But by extending his kingdom to the realms of art a King can secure his needed superiority over the common man, and be sure that his position will be strengthened and not weakened with the passage of years. This is what King Albert is doing with the aid of his clever and amiable Queen, and already it is easy to see that his policy is sound.

Perhaps this is hardly in a holiday tone, but I have been very much impressed by the hopeful spirit of the Belgian artists under the new régime. Everywhere I am told that Belgium is going to do big things in art, now that she has an opportunity to win free from the tyranny of the French critics. This is so different from the permanent gloom that envelops all those who cling to the ideal of high artistic endeavour in England that my spirit is infinitely refreshed. It seems that a select public of about two thousand settles the fate of works of art in Brussels, and that hitherto this body of amateurs has been united in its neglect of native art. Now all this is going to be altered, and poets and painters, musicians and architects go singing to their work.

To-day is a perfect blue day of spring, and as I finish this in a café on the boulevards the sap is rising in the trees, and every pretty girl who passes has a smiling face. I like writing in cafés because there is good literary pre-cedent for it, and also because to my ear there is no music in the world so soothing as the murmur of human voices. Probably most of the people who sit round me as I write are saying things of no importance, but the united effect of their voices is tuneful, and curiously like the sound of a small brook running over pebbles. In the aggregate men and women are pleasantly childlike. Every time a brass band passes (which occurs about every five minutes in Brussels) everybody stands up to see it go by. They look regretfully at their half-finished bocks, as if they wanted to go out and run in front with the other children.

A gentleman who is sitting at my table, and who had been watching my pen with an almost embarrassing interest, raised his glass a minute ago with a genial "Hurrah for England!" for the English are very popular in Brussels since the fire at the Exhibition. I was not to be outdone in politeness. "Hurrah for Albert, King of the Belgians," I cried, "and King of the Belgian artists!" The gentleman, who is clearly bourgeois, is still looking at me with approval, so it is apparent that the revolution has begun, for surely it is but a step from being pleased with such a toast to spending your money on pictures and books of verse.

SPRING JOURNALISM

ONE of the reasons why our popular newspapers are so monotonous is that they take no real account of the seasons. They do not reflect the glad unrest of Spring, the lavish fulfilment of Summer. They always appear to have been written by disillusioned business-men, whose style smells of faded poppies, forgotten among the autumnal stubble. The writers of leading articles show no disposition to frolic in the Spring, and in this—if leading articles are indeed written by human beings—they do wrong to their natures. For the man who can arrange his words in sounding periods during these first delightful blue days is capable of worse crimes than split infinitives. This is the season of the year when the yew peacocks in our gardens thrust out green branches and look for a moment like trees; and in the same way the wise man will now permit his cultured phrases to burst their strait-waistcoats and look for a moment like words. It is true that we have laboured over them all the winter-time, and set them down one by one with pride in our pocket-books. But now, when Nature is out of breath with running and the marble-topped tables are sprouting like mushrooms on the pavements, they seem inadequate. Our wintry ingenuities will not suffice to express a tenth part of our spring-tide flood of emotions. Like a schoolboy leader in a paper-chase whose bag is stuffed with fragments of torn dictionaries, we wish to scatter our words by handfuls, imitating in our humble human way the careless profusion of Nature and Mr. J. L. Garvin.

Very few people realise how much easier it is for a writer to be wise than it is for him to be cheerful. To be wise in a journalistic sense all that is necessary is to stand a platitude on its head and appropriate the small change that drops out of its pockets. To be cheerful on paper is a harder matter, for it demands either an extraordinary ignorance or an extraordinary knowledge of life. It is especially difficult to express this insane cheerfulness of Spring, for this is a lofty joy if you will, but it owes its position to the fact that it has clambered on the shoulders of sorrow. Like a child with toothache at its first pantomime, it laughs the louder because it is ever on the verge of tears. If you remember the Autumn, these young green buds are the saddest things on earth, for they, too, mark only another degree of decay. And yet, in spite of the fact that our new youth is the briefest of illusions, these are days when everything in the world that is not utterly broken and defeated claims happiness as a right; and as for all but the very greatest happiness is a confusion of ignorance, it is inhuman to expect journalists to be wise on this earth new painted with tender blues and greens. In a month or two, when the children have picked all the primroses and the motor-cars have covered the hedgerows with dust, it will be possible, perhaps, if the roses are merciful and the strawberry-crop fails, to write about the weighty problems that do not really matter with a becoming gravity. But what manner of man can think of Tariff Reform in a wood paved with anemones?

This is by way of being an apology, for I would certainly have written eruditely and unreadably on the proposed Flamandisation of the University of Ghent, if only the Spring had lingered a few more days on the way. I have discussed this important problem with a hundred persons; I have read a score of newspaper articles on the subject; I have the arguments and facts of both sides at my finger-tips; but now that Spring is here I have an unreasonable desire to write about something else, if only the expression of pleased astonishment on the faces of babies under six months old who feel the warm sunshine for the first time. My notebook emphasises the change. A few days ago I was cynical enough to reflect that "to regret that the days of our thwarted and uncomfortable youth are over is the only consolation that old age affords." Yesterday, moved to sentiment by the generosity of the season, I noted that "if it be true that in our dying hour we live again all the pregnant moments of our life, that hour for me will be a lifetime long." Not only the mood, but, quite unconsciously, the style has altered. With the omission of one word the second reflection becomes three lines of intolerable blank verse. That is what the Spring does for journalists.

Nevertheless I might have succeeded in writing about the higher Flemish education if I had shut myself in a cellar instead of foolishly seeking out one of the most beautiful places near Brussels. At Boitsfort the forest begins, and there is a little lake there in whose waters you can see a drowned village with white walls and red roofs. I sat in the paved courtyard of a café at the water's edge, and looked at the glorious duck-pond, and at the blues and purples of the forest beyond, and straightway forgot all about my stodgy essay. My drowsy kingdom was shared by a thoughtful waiter, who was obviously under the influence of the sweet oppression of the afternoon, and fed the ducks with French bread to keep himself awake. Also there was a dog who brought an enormous piece of wood to my feet and asked me to throw it for him. The beam looked as if it weighed at least three pounds, and to have thrown it on to the cobbles would have been an act of sacrilege against the tranquillity of that peaceful place. But the dog had appealing eyes, so I tried to bribe him vainly with sugar. At last, after he had picked up the piece of wood and dropped it again three or four times to convey what he wanted to my obtuse intelligence, he carried it away in disgust. I hope he only thought that I was stupid, and not that I was unfriendly; but, unlike cats, dogs are not reliable in their reading of human motives. I would have liked at the moment to have apostrophised him after the unsophisticated manner of the Flemish school of fiction. "Oh! dog," I would have said, "I should very much like to serve you by throwing that great piece of wood that you carry so cleverly across the courtyard, but I will not try to conceal my fears from your moist and eloquent eyes. I am afraid of the reproaches of the waiter, roused abruptly from his hour-long dreams. I am afraid of the echoes which would fill my ears with the mortal anguish of the murdered silence, but most I am afraid of a small baby who has just been hushed to sleep with some difficulty behind that open window. Being a café dog, it is perhaps natural that you should not care for sugar. I have heard that the employés at the great whisky distilleries always get drunk on beer. But if you care to stay here with me I will tell you all I know about the proposed Flamandisation of the University of Ghent." Long before I had finished composing this address the dog was out of sight.

Before me on the table there lay some blank sheets of paper and an empty coffee-cup. I dipped my pen in the ink three times with enthusiasm, and then balanced it on the saucer. It occurred to me to speculate as to the sensations of a tree in the Spring. First, it seemed to me, it is woken from its Winter sleep by a spirit of restlessness that by degrees takes the form of an intense irritation throughout the bark of the tree. I realised this stage so vividly that I know that old trees tell the young ones not to scratch. Afterwards the tree feels little threads of pain running through its channels, and these become more and more frequent, till the tree aches in every branch, and the image of each remotest twig is etched on the consciousness of the tree by suffering. Then, slowly at first, but afterwards quicker and quicker, each breaking bud brings relief, till long before the last bud has popped the whole tree is singing with pride of its great achievement. Some trees look upon their leaves as umbrellas, some as hats, and some as wearing apparel. It seemed to me that it would be a breach of manners to mention the Winter in the hearing of this last kind of tree.

But still the paper was blank and white; still my great essay on the proposed Flamandisation of the University of Ghent remained unwritten.

FRENCH OR FLEMISH?

IT is probable that the truest history of a nation is always to be found in its Art, if we study it with discrimination, for whether he seeks them in himself or in his neighbours the artist does undoubtedly register the emotions and opinions of his day. Therefore I think I need not apologise for approaching the burning question of the hour in Belgium through the medium of an artist's personality. It is a fact that I shall never be able to discuss the rights of the Flemish section of the Belgian population without thinking of M. Georges Eekhoud.

A few weeks ago I heard M. Eekhoud lecture on Lorenzaccio, Alfred De Musset's timid Hamlet, and after the lecture was over I was introduced to the lecturer and spent the rest of the evening in his company. I must confess frankly that I was disappointed. I had been told that, with Maeterlinck, Albert Giraud, and Camille Lemonnier, he was in the front rank of Belgian men of letters. I had heard stories of a youth spent in revolt against authorities and the conventions they support. I had heard of a decoration boisterously declined; in this country of cheap ribbon he is probably the only writer of any note who is not decorated. I had been led to expect a wild revolutionary; I met only a tame Professor. He had kindly little eyes and a courteous manner, but he clearly belonged to the fatal class that draws its opinions from books rather than from life. Equally clearly he was Flemish rather than Walloon, German rather than French.

There remained his books, and here a surprise awaited me. Side by side with sketches of a naïve and almost infantile sentimentality I found studies of rare emotions made with the sureness of touch of a master. I do not know that I have ever seen such contrasts within the walls of one book as are to be found in *Mes Communions*. "Climatérie" is the story of two boys at a Swiss school, of whom the psychology recalled to me those long days of my childhood when I had nothing better to read than *Harry Milner* or the *True History of Sandford and Merton*. These boys wept the same tears and behaved in the same romantic manner as the futile creations of Mrs. Sherwood and the eccentric Day. Yet in the same book there are such things as "Appol et Brouscard" and "Le Sublime Escarpe," sketches of a brutality of morals and emotion that would have made Mrs. Sherwood turn in her grave. The same contrast is to be noticed in *Le Cycle Patibulaire*, but in a modified form, for here a greater skill of expression has almost succeeded in refining the sentimentality to terms of sentiment. It is possible to read such a pleasant fancy as "Le Jardin" without feeling like a boy who has stolen a pound of chocolate; while, on the other hand, such a story as "Hiep-Hioup!" the tragedy of a gamekeeper whose noble violence of love awakens a genuine hatred in the breast of his malodorous Mary Fytton, lingers in the mind as a masterpiece of strong emotions. *Le Cycle Patibulaire* is a book that no one who is interested in French literature can afford to neglect.

Physically and intellectually the Flemish race is undoubtedly of a low type, moved by that ineloquent brutality that finds admirable artistic expression in Camille Lemonnier's *La Mort*. Under the influence of education this brutality, which might be described as unintelligent hatred, becomes softened to a sentimentality that is assuredly unintelligent love, and has been fully interpreted in Flemish by Henri Conscience. But this metamorphosis, in itself by no means surprising, does not account for the phenomenon of M. Georges Eekhoud, who is at once a rebel against conventions and a sentimentalist, which implies that he has accepted the most false of all conventions. To my mind the explanation of this paradox becomes simple when we look at the postage-stamps of Belgium, which are printed in two languages. Anyone of exceptional intellect who is born of Flemish blood must be subject to two very strong influences, mutually antagonistic; most Flemish artists settle the problem by becoming violently French, like M. Maeterlinck. A few feel the calls of patriotism and endeavour to make something of the dubious Dutch dialect that serves them for a mother tongue. M. Eekhoud must have hesitated between these two points until at one time he enjoyed the doubtful advantages of a dual personality. There was M. Eekhoud, the lover of passion and youth and beauty, the leader of a forlorn revolt against the follies of civilisation, the creator of wild and terrible tales. But there was also Herr Eekhoud, the timid student of books and dreamer of tearful, sickly-sweet romance, who must surely have suffered torments of remorse for the unruly deeds of his turbulent *alter ego*. All that is best in M. Eekhoud's work was produced by the reaction of French culture on his mind, and if, as a whole, his work is disappointing, it must surely be because he hesitated to throw sentimental Dr. Jekyll overboard early in his career. When I saw Professor Eekhoud smiling benignly at the fatuities of his bourgeois students, I felt as if I were assisting at the funeral of Mr. Hyde, the man of genius.

There are four Universities in Belgium, and in all of them the instruction is given in French. But the Democratic party is now moving to have the University of Ghent transformed into a Flemish University—so once more we have the spectacle of democracy seeking to bring about reactionary changes. This movement is really reactionary, going back at least as far as the Tower of Babel, for it is a deliberate effort to foster the continuity of the Flemish tongue by artificial means. Every intelligent man in the country talks French as a matter of course. But as the majority of the Flemish are too stupid to learn any tongue but their own ignoble patois, the democrats are anxious to burden a certain number of students with the same disability as the general mass of the uneducated. It is pretty enough to talk sentimentally about the mother-tongue, but if the children can speak a better language than their mother it is surely desirable that they should do so. This would seem an obvious truth, but it destroys nine-tenths of the arguments of the *flamingants*, as they are called. In two generations Belgium would become a French-speaking— and, what is far more important, a French-thinking— nation; but now we have the miserable spectacle of a number of clever men labouring to prolong the present antagonism of speech and thought, for there is not the slightest possibility of Flemish ever being the language of the nation as a whole. If democracy is always going to be so little intelligent, we shall soon long for the coming of a new prophet to save the people from being overwhelmed by the handicap of their rights.

This is one of those artificial movements which is started as an intellectual exercise, continued as a habit, and which ends by becoming a passion. I suppose the *flamingants* will have their University sooner or later, though there is at least a doubt whether they will be able to find any students willing to be taught in Flemish, save, perhaps, in Holland and South Africa. There is a story of a State-paid Professor of Flemish elocution who held his appointment for ten years without ever finding a single pupil. When the inspectors announced their periodical visits he had to hire pupils at five francs apiece to come and listen to his lectures!

A University run on those lines would perhaps be the most satisfactory termination to a foolish crusade, which suggests, nevertheless, certain dangers to those who are interested—and England surely not least of all—in a solid and united Belgium. We have seen the unhappy results of the fostering of race-differences in our own relationship with Ireland.

THE FAILURE OF THE CROWD

IT is a regrettable fact that nearly every one objects to
spending money on the beautiful when it is not disguised
as some form or other of the useful. People are willing to
purchase old chairs that they dare not sit on, or grandfather's clocks that have stopped for ever, but they will not
buy a book of modern verse, not even to throw at a cat.
In England we are apt to suppose that they do these things
better on the Continent, but it is not true. I am told that
the artists of Belgium have to go to Buenos Ayres to sell
their pictures;* I dare not ask the name of the place where
the painters of Buenos Ayres find a market. But the fact
remains that in the advanced state of civilisation which we
now enjoy the man who knows how to carve hat-stands
will find it easier to make a living than the man who knows
how to carve flesh and blood out of rocks. When reactionary æsthetes like myself object to this condition of things,
they are met with the argument that a nude statue is of no
use as a hat-stand; but this is only true because our hats are
atrociously ugly.

We all know the collector of pictures who tells them
apart by the prices he has paid for them; but, while we find
him amusing, we must remember that the majority of men
and women always ask the price when they are shown

---

* Middleton seems here in a fair way to deny his assumption
(made some weeks previous in *The Hope of the Artists*) that the
Belgian painters went "singing to their work."

On mature reflection it may be that he found he had been too
sanguine, and so with this new expression availed himself once
more of the luxury of owning that he had made a mistake.—J. G.

something beautiful, and that their judgment on its merits is largely affected by the answer to their question. I have often pondered on the possible experiences of a man who should steal half a dozen Old Masters from the National Gallery, and should try hawking them round the suburbs at 5s. each. Unless he happened on the one man in ten thousand who knows something about Art, I believe he would starve to death before he succeeded in selling an un-framed picture of real merit for 5s. in Tooting or Raynes Park. All of which is merely a long-winded method of stating the impression that it is only the very exceptional person who cares about beauty at all.

I found striking evidence of this at a great fire which occurred at Brussels two or three weeks ago. I was down on the boulevards interpreting for Easter-lost Englishmen when I looked up and saw a red bud breaking in the midnight sky. It was clearly too late for a sunset and too early for a dawn; so, with what I understood to be journalistic *flair*, I took a tram to the scene of the conflagration. An enormous stone town-hall, built in the elaborate style of the *Renaissance flamande*, was burning cheerfully from one end to the other; but what lent special piquancy to the spectacle was the fact that the whole building was closely enmeshed by blazing scaffolding-poles, so that it looked like a huge set-piece. Every now and then one of these poles seemed to leap up like a monstrous rocket, to fall fifty feet or so on to the pavement below. I have seen many fires in London, but I have never seen anything nearly so beautiful as this. The firemen would have pleased Mr. Max Beerbohm, for there were enough of them to be picturesque, while it was palpable that nothing they could do would make the smallest difference. When I had watched this noble pageant for an hour, while the fire burnt ever brighter and brighter, I felt that I should choke if I did not express my enthusiasm to somebody, so I poured it on to my neighbour in the crowd. He listened to my praise with a look of horror on his face. "Mon Dieu! monsieur," he cried, "it will cost a hundred and fifty thousand pounds!"

For a moment I could hardly believe my ears; I could hardly believe that any one would be so cynical as to weigh the price before that palace of leaping fire and under those heavens gladdened with a miraculous birth of stars. Then with a sinking heart I became aware that the whole crowd was assessing the cost of the spectacle in millions of francs, and that I was probably alone in realising that we were face to face with the ideal beauty, that elusive goddess whom some of us fare so far to meet. When I picked up the newspapers next day and found them all weeping francs, it became clear to me that the town-hall of Schaerbeek had burnt for me alone, save that perhaps here and there in the crowd there had been a small boy or two young enough and wise enough to know that this loss was really a tremendous gain to those whose eyes were not blinded by cupidity. How often our pleasure in a fine play has been marred by the stupidity of the audience!

It has been proved clearly enough that the fire was due to the spirited action of an incendiary, but there is no particular reason to suppose that his identity will be discovered. I imagine that it will be ascribed in turn to the well-known malignancy of the Jews, the Jesuits, the Socialists, the Flamingants, and the Pan-Germanists; but if I were concerned for the discovery of the miscreant I should advise the police to search the ranks of the artists. Or perhaps it was an amateur musician, some mute, inglorious Nero—in any case I should say that there is one man in Brussels who feels that he has been a success where so many fail. He has achieved the creation of the beautiful, and, though the child of his spirit only lasted a few hours, he doubtless knows that beauty is not to be measured in terms of years.

The crowd is not only unable to appreciate beauty when it meets it—that, if you will, may be held to call for a special education—but it is not even capable of knowing when it ought to laugh and when it ought to weep. I have been studying the audiences at cinema theatres lately, and I have been uniformly horrified by their emotional cynicism. The so-called pathetic dramas at these entertainments are as utterly remote from life as anything could very well be. They are like the tales a morbid child invents for its own amusement, and while they are perhaps in doubtful taste, they certainly do succeed in exhibiting the more artificial sorrows of civilised society in a humorous light. Grief wears a fantastic mask, and the world is turned upside down to add to its excesses; but the audience never fails to weep at these audacious parodies. On the other hand the so-called comic scenes are little tragedies presented with a remarkable realism. They uniformly represent the sufferings of the individual set down in an unfortunate environment, and with psychological accuracy they emphasise the fact that the failure of one man imperils all society. A thief, perhaps, is pursued by justice and in his flight brings ruin to a hundred honest tradesmen; another man in his efforts to escape from a false position brings a whole city toppling about his ears. I confess that when I hear a crowd of men and women screaming with laughter at these spectacles I am repelled by such perversity of feeling. Surely it is permissible to laugh at our own misfortunes, but not at those of other people.

Yet, as a matter of fact, the crowd never laughs at itself. There is a hydrophobia scare in Brussels, so when a dog entered a café the other afternoon, and, after running round half a dozen times, dived into the cellar with a cascade of bottles, I was granted a delicious picture of fifty men and women clambering on to chairs and tables. This is where the laughter would have begun at a cinema entertainment, but I noticed that nobody laughed. Later on, when two gendarmes armed with swords descended into the cellar to deal with the culprit, the mirth was uproarious. Yet it seemed to me that the situation was not very amusing either for the gendarmes or the dog, and that the men and women in the café would have been more discreet if they had waited to get their colour back before indulging their curious sense of humour.

THE NEWSPAPER HABIT

PERHAPS one of the most striking differences between the national life of the English and the Belgians is the fact that the average Englishman reads the newspaper and the average Belgian does not. I do not think that there can be any argument as to the truth of this. I have found myself that by running through the Belgian newspapers every day—a feat that can easily be performed in half an hour by anyone who has been brought up on the *Times* or the *Daily Telegraph*—I am better informed on current events in Belgium than any of the Belgians I meet. In this country, which in many respects is strangely primitive immediately below the surface, the gossip of the cafés and the streets is still the principal medium for the transmission of news. It would seem, however, that the days of this enviable freedom from the tyranny of the Press are numbered; some of the newspapers claim large circulations, and it is apparent that many Belgians make a practice of buying the newspapers though they have not yet acquired the vicious habit of reading them. They probably do not realise the risk they run in introducing these masses of print into the quietude of their homes. It may be granted that they have not the smallest intention of looking at them; but sooner or later—on a wet afternoon, perhaps, or in a moment of ennui—they will peep between the folded leaves and read an interesting paragraph concerning a thunderstorm in Colombo, or the latest telegram as to the defalcations of an omnibus-conductor in Nuremberg. From this it is but a step to the reading of leading articles and the rapt perusal of the advertisement columns, which are delights more insidious than alcohol or opium.

This aimless reading of daily newspapers is without doubt the most serious intellectual vice of modern England, although, like most important vices, it masquerades as a virtue. To take an interest in our country and in the doings of our fellow human beings is among the most obvious of our duties; but a critical examination of any copy of a modern newspaper will convince the unprejudiced observer that it is neither patriotism nor a broad spirit of humanity that inspires the supporters of our daily press. The newspapers cannot be blamed for endeavouring to give their readers what they want, and when we find that nine-tenths of their space is devoted to the sensational and the trivial we are justified in supposing that nine-tenths of their readers like that kind of thing. The trivial satisfies their curiosity, the sensational satisfies their lust for adventure, and the newspaper as a whole satisfies their too easily satisfied desire for culture. This is the enormous responsibility that the modern newspaper is apt to accept a little lightly— that with the large majority of its readers it takes the place of all other reading matter. It must be at once a Bible, an encyclopædia, and a hand-book to politics; a cookery-book, a treatise on popular science and a sporting guide. It must be the Hundred Best Books, a child's Guide to Knowledge, and a Peerage; a text-book on botany, astronomy, and natural history. It must be sister to the moon in eclipse, and little brother to the giant gooseberry. It must be newer than the guide-book of the tourist, and older than the rocks among which he sits. It must know how to reconcile a high moral tone with its functions as a romantic Newgate Calendar, and play the judge and the criminal with an equal grace. It must defend the rich from the poor, and the poor from the rich, with a fervour that fails when it is not interesting. It must know how to estimate the value to humanity of passing events; a hundred columns for a good murder, six columns for the speech of a politician, and a quarter of a column to herald the appearance of a new masterpiece in art. It must rake the gutters of the world for crime, and be swift in chronicling accidents and disasters. It must condemn vice with vehemence, and strangle virtue with platitudes. It must deride minorities, and congratulate majorities on reflecting its opinions. It must be registered at the General Post Office as a newspaper, and must be large enough when unfolded to serve as a tablecloth for the lower classes.

Is this tirade exaggerated? At all events there is nothing in it that I regret except perhaps the reference to a famous and irritating passage of Walter Pater. It is generally agreed that the daily newspapers of England are the best in the world, and it is worth anybody's while to live abroad to avoid them. I speak on this point with the emphasis of a momentarily-reformed drunkard, for I confess that when I am in England I am as much the slave of this vice of newspaper reading as anyone else. It is the mark of the newspaper inebriate that he does not very much mind which newspaper he reads, and that he reads them from one end to the other—politics, sport, City news and advertisements, with equal interest. To help him in this he brings a curious cunning to bear; he takes certain racehorses and politicians under his protection and is pleased when he finds a mention of their names. He makes friends with Steel Commons and Canadian Pacifics because they have a lively nature, and he watches their movements in the market with genuine excitement. He observes the stammering histories of the agony columns, and the normal dishonesty of advertisers in general. He reads the serial stories; indeed the passion for reading bad novels in arbitrary instalments is one of the most marked symptoms of the vice, and must not be mistaken for commonplace insanity. Your true newspaper-reader is best pleased when he can begin the serial in the middle and read every second instalment to the end. He does not wish his intellect to be disturbed by the significance of things. He seeks the tranquillity of words, words arranged in grammatical sentences that convey nothing in particular to his somnolent mind. When he is in a fantastic mood he seeks diversion in printers' errors, and sometimes he has been known to make a collection of journalistic *clichés* in a small black pocket-book. But it is to the leading articles that he returns like a child to the lap of its mother. There, at all events, he is secure from the noisy irruption of ideas, the desires of ambitious thinkers, the disquieting audacities of youth. There he may drowse in the land where it is always the day before yesterday, lulled by a tide of words to which the most morbid reader can attach no human significance.

This absorbed reading of daily newspapers is a vice, because it rather provides a substitute for life than contributes to our enjoyment of it. It helps us to pass the hours, but it does not make us wiser either by precept or experience, and, at the end, we are only so many hours poorer without any spiritual or mental compensation. Few people realise how much time they waste in nodding sagely over the morning papers. Let them lay the habit aside for a week or two, and they will be astonished at the lengthening of the days, the growth of the period that separates lunch from breakfast. Let them at the same time lay aside the illusion that there is generally something important to be found in the newspapers if you look for it long enough. They have only to ask themselves every morning after they have finished the paper what they have gained by its perusal to be convinced of the emptiness of this theory. There is hardly ever anything in the daily newspapers that we are the richer for knowing; and for the most part men and women read them for that reason.

So when a week or two ago a Belgian novelist told me that he thought newspaper-reading was increasing in Belgium I did not congratulate him. On the other hand, I told him that in England the daily newspaper is killing the magazine, the review, the novel, the short story, and the drama; that it has already killed poetry and made politics impossible for a sane man. That it flings literature to the professors, and painting to the Royal Academicians. That it labours to confirm the common mind in its vulgar self-satisfaction, and is the avowed enemy of all that is original or noble in modern thought.

"But you have the best newspapers in the world!" exclaimed the novelist. And the queer part of it is that I honestly believe we have.

LITERARY PAPERS

STEVENSON AND "TREASURE ISLAND"

IT is a pity that schoolmasters do not make a point of discovering the private literary tastes of their pupils, in order that we could form some general idea of what boys really like to read. Such an inquiry must be conducted tactfully; the only lists of the kind that we have seen were suspiciously priggish. It is true that there are boys who like Scott and Dickens, but it is safe to say that the average boy of twelve or thirteen cares neither for one nor the other, or at all events, given the opportunity, prefers Henty or Talbot Baines Reed. Yet, while we may acknowledge that boys do not accept our adult standards of criticism, it must not be inferred that they do not possess any of their own. A bookish boy will read anything if the supply of books is limited, but he will like some books better than others, and the most sophisticated of critics has no firmer ground for his judgments than that.

That the critical instinct of boys is sometimes subtle in its workings may be seen from the classic instance of *Treasure Island*, which entirely failed to capture the hearts of the juvenile readers of *Young Folks* when it appeared as a serial in that periodical. Indeed the editor had to defend it, in reply to criticisms of the earlier instalments. In revenge the *Black Arrow*, surely Stevenson's worst book, proved a great success with the same body of readers, a preference which should reveal to the thoughtful writer the enormous difficulty of estimating the probable popularity of books written for boys. The conscientious critic should be panic-stricken at Christmas-time, when he is faced with

the usual deluge of juvenile literature, for he is about to adventure in an unknown land. A musical critic set down
suddenly in Barnard's ring at Epsom to write an account of
the Derby for the Newmarket touts would be in a position
no more embarrassing.

What was it in *Treasure Island* that the readers of *Young
Folks* did not like? If we could find a satisfactory answer
to the question we should be nearer to an understanding
of juvenile standards of criticism. Offhand, though we
should not have thought of bracketing it with *Tom Sawyer*
and the *Iliad*, like Mr. Andrew Lang, we should have said
that *Treasure Island* was the best boys' book that had
ever been written. Pirates, treasure, a desert island, some
good fighting and a boy hero are the elements that we
should seek in a model work of that description; and
though we do not credit the young with any taste for style,
they should surely appreciate the romantic spirit and un-
failing energy with which Stevenson's tale is told. He
avoided, too, the heavy-handed morality that proved the
undoing of Dean Farrar, and even, from a boy's point of
view, of Thomas Hughes. Virtue triumphs, but so, to a
minor extent, does the principal villain—that very finished
ruffian John Silver—whose character drew its inspiration,
we are told, from the "maimed strength and masterfulness"
of the poet Henley, and with whom Stevenson had clearly
fallen in love himself. An omission in the story that the
author lamented would not probably occur to the mind
of a boy. "The trouble is," he wrote, "to work it off
without oaths. Buccaneers without oaths—bricks without straw. But youth and the fond parent have to be
consulted." Another omission, that of female characters,
was in joyful obedience to the wishes of the boy on
whom he tried the earlier chapters, and here he was undoubtedly right. Yet the readers of *Young Folks*, those

bizarre and nameless critics, refused to hear the charmer's voice till he changed his pipe and gave them the *Black Arrow*.

Boys are ineloquent critics, and this heightens the difficulty of understanding their literary preferences; so that we are forced to fall back on theory to account for the failure of *Treasure Island* in serial form. Perhaps the most notable difference between that and the average book for boys lies in the fact that Stevenson's characterisation is more than skin deep. His hero, Jim Hawkins, is a real boy, and not one of the super-boys who lead armies and drive motor-cars across the pages of most boys' books. Admitting that Jim does heroic things, it is nevertheless true that Stevenson has robbed him of the normal heroic glamour. The grown-ups in the book do not turn to him for orders or acclaim him as a genius. We are made to feel—indeed we are told —that his splendid achievements are due to luck rather than judgment, and he emerges from his adventures without a halo. Now, doubtless this study of a boy is faithful in terms of life, but this is not the kind of part that a boy would choose to play in his dreams. In the imaginary world of youth a boy triumphs over difficulties by superior skill and intellect, and not by luck, and his triumph is immediately recognised by old and young alike. Instead of adding a new kingdom to this world, *Treasure Island* is a shrewd blow at this fundamental law. It suggests that it is possible for a boy hero to be thoughtless and even foolish, and is a manifest denial of the truth that a boy can do no wrong in the world of adventure.

Again, though the adult mind finds John Silver a convincing and sufficient villain, it may be doubted whether he is acceptable to the young as a type of pirate captain. He is smooth-tongued and hypocritical, and he achieved by guile the ends that a proper pirate captain would have attained by force. It is a pity, for it cannot be denied that his ferocity is genuine when he doffs his ignoble mask. Flint or William Bones must have played the part with a better grace; in fact, from all we learn of Flint he must have been a model pirate, and all the lesser ruffians of *Treasure Island* fall to talking of him when they want to make our flesh creep. Their villainy is merely the shadow of Flint's, and tender youth, with a mind tuned for deeds of violence, may well imagine that the book begins too late. *Treasure Island* is well enough, but where is the tale of Flint's adventures? That is the book that a healthy-minded, blood-thirsty boy would wish to read.

Doubtless in humanising his characters, in making his boy-hero a mere lifelike boy, in sketching his pirates as the cowardly, clumsy ruffians they were in real life, Stevenson was at variance with juvenile conceptions of adventure; and yet the story is so good that the coldness of those early readers remains a mystery. *Treasure Island* was begun at Braemar in August 1881, and at the same time Stevenson was writing some of those graceful notes of childhood that were afterwards gathered into *The Child's Garden of Verses*. In our experience these never fail with young children, who find in them a straightforward expression of everyday emotions, where grown-up people find poignant echoes of the rapture and enchantment of their lost childhood. When a child in our hearing called them "sensible" we realised the measure of the poet's success. From the lips of children he would have desired no other praise.

Intellectually boys are hard to reckon with, for in most of them the child's imagination is giving place to the materialism of a healthy animal, so that side by side with the credulity of inexperience we find a scepticism founded on cheerful ignorance. A boy may dismiss the novels of Scott as "rot" and read a halfpenny legend of Deadwood Dick, the Dime Detective, with interest and pleasure. But we must not on this account deny him the possession of a critical faculty. He knows what he likes, and that is the beginning of all criticism.

STEVENSON AND "LAY MORALS"

WHEN we reflect that seventeen years have passed since Stevenson's death,* we cannot but think that Time, prince of destructive critics, has dealt very gently with the reputation of that distinguished writer. This is the more remarkable in view of the fact that during his lifetime Stevenson was lavishly over-praised, or perhaps it would be more accurate to say, was studiously praised for attributes that he did not possess. By his contemporary friends Stevenson was regarded as an inspired writer of romances and the possessor of a fine prose style, but it is becoming increasingly clear that he was neither one nor the other. His stories were carefully planned, ingenious, entertaining, but they lacked that speed, that breathlessness, that prevents the reader from noticing the machinery that drives the wheels of romance. It is only necessary to set *Kidnapped* or *Catriona* against one of the earlier romances of Mr. Stanley Weyman, to realise how little Stevenson was gifted in this manner of writing. It is another instance of a Hamlet seeking to create Hotspurs, and in consequence we feel no surprise on recognising the anxious features of our Scotch moralist under the tattered finery of Alan Breck. Stevenson was far too much concerned in the struggle between his vagabond temperament and his Puritan conscience to devote himself whole-heartedly to love and fighting and adventure as a good writer of romances should. Nevertheless he was attracted to this kind of composition, partly, we fancy, because being sprung from a distinguished family of

* Written May 1911.—J. G.

engineers he thought he would find himself in the literature of action, and partly because throughout his life he retained the little boy's love for toy swords.

As for his style, it had every merit but that essential ease which every writer must retain, even while he is learning to keep it under control. His picturesque sentences force the reader to be conscious of the ingenious hand that wrote them, and his careful mannerisms prevent his books from achieving an existence independent of his personality. While we pause to admire his sly Scotticisms, his judicious derangement of epithets and the poise and rhythm of his phrases, the story not unnaturally falters; and it is for this reason that we prefer his essays, where an individual and self-conscious style is an advantage, and his letters, where he often wrote as happily and carelessly as a schoolboy, to his romances which go with a verbal and metaphysical limp where they ought to carry us off our feet, and at best only attain to the crippled agility of a John Silver. Edmund Gosse, we believe, has somewhere expressed the opinion that it is by his correspondence and his essays that Stevenson will live. We would certainly add his poems—the most original section of all his work and oddly underrated by most of his admirers—and two or three of his short stories to the list. In such a story as *A Lodging for the Night* his vividness of imagination and his sympathy with the vagabondage of Villon have enabled him to achieve the necessary illusion in spite, it might be said, of his quibbling turn of words.

But all this is to miss Stevenson's true value for his readers, which lies in the autobiographical nature of all his work rather than in any merit he may have possessed as a creative artist. Like Pepys, he was his own Boswell, and whether he set out to write a romance, an essay, or a poem, he always ended by writing about himself. He is one of those writers whose personality appeals to us more than the particular manner in which they seek to express it, and it is natural that his work should be judged by the worth and interest of the character therein revealed. And here, happily, we are on more grateful ground. For after all the confessions that crowd the pages of his books, after the many criticisms of his friends and his enemies, he still lives for us a gallant and lovable figure of a man. His popularity may be held to reflect the broad humanity of his nature; and just as it has been said that we all have something of Willoughby Patterne in us, so it is to be hoped that we all have something of Stevenson in us as well. For he was above all things a brave fighter, and if we must agree with Henley that, in Stevenson, Jekyll never wholly succeeded in overcoming Hyde, we may take pleasure in the fact that both sides of his nature fought with superb courage. He fought his ill-health, and even more he fought the effects of his lamentable Scotch upbringing, better calculated to produce Cabinet Ministers than men of letters; and if these were not the chivalrous opponents his romantic nature would have chosen, for us his courage is not the less admirable. All the evidence goes to prove that it is easier to lead an army into battle than to endure the toothache, and Stevenson's battle-fields are only petty in the eyes of the unintelligent.

Judged from this standpoint, as presenting the inner life and aspirations of a human being sufficiently typical to be of interest to us all, nearly the whole of Stevenson's work is important, for the man is as much displayed in his fragments and his failures as in his finished works. It is on this account that we are prepared to welcome the publication in *Lay Morals and other papers* of much immature work that might seem in the case of another writer to be impertinent. It contains the first unrevised chapters of a projected treatise on ethics, a few early essays of no special merit, the opening chapters of three unfinished romances, and the famous open letter to the Reverend Dr. Hyde on Father Damien—a letter which we seem to remember Stevenson afterwards regretted having written. Hitherto these papers have only been available in the two fine collected editions, and lovers of Stevenson who have bought his books one at a time—as lovers generally do buy their books—will be glad of the opportunity to complete their collection. *Lay Morals* is Stevenson with a vengeance in his most didactic mood, and might almost have been written by any one who had a thorough knowledge of his work. As for the other papers, we confess to a partiality for the outspoken disgust of the letter on Father Damien, while *The Great North Road*, though not to be compared with the masterly fragment of *Weir of Hermiston*, looks as if it would have developed into a pleasant, boyish yarn.

The essays are interesting, as showing from what unpromising materials he derived his ultimate style—by playing, as he told us with unwise candour, the "sedulous ape" to Hazlitt, Sir Thomas Browne, and a number of others. It is true that every author has to learn to write, but we have always felt that with Stevenson the process was too conscious, that he was not, in the fullest sense of the word, born to be a writer at all. His papers on the art of writing compete for futility, in our opinion, with Poe's well-known essay on the same lines; and while we may credit Poe with knowing better than he wrote, there is, unfortunately, no reason to doubt Stevenson's sincere belief in his disastrous theories. Nevertheless, by force of character, by sheer hard work, and especially by aid of his enthusiastic interest in himself—an interest that it would be unjust to call vanity— he won for himself an enviable position among the men of letters of his day; and that day is not yet over.

J. M. BARRIE AND "PETER PAN"

IT is given to few artists to become "classic" in their life-time, but this is the fate which appears to have befallen J. M. Barrie. Let him but alter a line of *Peter Pan* and the great theatrical clubs of London murmur in their perpetual sleep. The names of the characters trip as lightly from the tongues of Londoners as those of the *Pickwick Papers*. In the saloon-bars of farthest Streatham they compare the various actresses who have played the part of Peter, and quarrel in their cups. But the wonderful thing about this sudden fame is that nobody seems to know what *Peter Pan* really is.

Perhaps a word of history might not be misplaced first. Probably the literary ancestor of *Peter Pan* is *The Child's Garden of Verses* and certain of Stevenson's essays. The philosophy of play it embodies is certainly that of Steven-son, as are the pirates, who must have served their appren-ticeship with the notorious Flint. Peter, of course, hails from *The Little White Bird*, and it is curious to notice how poorly he has succeeded in effect in his task of never grow-ing up. In that volume he was one week old (Mr. Rackham made him rather older), but by the time the play appeared some two years later he was at the least fourteen years of age! At the same rate he is thirty-five this Christmas (1907), a nice age, but hardly boyish. Wendy and Mrs. Darling are, of course, identical with Mary, Babbie, Grizel—or shall I say, briefly, Margaret Ogilvy? Smee, the kindly pirate, with the mild manners and the sewing-machine, is evidently drawn from the model of a non-combatant, it may be an aunt or nurse herself, who is impressed in order to swell the numbers of a pirate crew, but insists on regarding the honour and peril of her appointment with the exasperating placidity of a grown-up. The lost shadow can be traced to Adelbert von Chamisso's "Peter Schlemihl," and the unconvincing Redskins to Fenimore Cooper. The two Darling boys, with the Carmelite Street names, are so natural that they must surely have been drawn from the life, though there is something of R. L. S. in the smaller one. Slightly is a brother of Corp in *Sentimental Tommy*, and Nana is an ingenious variant of the ordinary burlesque pantomime animal.

So far for Barrie's materials, but it is when I come to consider what he has expressed with them, that I find myself at variance with the general idea. I am accustomed to hear *Peter Pan* described as a children's play or as a fantastic thing full of humour and laughter; but in my view *Peter Pan* is no more a child's play than *Gulliver's Travels* is a child's book, and it is the most deliberately conceived and carefully developed tragedy I have ever seen. It is the tragedy of the relationship between children and their parents which Barrie has developed fully and remorselessly, showing the effect of the widening experience of children as they grow up, both on the children themselves and on their parents; and by the fine conception of the rebel Peter Pan, who refuses to obey the iron law that makes nurseries sad places for the far-seeing, he has added the last touch that was needed to make the tragedy complete. For he has shown that it is inevitable.

A very few words will suffice to prove this if we examine the course of the play. In the first scene Barrie has commenced by drawing us as happy a nursery as it is possible to find. We see that the mother understands her children and the children understand their mother. There is, moreover, the nurse Nana, sufficiently affectionate, but firm when it comes to such important matters as baths and bed-time. Only the father conveys a suggestion of the coming trouble, for having a more shallow nature than the others, he is already reduced to prevarication in dealing with his children. But the first part of the play ends lovingly with the mother's good-nights. And then the children go forth. In real life, it may be, they go to school or to stay at some house where the children are older, but there, as in the play, they leave their nursery to take part for the first time in adventures that they do not share with their mother. It would be unwise, perhaps, to trace the symbolism too far in examining their adventures in the Never Never Land. The pirates, the redskins, the mermaids are but the possi-bilities of the world as it presents itself to a fresh and im-aginative mind. Things half seen, stories half remembered, serve as the threads from which to weave a bizarre but beautiful tapestry, from which experience tears a fragment every day of a man's life. But meanwhile, while her chil-dren are gathering new impressions and glorying in their wings, the mother waits at home for them to return. It is hard for her to relinquish her kingdom, it is difficult for her to acknowledge that their allegiance was of an evanescent character. And when at last they do come back, when the new game has a little palled, she does not at first realise that their new love, if no less sincere than the old, is more intellectual and less natural. Their lives may no longer be a fragment of hers, for between the mother and her chil-dren there lie experiences, though they be but trifling, know-ledge though it be almost unconscious, that make the old simplicity impossible. Her children have grown up.

This is the tragedy, alike for mother and children, which Barrie has expressed so well. Peter himself, the child who never grows older, we know too, though the Never Never Land, where he leads his adventurous companions, is, as far as we can see it, a place of grass and small white stones.

There is one character more in the play who calls, perhaps, for notice, and that is Liza, described as "The Author of the Play." Apart from her duties as house-maid—or is it general servant?—to the Darlings, she makes two noteworthy appearances on the stage, and on each occasion we feel that she is present there in her character as the author of the play, mocking at his own inventions. Surely this is the most bitter conception any man ever had. We recall the termination of *Vanity Fair*, where Thackeray writes, "Come, children, let us shut up the box and the puppets, for our play is played out," but there is a distinction between the two cases, for Thackeray's was certainly mockmodesty, while I feel sure that Barrie's is not.

Truly it is difficult to write masterpieces, and an author may be forgiven if he sometimes turns against the gods who represent so hard an ideal. But still the goal lies not through bitterness, but rather along the "Road of Loving Hearts," as Barrie knows well. And it is because he has been content to follow that road that he has been able to give us *Peter Pan*.

LADY NOVELISTS

LADY novelists may be divided into three groups: the Fantastic, the Naughty, and the Domestic. There are certain features that these groups have in common, and particular qualities in each group which the others do not possess, and it is concerning these features, and not the charming women who are responsible for them, that I propose to write. In the first place it may be said about them all, that they tell fibs about the things they know, and the truth about the things of which they are ignorant. When they know anything too well to fib about it, they put rows of dots like this . . . . . in order to annoy their readers. It should be borne in mind that each of these dots means a solitary blush on the part of the lady who puts it on the paper. Again, it is a point of honour with women who write to know nothing of spelling, punctuation, or grammar. They leave these things to the "printer-man," as to worry about them would interfere with their inspiration. Inspiration is a habit of writing quickly on both sides of the paper. A flow of inspiration is half an hour with a fountain pen. The "only piece of real inspiration I ever had" is something the publishers won't accept. A sudden inspiration is a plagiarism. When we come to the group I have called "Fantastic," we are faced with the consideration of by far the most numerous type of woman's novel. The dear ladies who write these books honestly believe that they are interpreting life literally, and that for adornment their volumes must rely on the soft glow that emanates from the eager hearts of young persons, breaking into a love that involves matrimony at the end of seven-and-sixpence worth of writing.

This form of art, which might be described as an effort to make the obvious improbable, appears to be eternal. Long ago in the days of the *Keepsake* they were doing this same thing; then, I believe, the hero wore whiskers, and the heroine's chief weapon was a kind of charming cowardice. To-day the hero is clean-shaven and has a jaw of American strength, while the heroine boasts a rare spirit and the manner of speech, half rude, half obscure, invented by Anthony Hope. But these are but surface details. The great heart of these books palpitates to the same old refrain, "Love, obstacles, marriage-in-a-church, love, obstacles"— and so on for ever. In manner there are small variations. To some is granted the advantage of local colour, others are enlivened with fragments of foreign languages, French, German, or Italian, or such useful Latin phrases as "*multum in parvum; magnum opum,*" and the like. And, of course, there are the subsidiary characters, the peasants, the servants, the wild young poets. The villain, I am sorry to say, is out of fashion at the moment, and the wicked baronet of my youth has become a sort of understudy to the hero, or sometimes even fills the part of hero himself. As a class, we feel that these books must be very much easier to write than they are to read.

The second on my list and the second as regards numerical strength, are the "Naughty" books. These are quite a modern invention, and are becoming more popular every year. Unlike the "Fantastic" books I have just described, they are usually very difficult to understand, and they are extremely full of dots. They start vaguely and end nowhere, but we know that we are on intellectual ground, because the hero quotes Nietzsche, and the heroine, in moments of excitement, steals from the works of Mr. Bernard Shaw. Still, it is certainly a relief to come to the geographically exact descriptions of kisses, which, apart

Q

from their context, would suggest the primitive way of eating an orange. It is impossible to read these books without feeling a bit of a dog, for the sweet girls who write them contrive to suggest subtly that they are going to be very shocking in a minute or two. The earnest reader only discovers the fraud when he has finished the book. They are not really naughty at all, these novels. They are colossal expressions of innocence, resembling in every way the sinful words which bad little boys chalk up on walls. They are not capable of doing anyone any harm; even their authors, I fancy, marry and settle down after a while, and in the meantime their books sell by hundreds. If they are fortunate enough to be black-listed at the libraries they sell by thousands. They are full of melancholy meaninglessness and we gather dimly that all the characters are wretched, but it is only when they are religious that we can accuse their authors of bad taste.

When I come to the "Domestic" group of novels, I feel that the lady novelists are on their least assailable ground. If women may not write pathetically about little boys' braces and little girls' hair-combs, and similar domestic trifles, I don't think they ought to write about anything at all. The Domestic novel is the ultimate expression of the sanctity of the family, and they are always written by elderly, unmarried ladies of good repute. These books cannot help striking a certain note of pathos, for we can watch the spectacle of the writer preparing a home for the man who does not come. Antimacassars on all chairs and chintz covers for the foot-stools, because men have clumsy feet. All the house is furnished with the same regard for his comfort; there are "priceless" cigars in the smoking-room, and two or three armfuls of lovable children in the nursery, there are dogs with kind sore eyes, and a cat named "Tib"; there are cheap Japanese ornaments for him to break when he is annoyed, and a residential staff of recording angels to blot out all his damns. At the top of the stairs stands a delightful woman, not exactly handsome, but interesting, with a darkly crooked smile and wonderful drowned eyes, and devotion that rarely receives its full allowance of praise until she is dead. Books of this sort cannot possibly hurt anyone, and only wicked baronets ought to be annoyed with them. If the men who strut through the chapters are very, very lovely, and the women perhaps a little too fond of getting kissed unexpectedly, it is, nevertheless, all pleasant and clean and wholesome, and we do not have to trouble ourselves with a wearisome search for motives. And considering it is a product of woman, this class of book is singularly free from dots.

CHESTERTON AND "THE MAN WHO WAS THURSDAY"

THERE are some men whose names, pleasantly inscribed on the title-page of a book or at the head of an article, fill the hearts of even a tired professional reader with a hardly describable emotion. There is something of expectancy in it, as when a man descends from the railway train at some little wayside station for the first time. He may be well acquainted with the sort of country he is going to see, he may have looked it all out on the maps; but there are the sun-blistered advertisements, the station-master's flower-beds, the hills and trees and little fields, and somehow the very blue sky becomes uncanny, it is all so new! There is something in this emotion also of fear, not the quick fear of street accidents or forgotten umbrellas, but the slow terror which lurks among the velvet chairs of dentists, and keeps the woods with Pan. We know these men, on whose operating tables we are about to lay our minds, can hurt us extremely if they have the will, and yet we gladly grant them the opportunity, for they can give us so much pleasure.

The truth is that these writers scorn to play games for the amusement of arm-chair readers; what they ask is that the reader should leave his mental island, and join them in a universal debauch of play. Now they will dance him down to hell to make mud-pies, now they will lead him up to heaven to fetch birds'-nests, and drag him from star to star in a triumphant game of hoodman-blind. After a while, if his heart is in the game, the sportive reader will come to understand these intellectual will-o'-the-wisps more or less. He will see that they always laugh when they are sorrowful, because they desire to be brave; he will see that they always cry when they are happy, because they cannot express their gratitude with mere human lips, made of flesh. He will find, in fact, that it is their pure and childlike simplicity which gives their utterances a twist of paradox in a very civilised world.

Chief among these mad lords of intellectual playing-fields I should place Mr. G. K. Chesterton, and of all his efforts to call a sleepy world to play, I esteem *The Man who was Thursday* the best. Once you have opened this book it is of no use to hide behind the nursery door or to feign a sudden interest in the sterile deeds of grown-up people. Rather you must out into the world with wild Master Chesterton to play until your clothes are torn and your braces broken and your breath lost for ever. Mr. Chesterton calls his book "A Nightmare" as a sub-title. Nightmare is a fine wide word, but only a child who has never had a nightmare would dare to use it, even in broad daylight. Mr. Chesterton would also have us believe that his book is an allegory, but he should have taken warning by the awful fate of Dean Swift, who sat down in a temper and wrote one of the best children's books that has ever been written. He thought *Gulliver's Travels* was a bitter satire, but the young people read it and found that it was a pleasant and imaginative work, full of agreeable details. So, I am afraid, the youthful-minded will find in *The Man who was Thursday* a delightfully veracious account of present-day life, written with spirit and charged with a hundred surprises. It is something like the *New Arabian Nights*, but more virile and much, much madder. Stevenson would have liked to have written four-fifths of it, but there was that in his Scotch blood which would have stopped him, even if he had chanced, by aid of his fairies, on Mr. Chesterton's extraordinary plot. It is as subtle as treacle, as probable as a dream. Yet in all the book women are hardly mentioned!

And this is one of the most curious qualities of the author's infinite zest for the romantic. It is only the manly toys that appeal to him: wine and food and fighting; and I seek in vain in his pages for such essentially romantic things as women's hand-bags, and the cropped curls at the back of a girl's neck. This is boyishness with a vengeance, but I cannot deny that Mr. Chesterton has a strong case. There were no girls on Treasure Island because girls are not really any good at playing; they have no stamina, and that, I imagine, is why there are no girls in *The Man who was Thursday* and none in *The Napoleon of Notting Hill*. The latter book contained Mr. Chesterton's scheme for a Utopia of violence: fine, manly, bloody violence; but in *The Man who was Thursday* we discover a kind of Utopia of fear. It is often but mock-fear of the same quality as that terror which children will affect in peeping into an untenanted house. But we know that a creaking board or the scuttle of a mouse in the wainscot will start them tearing down the grassy drive in a veritable panic, and in the same way I feel that a trifle would set Mr. Chesterton's characters screaming with ugly fright. It is this sense of shadowy terrors that gives the book its undoubted power, for the author first bids us become children and then leads us into a world full of darkness and unknown things. We may tell ourselves that these terrible shadows are trees and men and houses, but the torturing doubt remains.

Mr. Chesterton, as I have said, believes his book to be an allegory, and in the last two chapters he makes a wholly unsuccessful effort to expound it. But while I utterly refuse to accept the author's explanation as to what his work means, I am not on that account the more prepared to explain what it means myself. It is extremely amusing, and sometimes it is terrifying. But for the rest, I had rather content myself with telling an allegory of my own.

In the city of London there was a great restaurant, and high up in the roof of it was a gallery wherein an orchestra played day and night to the folk who swallowed their meat and drank their wine down below. The customers could not see the orchestra, and it was not considered etiquette for the orchestra to look at the customers, and as these latter were too busy eating and drinking to applaud, in course of years the musicians forgot all about the ordinary people in the restaurant, and lived very happily in a world of mutual admiration. Until one day, a little boy eating ices in the midst of the grown-up people, got up and clapped his hands, partly from admiration for the playing of the orchestra, and partly because he wished to make a noise of his own. The musicians were roused from their harmonious dreamings by this unwonted tribute, and fell a-quarrelling as to its due division. From quarrelling they fell to beating one another on the skulls with their violins, and so ultimately they found disaster.

So far for the allegory, and now I will venture on the application, with which anyone is at liberty to disagree. I own that it is partly prophetic. My beloved (as they say in the *Gesta Romanorum*), the restaurant is the intellectual world, and the folk who eat and drink in it are the ordinary people like you and me. The musicians are the present-day prophets, great and wonderful men like Bernard Shaw and H. G. Wells. But the little boy who claps his hands is G. K. Chesterton.

MR. CHESTERTON CONSIDERED

PROBABLY when the literary history of the present age comes to be written, few figures will cause the honest historian more tribulation than that of Mr. G. K. Chesterton. In him I recognise a clear-cut and amazing personality, a happy and subtle controversialist, and a writer of elusive but undoubted gifts. But others, with whose criticisms I am usually in agreement, find in him at most an able journalist, capable of being extremely dull and endowed with a number of vastly irritating mannerisms of style. And the trouble of the matter is that while I cling desperately to the idea of Chesterton, while Chestertonics are for me the only true restorers of the lost laughters of spring, I am not quite sure that these candid opponents are wrong. Where is the greatness of Mr. Chesterton (I repeat that I think he is great), fully expressed in his writings? I think that there are passages in *The Napoleon of Notting Hill*, but there is unhappily a deal of journalism in that fantastic book; there are sentences in his essays and even more journalism; there are colour and wonder in his verses, but for Mr. Chesterton, Parnassus is formed as narrow as a church steeple, whereon Pegasus balances himself like a weather-cock, and not as the broad and comfortable mountain of our dreams. There was an admirable book on Browning, which yet was only a book on Browning. Can it be possible that when Mr. Chesterton defends the ephemeral, as he does in the first essay of *All Things Considered*, he is really defending himself?

And yet after I have made this handsome acknowledg-
ment of the strength of the position of those who are
irritated or wearied by Mr. Chesterton, I can still believe
in him as a figure of considerable literary importance. If
he has not yet produced the big book, I think it is rather
the fault of his age than any fault of his own. For these
are days when our writers love to preach and to prophesy,
and no man can hope to make good art until the sands of
his pulpit hour-glass have run down. Mr. Chesterton has
always taken himself too seriously, and so he has never
taken his work seriously enough. The mistake is pardon-
able, for Mr. Chesterton is a very good thing; but person-
alities count for nothing until they have been expressed
in art, and the romantic novel which I believe Mr. Chesterton could write grows dusty on the shelves of his imagination, while he tells his readers credible things in incredible
terms. Yet all this moralising belongs to an age of life
which Mr. Chesterton should have left behind by now;
the age between the glowing recklessness of boyhood and
the dispassionate zest of manhood, the age which we call
callow, intolerant or youthful, according to our moods.
And so I am afraid that Mr. Chesterton, who shall be
romantic, has not at present either a real pirate-ship
or one perfected in dreams, but only some quite un-
important theories as to the moralities of pirates. And
if a healthy boy were to confront him with the facts
of the case, he would not scruple to pillage the South
Seas to deck Battersea with their fantastic golds and
crimsons.

So when I come to examine Mr. Chesterton's latest book
of essays I find him posing outrageously as a journalist, a
part which, personally, I do not think he fills very well.
Mr. Chesterton says in effect that he will write about hats

and politics and phonetic spelling, but in practice he always ends by writing about G. K. C. and the Eternities. In this way Mr. Chesterton's essays remind me of a pious game of my childhood, which consisted in persuading someone to think of some natural object, and then tracing its origin triumphantly back to the Deity by means of a series of questions. The problem lay, as far as I remember, in choosing some object which postponed the culminating expression of faith as long as possible, and with all reverence, I think it may be said that Mr. Chesterton is an expert at this game. Further, it seems to me that in seeking the obvious in subtleties he sometimes misses it altogether, and is either unintelligible or frankly wrong. And for all his optimism and healthiness, Mr. Chesterton's essays remain inhuman. He can tell you all about a man's thoughts and motives and emotions, but he cannot talk to him in a Lamb-like manner about the weather. His little papers are too intellectual and not bloody enough for my taste, and I feel somehow in reading these essays that life is made up of trivialities, trivialities which Mr. Chesterton can find stimulating and important, but which would, if we were to accept his philosophy, make life wholly ridiculous to normal minds.

And now I find that I have nearly reached the end of my essay without having accomplished the appreciation which I had intended to write. But it must be remembered that criticism is, for all our cunning, a relative matter, and that I have paid Mr. Chesterton the compliment of considering him largely from the point of view of his possible legacy to posterity. I firmly believe that he has not yet given us of his best (though of his latest book, *Orthodoxy*, I hear great things, and hope to think greater), but I owe him a debt of gratitude for the books he has given us, and I must confess that I have found many wise and suggestive observations in *All Things Considered*, and that it is moreover frequently extremely entertaining. But I wish to have an opportunity of praising the big book before I go to join my dreams.

FRANK HARRIS AND HIS GLASSES

I SOMETIMES wonder whether we are sufficiently grateful
for our national birthright of self-satisfied stupidity, which
has produced, in revolt, all or nearly all that is good in
English literature. "Nature hates mind," said Wilde, in
Intentions, and in this respect the English are Nature's most
faithful children. All our favourite English institutions,
our laws, Members of Parliament, newspapers, judges,
educational systems, and domestic dogmas, are venomous
symbols of this consuming hatred. Even the Socialists, who
might be presumed to have revolutionary intellectual
tendencies, are at pains to flatter the popular stupidity.
    It is not part of my purpose here to defend or attack
anarchy; but it is certainly worth while to show that it
is a reasonable position, if not the only reasonable position, for a man of intellect to adopt, who is unfortunate
enough to be in touch with his age in material matters. It is
given to few to dream with Blake, and for the rest there is
no compromise between the anarchy of Shelley and the
complete cynicism of Anatole France. Our modern civilisation is intellectually putrid, and if you cannot ignore it
you must hate it, or crown it with scornful laughter. And
here, if they had chosen to see it, lies the explanation of the
extraordinary realism that startled the reviewers of Frank
Harris's amazing novel, *The Bomb*. Of course, Frank
Harris could describe the spiritual and physical sensations
of the Chicago anarchists, for, living as he does in twentieth-
century England, he must have flung a hundred bombs in
his dreams. He has heard the explosion, and seen the
bruised bodies of fools lying like mud on the roadway,

and thereafter he has felt the inevitable reaction that leads even the sternest intellects to pity the wantonly ignorant at times. "Forgive them, Lord, they know not what they do!" But it is a hard saying in the country of the Police Commission, and the Albert Memorial, and the cheating spirit of vengefulness that men call English justice.

But it is just this spirit of pity that underlies the bitterness of *The Magic Glasses*, Frank Harris's remarkable short story. It is a story that Hans Andersen might have conceived, but, as it is hardly necessary to tell readers of *Elder Conklin* and *Montes the Matador*, its treatment by Frank Harris is as far removed from the washy sentimentalities and niggling satire of Andersen as the blank verse of Shakespeare is from that of Dryden. There is a phrase of Browning's that always recurs to me when I read anything from Frank Harris's pen, "It's as if I saw it all!" *The Magic Glasses* is not only a very fine story; it is also a true story, and he has told us exactly how it all happened.

In this I shall not attempt to follow him. Indeed, I shall content myself with giving a bare outline sufficient to enable the reader to grasp the general drift of the story. An old optician, named Penry, has been charged by the police with obstructing the traffic by selling glasses, and, when that charge fails, with fraud. It seems that he has induced a man called Hallett to buy a pair of glasses for a sovereign, on the ground that they will enable him to see the truth. Hallett, the type of bumptious and ultimately successful English tradesman, can see nothing through the glasses, and wants his money back. Penry says there is no fraud; that the fault lies with Hallet, who has no eyes for the truth. With nine magistrates out of ten Penry would have been committed for trial at this point, but he is fortunate in having met the exception, and persuades the magistrate to try his glasses himself. This the magistrate does, and

sees the faces of the men about him become unspeakably
villainous, "and the worst of all are the solicitors." For a
while he is inclined to accept the statement of the accused,
until, at the suggestion of a solicitor, he looks at his own
image in a mirror. For a moment he is silent, and then he
commits Penry for trial.

Here, even if the story went no further, we have a moral
as strikingly conveyed as is the eternal duality of man in
Dr. Jekyll and Mr. Hyde. But there is more, much more.
We have the account of how Mr. Penry came to make the
glasses, an account so convincing that, when I read it, I
wondered why no one had hitherto made such glasses;
we hear of the commercial ruin that would inevitably overtake any man who devoted his life to the discovery of the
truth; we catch an enchanted glimpse of the old man, of
whom alone the soul is noble enough to bear the test of
the merciless glasses, pursuing his ideal, undaunted by the
buffetings of a world of fools. He has made glasses that
will reveal the appearance of men and things as they are;
now he would fain discover the ultimate truth, their likeness as it might be revealed to the eyes of higher beings. I
cannot pretend to convey any suggestion of the ingenious
beauty of this part of the story. There is one description
of Dante Gabriel Rossetti, "pouring out truths and thoughts,
epigrams and poetry, as a great jeweller sometimes pours
gems from hand to hand," that must serve to suggest
the passionate realism of these pages.

In Penry's second trial we have the culmination of this
bitter comment on our admired and coveted earth. Once
more we meet the uncultured venom of Hallett, loathing
the thing he is not clean enough to understand; we have a
new witness, a Canon of Westminster, who finds the message of the glasses blasphemous, and wins the British jury
readily enough with his greasy eloquence. We have

alleged witnesses to the character of the defendant, tradesmen who can only say that he was respectable before he
neglected his normal business of optician. Penry himself
cannot influence an unfair judge and a jury that has made
up its mind, and the case seems over, when he challenges
the judge to let him try the effect of the glasses on a little
girl, the daughter of the judge, who is waiting in a room
behind the court. The judge agrees, and the little girl puts
on the glasses. Like the magistrate before her, she looks
about the court and finds all men save Penry, ugly. Last of
all she looks at her father, and tears the glasses off her face
indignantly. Then Penry gives her another pair of glasses,
and bids her look into the future. She sees a cold, white
place, where there is no living thing and after that she can
see no more. Even a child may catch no more than a scant
moment of the grave that shall bury this. The story ends
abruptly, with Penry's death in prison.

Even in the mangled form to which I have been compelled to reduce it, the reader can hardly fail to appreciate
the simplicity and directness of the criticism of life, that
gives *The Magic Glasses* that spiritual power to which
ordinary fiction cannot hope to attain. For, as I have said
above, the thing is true. Frank Harris has not merely
suggested that through a pair of magic glasses the face of
civilised man would seem frightful. He has given, as it
were, one terrible momentary glimpse through the glasses
themselves, we have seen the little lewd maggot puffing
and creeping behind the mask of civilised humanity, and,
like the child of the judge, our minds are aghast at the
spectacle. How shall we endure this world of ugly faces,
this place of low ideals and muddy souls?

And yet, as I have said, behind all the bitterness of *The
Magic Glasses* there sounds a note of pity. It would have
been easy to show the world, as Anatole France has shown

it in *L'Ile des Pingouins*—a place beyond hope, where folly and baseness writhe in the mud for dominion. But in the narrator of the story, who bails out the old man from motives of compassion, in a labouring man who, though he thinks he has been cheated, refuses to give condemnatory evidence against him, even in the child starting in dismay from the repellent face of her father, Frank Harris has suggested the light moment of valour, the passing breath of love, the last pride of humanity that in the end shall conquer all the cunning of our civilisation. We have made our lives a lie, a stupid lie, but we cannot quite kill our souls. After all, there is something in most of us that we have not made ourselves. But who will flog this age of idiots into understanding that that is all we have?

If I have failed to convey that *The Magic Glasses* is a very great story indeed, then I will assure the reader that it is my pen that is at fault, and not my judgment. Frank Harris has shown us before that he stands alone as a writer of short stories. So if I say that *The Magic Glasses* is as good as he has given us I need say no more. And to the critic who thinks it criminal to praise a man in his own house,* I say "Peace." For I have seen the face of that critic through *The Magic Glasses* and I feel concern for his soul.

* Published in *Vanity Fair*, then under the Editorship of Frank Harris, March 31, 1909.—J. G.

FRANK HARRIS AND SHAKESPEARE

"The play's the thing"; really, there are times when the most hackneyed of quotations is justified by its aptness. The controversy between Mr. Frank Harris and Mr. Bernard Shaw has been extremely interesting, but it is to be regretted that as a consequence the critics of our contemporaries have for the most part devoted themselves to the discussion of Mr. Harris's spirited introduction rather than to the appreciation of the play itself. To our mind, the problem has assumed very simple terms. Mr. Shaw has admitted that he had read Mr. Harris's play, and, being possessed of considerable critical acumen, he should have realised that he could not better it. Knowing that there was an admirable drama of Shakespeare in existence, he should have hesitated before writing his ineffective skit. On the other hand, Mr. Harris, who seems to produce a masterpiece every time he returns from the south of France, can afford to be generous. Having reduced our Shakespearean professors to anonymous lamentations, he might have spared poor Puck, nut-eating, Jaegar-clad, uncomfortable Puck, who never harmed anybody save perhaps certain archdeacons, fallen unwarily to reading his periodical letters in *The Times*.

In a play of which Shakespeare is the protagonist, we have the right to demand not merely the ordinary dramatic qualities, but also that the portrait of Shakespeare should be satisfying in terms of truth and sympathy. We need hardly say that the author of *The Man Shakespeare* has not failed us here; that memorable book is surely the classic proof of the fact that all true criticism is founded on love,

R

and in the gentle, lovable features of the Shakespeare of the play we recognise with a thrill quickened by the dramatic atmosphere the man Shakespeare who spoke to us with so clear a voice from the pages of the book.

And in one respect Mr. Harris's task in the later work was the harder. It would have been so easy, it must have been so tempting, to sacrifice the truth of the portrait in order to make Shakespeare one of those heroic figures for whom our blind zest for the romantic has made us greedy. It must be remembered that the story of the Sonnets which gives the play its main plot shows Shakespeare in the guise of a betrayed and outwitted lover, a situation which moves most men to laughter rather than sympathy. Mr. Harris has not abated one jot of his humiliation; we see the poet's first passion for Mary Fytton quickly fanned into flame by her half curious, half careless, wanton acceptance of his love. This was not the kind of wooer to whom Mary Fytton was accustomed; she preferred the eloquence of deeds to poor Shakespeare's elaborate expressions of his passion, but she appreciated the charm of variety, and on the whole she was kind to Shakespeare, if it be kindness in a woman to stimulate the passion of her lover. She made even less to-do about yielding to Herbert when that brilliant young man had leisure to covet her and betray his friend Shakespeare; if anything were needed to increase Shakespeare's humiliation, it would be the almost careless readiness with which his friend and his mistress betray him. But Mr. Harris has emphasised rather than concealed this aspect of the tragic story. How, then, it may be asked, has he made Shakespeare sympathetic?

The question can be answered easiest by contrasting the character Shakespeare with one of the other characters, Herbert, for example. Herbert is a magnificent version of what we may call, in no spirit of condemnation, a woman's

hero. He is dashing, impudent, resourceful, and unscru-
pulous. He is extraordinarily successful with women, although (or perhaps because) his conception of the relationship of the sexes is hardly nobler than Montaigne's. He is
amicable to men, and clever enough to appreciate the value
of Shakespeare's friendship. Such a man will go far in a
world of men, and farther still in a world of women. Shakespeare, on the other hand, is the dreamer, gentle, affectionate and sincere, mistrustful of action, and loving to "unpack
his heart with words." For him, as for his own Romeo,
passion is the mother of beautiful phrases, although women
hate beautiful phrases, finding them but too successful
rivals of their own physical charms. All but the very rarest
and noblest of women prefer the Herberts to the Shake-
speares, if the choice is forced upon them. Mary Fytton
found Shakespeare interesting enough though rather
wordy, until Herbert called her; then she had to go.

It is the inevitability of the betrayal that saves this great
play from being too painful for lovers of Shakespeare to
read it with enjoyment. We feel that the characters are
helpless in the clutch of circumstance; Shakespeare must
forsake his gentle Violet to serve the white wanton;
Herbert must cheat his friend; Mary Fytton must accept her
brief hour of Herbert's favour, with perhaps a half-regret-
ful glance back at her poet, the noblest and maddest of all
her lovers. They are all the servants of Destiny, and it is
our sense of this that makes it possible for us to endure the
poet-dramatist's humiliating defeat in the merciless tourna-
ment of love. The noblest part of Shakespeare was not to
be known by Mary Fytton, since we can only judge others
by our own standards; we may doubt with Mr. Harris
whether it was known by any of his contemporaries, save
perhaps Ben Jonson.

It is just this noblest part of the man—we may call it his

genius—that is present, as Mr. Shaw admitted, in the Shake-speare of Mr. Harris's play. Whether we meet him among his fellow dramatists at the Mermaid and the Mitre, or in the bitter-sweet company of Mary Fytton, or in the last sad scene on his death-bed, we are always conscious of that in-definable magnetism that is the true halo of great men. Yet for all his greatness he is supremely human; witness his attitude towards Chettle, the delightful prototype of Fal-staff, who writes to him for money with which to pay his tavern reckoning. Jonson reproaches Shakespeare with squandering his money on a man who deserves it so little. Shakespeare replies: "I owe him what money can never pay . . . his jokes and humoured laughter. He warms me with his hot love of life, and living." This in the blackest hour of his passion, when the knowledge of his betrayal has failed to lighten his servitude! Was ever a man more humanly lovable?

The scenes between Shakespeare and Mary Fytton are really astonishing, and make us regret that we have not heard that the play is going to be performed. There can be no mistaking the quality of these love scenes. Mary Fytton is superb; the finest figure of a passionate woman that our drama has known since *Antony and Cleopatra*. That Mrs. Patrick Campbell should have been eager to play the part is in no way astonishing, though creditable to her artistic courage. Herbert, too, as we have suggested, is completely successful. His impudent quickness in flattery of Queen Elizabeth is admirable; so, too, is his little quarrel with Raleigh. If we are to interpret a certain passage in the Introduction as being an explanation of the scenes wherein Chettle and many of the dramatists of the time are intro-duced, scenes which might be held to lie outside the main current of the play, we can assure Mr. Harris it was not needed. The scenes themselves have such intrinsic merit, and display such an intimate knowledge of the life of the period, that for our part we could not spare a word of them. The setting is all worthy of the picture.

But after all the play stands by Shakespeare, and he satisfies us wholly. Mr. Harris has not merely drawn the figure of a great man and made us feel that he is great; that he had already done in *The Bomb*. But now he has drawn the figure of a great man and made us feel that he is Shakespeare, and in accomplishing this task he has written a great play. We have not hesitated to praise this play without reservation; we know that in this we are doing honour to ourselves rather than to Mr. Harris. To the man of genius the pride of good work accomplished is the sufficient reward; this is fortunate, for in England he rarely gets anything else.

THE ART OF HILAIRE BELLOC

On my table there lies a half-written, and, I trust, tolerably sincere, article on the decay of the essay; yet here is the third volume of essays within a month to deserve something more than railway-carriage attention. Of the art of Mr. Max Beerbohm and the extraordinary ingenuity of Mr. Gilbert Chesterton I cannot sing here; but, before I consider Mr. Belloc's *On Everything*, I should like to congratulate Messrs. Methuen on the pleasant little series to which that book belongs. If anything can restore the lost popularity of the essay, these little volumes, pleasant to handle and read, and costing a nominal crown-piece—an actual three-and-ninepence—should have that desirable result. So much intelligence is squandered on modern journalism that it is really necessary that we should possess the best of that journalism in durable form. And on the jaded reader these significant books should fall like summer rain, after the consuming drought of sensational stories that do not thrill, modern novels that are not new, and slip-shod biographies of persons who do not matter.

For the most part, Mr. Belloc informs us, the essays included in his volume appeared in the *Morning Post*, and at times I wished that he had been more specific, for some of his little papers must have seemed devilish queer to the readers of that admirable journal. It is not that he does not possess the "tone"—for he writes ever with a very gentlemanly pen—but that he is essentially a Liberal, and is thereby compelled to direct keen thrusts at objects very near to the truly Conservative heart. So that, having a curious mind, I was led to wonder while turning the pages whether this essay or that had appeared in the *Morning Post*, or whether it was among those added to the number to give righteousness to the whole.

In one respect I could wish that Mr. Belloc were not so well suited to be literary editor of the *Morning Post* as he certainly is. For, in spite of his years as an artilleryman in the French army, in spite of his experience of men and hills and lonely places, in spite of his love of red wine, I feel that Mr. Belloc is still an admirer of academic knowledge. How otherwise could he write scornfully of a man who "exposed and ridiculed the legend of the Girondins, but throughout his remarks pronounced their title with a hard *g*"? It is true that the man he is ridiculing was himself an Oxford don, but the serious thing is that Mr. Belloc should think that this mispronunciation affected the value of the argument. I do not wish to emphasise the point, but this Oxford contempt for the man who forms his judgments intuitively, rather than by aid of a knowledge of facts, crops up again and again in the book, and makes much of Mr. Belloc's work hard and unsympathetic. Facts are queer things, and I doubt whether they are much good to anybody; they set limits to the imagination, itself surely the soaring spirit of man, and in compensation they give him I know not what—self-assurance, perhaps, and the power to concentrate—something a little earthy, I suspect.

Mr. Belloc knows too many things to be a wholly delightful companion, and he sets too high a value on that knowledge to be deeply wise. He has, I think, a genuine admiration for simplicity, but the facts he has collected about human nature force him to draw men and women from the outside. There is one great chapter in *Emmanuel Burden*, where the old man goes home to die, in which Mr. Belloc seems for once to have slipped into the skin of his character, and the result is one of the really fine things in modern literature. But normally he is the clever child in the corner with a slate and a rather cruel pencil, and, in consequence, his satire almost invariably fails through lack of sympathy with his victims. Mr. Belloc hates Jews and company promoters and Union-Jack imperialists—all things quite important enough to hate—but, instead of using their virtues to emphasise by contrast their vices, he changes their virtues into vices of hypocrisy, and leaves them incredibly wicked. *Emmanuel Burden,* save for that one splendid chapter, is a kind of intellectual nightmare— a vision to make timid thinkers scream, and the devil himself would scruple to use it as convincing evidence of the evil of modern finance.

Fortunately, in his latest volume, Mr. Belloc has succeeded in keeping his black beasts under control, and he would be a very foolish Conservative who neglected to read *On Everything* because its author was a Liberal M.P. with sound views on the licensing question. The thirty-nine articles therein collected, if they do not deal with everything—Mr. Belloc knows too much for that—certainly cover a great deal of ground and display a pleasing variety of treatment. I like Mr. Belloc best, not as a satirist, but as a lover of simple men and simple places, and as a teller of unpretentious parables. "The Barber," to my mind the pleasantest thing in the book, shows Mr. Belloc combining these two qualities. There is also some quite agreeable farce, and at least one paper, "On An Empty House," is sentimental in a restrained way. A few suggest the influence of Mr. G. K. Chesterton, though Mr. Belloc's fettered enthusiasm for the things he likes is at the other end of the world from Mr. Chesterton's *enragé* common sense. They have a way of liking the same things for different reasons.

My general title must be my excuse for referring

briefly to Mr. Belloc's other work. He has written wisely on Paris and London, and the French Revolution. He has written two satirical novels, *Emmanuel Burden, Merchant,* and *Changes in the Cabinet.* He has written a good travel-book of the intimate personal kind in *The Path to Rome,* though Stevenson's supremacy in this *genre* remains unchallenged. There were pleasant things in *Hills and the Sea,* a previous volume of essays, and there was a volume on Algeria, full of colour. All these things—and there are others—constitute a very creditable output of work—books of the kind which a man is glad to have in his bookshelves, and does not allow to grow very dusty. And even then the tale is not complete. Mr. Belloc has written a number of poems, and these have never been collected in volume form, and it may be doubted whether there is any living poet so considerable of whom the same may be said. If anyone doubts this let him read Mr. Belloc's poem, called "Sussex," in *The Open Road,* the first bright flower of Mr. Lucas's growing garland of anthologies. It is strangely different from Mr. Kipling's poem on the same happy county, but it is very good nevertheless. Rumour of Mr. Belloc's biting doggerel "among his private friends" suggests that he has another talent, even rarer, perhaps, than the gift of writing musical verse. His lighter nonsense poems are happily known to us all, but the more pungent of these, in which he assaults the Union Jack Imperialists, company promoters, and Jews, will probably, in the present state of English letters, never be revealed to us. It is our loss.

On the whole, Mr. Belloc stands pretty well for the modern spirit in English letters. He is purposeful in thought and act; he has no fond delusions as to the value of art; he acknowledges the æsthetic charm of the fallen years, and yet believes in progress. He is sensible, in the modern meaning of that word, and I should think he despises men who sacrifice their power of action for dreaming.

I sometimes wonder whether, when the literary historian comes to sum up the latter years of the nineteenth and the earlier years of the twentieth centuries, he will recognise that those years included a definite literary movement and a definite literary revulsion. The critics are apt to underrate the importance of the movement a little narrowly connected with the Yellow Book, just as they are apt to exaggerate the importance of the propagandist tendency in literature to-day. Wilde and Beardsley, Dowson, young Mr. Symons, and the rest of them, were by no means members of a common school, but they did share the belief that the creation of beauty was the all-sufficient purpose of the artist's life. In their negation of this principle I would class together, not merely Mr. Shaw and Mr. Galsworthy and the useful dramatists, but Mr. Belloc, Mr. Wells and Mr. Chesterton as well. What the end of it all may be, the years, perhaps, will prove. Meanwhile, you may choose between the sweet, twisted smile of Ernest Dowson and the rather truculent Jaeger-men of Mr. Shaw, between *Intentions* and *On Everything*. Or, if you have catholic tastes, you can read them all. Certainly, Mr. Belloc's little book is interesting, and, at times, very nearly something more.

THE GENIUS OF A. E. HOUSMAN

POETRY is the highest expression of human emotion, and, as our emotions are of many different kinds and degrees, it follows that there are many different kinds of poetry. This is trite enough for the top or exemplary line of a copy-book, but it would be no ill thing if every article about poetry started with some such maxim, in order to remind the dogmatic reader that, while no doubt the very best poetry is rare indeed, there is quite a large amount of real poetry in the world, *great stuff* as a friend of mine would call it. It's a fine thing to appreciate Keats and Swinburne, but it is a great mistake to burn all the other poets in their honour. Yet this is what many critics are ready to do cheerfully enough. I showed the *Shropshire Lad* to a man the other day, and he looked at it and praised it, as everyone will have to praise it sooner or later. "But," he added, "you can't compare this sort of thing with the poetry of Keats." It's quite true; I can't. Mr. Housman can no more write like Keats than Keats could write like Mr. Housman. But, as I ventured to point out to my critic, there are other flowers beside the rose, and to be catholic in one's appreciation of poetry is not to deny a preference for the best. To me Mr. A. E. Housman, within his rather limited range, is as good as it is possible for a man to be. I would not compare him with any of the great immortals, because he himself has that individuality of expression that makes for immortality. He derives, it might be stated, rather from A. E. Housman than from anyone else, and beyond that I would seek among the simple ballad rhythms that we all inherit with our blood and in the pregnant earth of

Shropshire itself for his origins. A thousand years ago men like Mr. Housman were making folk-songs, and it's as something of the nature of twentieth-century folk-songs that his poems make their appeal to us to-day.

I have referred above to the rather limited range of his poems, but in truth the word is absurd. It would be truer to say that he has such intensity of utterance, so great a concentration of expression, that his pen, or, perhaps, I should say, his voice, deals only with what to him are the essentials of life. Death and hate and love, the bitterness of friendship, the torturing echoes of dead years, murder and suicide, and the hangman's noose are his themes, and over all there broods the sorrow of the Shropshire hills. To me he conveys a message of intense scepticism, hopeful only in the moment, bitterly regretful of the past, deeply mistrustful as to the future. I know of no poet, not even "B. V." Thomson, whose outlook on life is so deeply melancholy. He examines love and decides:

> His folly has not fellow
> Beneath the blue of day
> That gives to man or woman
> His heart and soul away.

He congratulates the unhappy suicide on having avoided the graver ills that might have resulted from continued existence, and he realises that in thinking lies despair and bids the world:

> Think no more; 'tis only thinking
> Lays lads underground.

And when he comes to consider his own state he can only sum up the whole sorry business of living with the bitter reflection:

Try I will; no harm in trying:
Wonder 'tis how little mirth
Keeps the bones of man from lying
On the bed of earth.

I am inclined to think that among contemporary poets
Mr. A. E. Housman is the only one who has sought in any
way to express the spirit of his age, by which I comprehend
the true spirit of the people, and not the lip-spirit of mobs
or still less the intellectual spirit that is sung by the few.
These are days of a deep and growing melancholy in relationship to eternal things, days when we are all tending to
a passionate belief in the necessity of faith, and are growing
less and less capable of achieving faith of any kind. A
consuming scepticism is in our blood, that leads the majority to accept desperate gods, the minority to beat their
heads against the walls of life, and cry pitifully for release.
It is the failure of our living artists to express this spirit
that has caused the almost complete divorce between
modern English art and the lives of the people. It seems
as though our artists can no longer see beneath the skins of
their fellow men and women, can no longer detect the timid
thought behind the blustering, meaningless word. And it
must be remembered that the common mind has always
relied, consciously or unconsciously, on the higher intellects for the discovery of its own ideas. What meaning the
work of the artists of to-day has for the common man I
do not know, but it certainly does not help him in his
search for his own ideas.

I am aware that present-day Englishmen are quite unconscious of their scepticism, but it seems to me to betray
itself in their every word and deed, and it is significant
that, at a period when they are notably heedless of poetry,
they have bought seven editions of the *Shropshire Lad*.* I

* This by November, 1909.—J. G.

have spoken about Mr. Housman's poems to a great many persons; but while I have found a few whose musical ear could not respond to the simplicity of their technique, I have found no one to condemn the disenchanted attitude towards life of which they are an expression. The truth is that few people are trained to detect tendencies in thought that they share themselves, and probably most of Mr. Housman's readers consider his poems as so many simple bird-songs from an English county, and are happily unconscious of the bitterness that finds a secret echo in their hearts.

Perhaps I have over-strained this point because it is one that is very interesting to me, and I am aware that my appreciation of Mr. Housman's poems is coloured, if not heightened, by my acceptance of his philosophy. But the *Shropshire Lad* needs no philosophical inquiries to prove its worth. Take this, for instance:

> High the vanes of Shrewsbury gleam,
> Islanded in Severn stream;
> The bridges from the steepled crest
> Cross the water east and west.
>
> The flag of morn in conqueror's state
> Enters at the English gate:
> The vanquished eve, as night prevails,
> Bleeds upon the road to Wales.

The beautiful first verses of a beautiful poem that I would like to quote in full. And this is one of the difficulties of my task; Mr. Housman is a poet of poems and not of lines, and that can be said of his poems which Swinburne could not bring himself to say of *Atalanta in Calydon*; the whole is greater than the part. Thus, I have marked seventeen poems to quote in full, and, if I carried out my intention my essay would take at least another ten pages. Fortunately, the poems are easily obtainable—you can buy them in a pretty little book for sixpence or a shilling—

and if I have not excited the reader's curiosity to that extent, so much the worse for the reader.

I find Mr. Housman best when he is handling a grim subject, and, outside one or two of the early ballads, I know nothing like the savage simplicity with which he outlines his rustic tragedies. There is the wonderful ballad on an execution at Shrewsbury jail, and the, to me, even more wonderful poem of the labourer who has murdered his brother:

> The sun burns on the half-mown hill,
>   By now the blood is dried;
> And Maurice amongst the hay lies still
>   And my knife is in his side.
>
>   .   .   .
>
> And here's a bloody hand to shake,
>   And oh, man, here's good-bye;
> We'll sweat no more on scythe and rake,
>   My bloody hands and I.
>
>   .   .   .   .
>
> Long for me the rick will wait,
>   And long will wait the fold,
> And long will stand the empty plate,
>   And dinner will be cold.

It is surely hardly necessary to point out how the naïve simplicity of the last line heightens the realism of the poem, and enables Mr. Housman to get an extraordinary effect in twenty-four lines. There is an even more striking instance of this simplicity in *The True Lover*:

> The lad came to the door at night,
>   When lovers crown their vows,
> And whistled soft and out of sight
>   In shadow of the boughs.
>
> "I shall not vex you with my face
>   Henceforth, my love, for aye;
> So take me in your arms a space
>   Before the east is grey."
>
>   .   .   .   .

"Oh, lad, what is it, lad, that drips
   Wet from your neck on mine?
What is it falling on my lips,
   My lad, that tastes of brine?"

"Oh, like enough 'tis blood, my dear,
   For when the knife has slit
The throat across from ear to ear
   'Twill bleed because of it."

Under the stars the air was light
   But dark below the boughs,
The still air of the speechless night,
   When lovers crown their vows.

This is surely convincing enough even when deprived, as space compels me to print it, of four of its verses. I should say that whether or not you can appreciate work of this character is simply a matter of temperament. To some people that penultimate verse might seem humorous in its frankness; to me it is simply terrific.

There are many other poems in the *Shropshire Lad* which I should love to praise here; especially the curious poem beginning "Be still, my soul, be still; the arms you bear are brittle," in which the poet almost succeeds in winning hope out of hopelessness, and the first poem in the book, surely the only good poem inspired by the 1887 or any other Jubilee. There is a poem like the Kipling of the *Barrack-room Ballads*, and as good; and another, won from the mirror of the waters, like the Stevenson of *The Child's Garden*, but better. And, lastly, there is a poem which acts as epilogue to the book, and gives us something of the poet's attitude towards his own work. I quote it in full:

I hoed and trenched and weeded,
   And took my flowers to fair:
I brought them home unheeded;
   The hue was not the wear.

So up and down I sow them
  For lads like me to find,
When I shall lie below them
  A dead man out of mind.

Some seed the birds devour,
  And some the season mars,
But here and there will flower
  The solitary stars.

And fields will yearly bear them
  As light-leaved spring comes on,
And luckless lads will wear them
  When I am dead and gone.

The poet's belief in the immortal element in his work is a belief always justified if it is sincere. I have tried to express my appreciation of Mr. A. E. Housman's work, but the task is impossible within the space at my disposal. I have left out a hundred things that I wanted to say.

S

LITERATURE AND BURGLARS

IN a less impatient age we should like to have reverted to an old and pleasant manner, and named this "Some Winter Thoughts on Burglars: being a Lament for their Little Culture and an Inquiry into the Origin of Picturesque Illusions." But the day has gone when an author would reveal his soul on his title-page, adorned with a border of grapes and sprawling Cupids. Authors to-day have forgotten the little arts by means of which eighteenth-century writers made their books as intimate as conversations. Printers are no longer lavish with their capitals, and the modern journalist does not plunge into italics every time he becomes excited. Our great-grandfathers had a wonderful gift for this sort of thing, and they were sometimes most human where a modern writer would feel bound to be most matter-of-fact. Johnson contrived to give his very admirable prejudices expression in his Dictionary, and even a list of errata might be made to convey something of a man's mind to his readers. Dreaming at a bookstall the other day, we found a little volume on the prevention of smoky chimneys, in which the list of errors bore this charming apology. "Sith Venus hath her mole and the Moon her spots, think it not strange if this little book hath its blunders." We felt as if we had shaken hands with the author.

This by way of digression, for which also there is good eighteenth-century precedent; yet our complaint against burglars can be stated quite simply. We would not be so unjust as to blame them for not fulfilling the wakeful nightmares of children. Nothing can do that, and the most conscientious burglar would weary at last of carrying a blood-stained knife between his teeth and twisting his features to a scowl of unassuageable hatred of the human race. Our grievance lies deeper. As an intellectual conception a burglar is a rather fine thing. The spectacle of the individual leading his gallant little forces to battle against the tremendous laws of his race is one that, even in defeating him, it becomes us to admire. But in practice they are only sordid pilferers with a soul that does not rise above tea-spoons stamped with the hall-mark of convention. One of those planetary visitors or Chinese philosophers of whom our ancestors were so fond would not fail to infer this from an examination of the London shops. Books, charged with the wisdom that is beyond price, stand openly on the pavement for any man to touch with his hand, but the diamonds in the windows of the jewellers' shops are guarded by little steel grilles. In a world where the thieves were men of culture this would have to be reversed. The jeweller would heap his stupid wares in barrels on the pavement, and we should peer at books through iron bars, under the watchful eyes of plain-clothes detectives. In such a world the police reports would really be as interesting as the newspapers appear to think they are. Perhaps when our habitual drunkards can quote their Omar, and our professional unemployables loll starwards with Tennyson's *Lotus-eaters* on their lips, English burglars will turn their attention to libraries and convince the common mind that since books are worth stealing they must also be worth possessing.

Outside fiction the ranks of cultured cracksmen are very thinly filled. For some reason or other, men of letters have generally preferred forgery. Possibly a milder term should be found for the venial exploits of Chatterton and Mac-pherson, but Wainwright, to whom both Swinburne and

Wilde have devoted papers, and Johnson's Dr. Dodd, the unfortunate author of the *Beauties of Shakespeare*, naturally occur to the mind in this connection. Villon was rather a cut-purse than a burglar, and the evidence as to Deacon Brodie's culture is not very clear, though in Stevenson's play he is educated, if not scholarly. We do not know that he ever stole any books.

In novels the educated burglar has become rather a nuisance, and the descendants of Raffles are as wearisome as are the offspring of Sherlock Holmes. We believe that Arsène Lupin had a library of stolen books, but they were selected rather for their rarity than for the merit of their contents. This is the test that we should apply to scholar-burglars. They should select their booty for its intrinsic and not for its monetary value, and they should form their libraries with far greater care than those who pursue the ordinary cheque-book method. We have not heard of a burglar of this character, but it is possible that he exists. If this be so, we admire his discrimination, and at the same time envy him his nocturnal adventures. We sometimes feel that nowadays books are too numerous and too cheap for those who obtain them so easily to appreciate their true worth. But with what pleasure must our scholar-burglar regard his library, where every volume recalls a glorious adventure! How often he has crept by night into the libraries of other men and turned his dark lantern from shelf to shelf while making his cultured and leisurely choice! Looking at other people's books is always a pleasant way of passing time, and sometimes, one fancies, dawn must have discovered him still hesitating between the merits of two rival editions, or held spellbound by the charm of some plump old quarto into which he has dipped too far. Being one of your true scholars who love to leave their books to posterity in proper trim, he handles books tenderly, and would scorn to use his jemmy as a paper-knife after the manner of library subscribers. Nor does he rob proud old books of their plates in order to extra-illustrate volumes of no merit, and thus preserve his memory for the profanities of book-lovers yet unborn.

Probably the nearest thing to this ideal burglar of ours is the hero of Barrie's *What Every Woman Knows*, who broke into a house, if our memory serves us, in order to study, but drew the line at stealing books. But the whole spirit of the devout book-lover lies in his possession of his treasures. He likes to have them about him, and to hear them and smell them at all hours of the day and night. It was for this reason that a distinguished book-collector of our acquaintance used to keep under his bed the three editions of Keats's poems that appeared during the poet's lifetime. When he could not sleep he would lean out of bed in the dark and stroke them, and be subtly comforted. It would have fared ill with the burglar who should have sought to annex these treasures; but ordinary book-lovers have no need for expensive first editions.

It is certain that the romantic burglar is almost entirely a myth, though the exploit of Colonel Thomas Blood, who nearly succeeded in getting away with the Crown jewels, and received a pension of five hundred a year from Charles II for his pains, is romantic enough for anybody, and provided a fitting climax for a life of which a brief account is to be found in the notes to *Peveril of the Peak*. As we have already implied, the life of a man who endeavours to obtain wealth dishonestly is no more romantic than that of a merchant who acquires it honestly. But it is difficult not to admire a man who makes, as Blood remarked complacently, a gallant attempt for a crown. Just as the highwayman and the pirate dwindle to insignificant and rather pitiful figures when closely examined, so, too, the average burglar is no more than the meanest and clumsiest of rogues when we put aside the splendid conceptions of imaginative writers. It is suggestive that in England we measure the relative guilt of housebreakers by the number of convictions that have been recorded against them, so that we must believe that our most dangerous criminals have spent practically all their lives in prison. The novelists will have it that the most dangerous criminals are those who habitually escape detection, a reasonable though apparently inaccurate thesis, unless it be admitted that in practice the cleverest burglars have a very short run for their money. And that is probably the truth of the matter, and, taking the *personnel* of our criminal classes into account, we are not sorry they fare so poorly. That a man should risk his liberty because he could live no longer without the lyrics of Herrick or the diary of Mr. Pepys would be an admirable thing; but we have no sympathy with the person who blunders into prison in a clumsy effort to steal silver teaspoons and plated vegetable dishes.

OCCASIONAL PIECES

THE MADNESS OF SPRING

IF we accept Johnson's definition of madness as a perturbation of the faculties, we must acknowledge that there is more than a conventional association between madness and the earlier months of the year. While the buds are breaking, the faculties of all of us are perturbed with a vengeance, and never a green leaf unrolls beneath the sky but one of us tramples underfoot the laws he has made for the guidance of his life. Sometimes our mania is clear to everyone, sometimes we are the most cunning of madmen, only wearing straws in solitude, and duly imitating the lives of our grandfathers before our suspicious neighbours. But, however this may be, we are all mad in the spring, and though their perturbations vary as widely as the new leaves, our faculties sing drunken songs together along the wind-swept streets of the world.

This is a period when it is very good to be young, and so I willingly sympathise with the madness of my friend Florizel, who drives about London looking for his lost youth in a taxi filled with children and chocolates. There are moments, he tells me, when this annual search seems to be crowned with success. Perhaps for an hour he recovers the forgotten ignorance of his early years; the children treat him with the genial rudeness of comradeship; he is patronised by ticket-collectors and policemen. But he goes home an old man. No less do I sympathise with the youthful and agreeable Hamlet, who staggers along the Charing Cross Road at this season with his arms and pockets filled with books. These are not, alas! the spoils of a conqueror, but the sacrifices of the vanquished, for every spring Hamlet falls in love, and madly sells his books for flowers and jewellery. His dream-girls are always of the practical kind, and their affection for Hamlet appears to pass with his library; but Hamlet loves the spring nevertheless. So too, I suppose, does Pericles, whose madness, however, fills me rather with envy than with sympathy, for to him the spring brings a passion for work that enables him to squander the summer hours at Lord's or the Oval like a capitalist. There is something immoral in being able to perform prodigies of work when all the world is stretching from its winter sleep. But so it is with Pericles, and his friends will know him no more until these delicious months are over.

In truth there is no harm in these vernal follies; they are only the fuller expression of that self over which our conventional cunnings have no control. Perhaps if we were honest and not quite so civilised we should dance blithely along Piccadilly every day of our short lives. Perhaps if we understood our neighbours better we should endue every night with the dreamy colours of our desires. As it is, it is only in the spring that we are willing to acknowledge the charm—I might almost say virtue—of wise excess. Over a certain section of one of the London parks there used to rule a policeman so dour that he never wearied of condemning himself for the frivolous character of his dreams. He felt that the midnight caperings of his spirit went far to counteract the rectitude of his conscious life, and over all his asceticism there hung a bitter consciousness of its futility. At last, on a golden day of spring, he proposed to and was accepted by a nursemaid of secure charms, and the kingdom of paradox knew him no more. He traced his fall to a bed of tulips.

But most cruel of all are the dealings of this wanton season with those of us who write about little things with

wide, splendid words. Never, it would seem, are our
emotions more trivial, never are the words with which we
hold them wider and more splendid. It is true that this
verbal insanity affects us in different ways. Me does the
coming of the almond blossoms afflict with adjectives—
great and gorgeous adjectives in merry companies—fallen
together by the chance of the road, but surely inseparable
thereafter. There is nothing to be done with these blithe
comrades but to enshrine them in notebooks and sigh a
requiem. For, fine as life is, there is nowhere anything on
the earth worthy of such epithets—and I lack my notebook when I wander in the city of dreams. Moreover, this
futility extends to the ideas themselves that are bred in our
minds during this happy, bitter season. On a fair morning
of spring I seemed to have discovered what really should
be done with H.M.S. *Buzzard*, that promising gunboat
which lies off the Embankment for the encouragement of
the naval volunteers. As in a vision, I saw her captured at
night by twelve decadent millionaires, hopeful of winning
the ultimate sensation by their piratical enterprise. Thereafter the tale pursued a pleasant and profitable course.
Their number raised to thirteen by the volunteering of a
romantic small boy, my millionaires diverted themselves
by singing sentimental songs to the tall white masts and
by scattering explosive shells like roses all over London.
Beaten at last by the invincible force of the British Navy,
they blow a magnificent hole in the bottom of the ship,
which sinks some three feet, it being low tide, and there
are god-like laughters upon the decks. Finally, I think the
survivors, being three of the millionaires and the small
boy, were to drift down the river towards the sea in a
leaky boat, talking pleasant philosophies as they went.

Here was a fine tale with never a woman in it, yet, nevertheless, it was of the spring. For when, in an autumnal

mood, I revisited the *Buzzard*, I saw that even the most decadent millionaire or the most romantic of small boys could not hold that wretched vessel for five minutes against a handful of marksmen. So passed my screaming shells, my armoured tramcars, my ploughed and reddened decks. Before the first puff of saner weather my visionary galleon sailed back to the harbour of dreams.

Yet withal, when the last joss-stick of winter dies in the room and the scent of the violets in the flower-girl's basket comes singing through the open window, it is only the more cowardly of us who quaff the cautious iron and quinine. Those of us who are lovers know that there are troubling days before us in this season of finite sorrows and infinite joys, and amateurs of pain as we are, we would not have it otherwise. It is enough for us, though our feet be lame and bleeding, that, from the grey morning and through the hot day and down to the cool time when the stars light up the sky, our love fares on. We may mock ourselves with speech of green-sickness and of faculties devilishly perturbed; we may turn a sorrowful eye on the morrow inevitably grey; but our hearts are for the spring.

THE PANTOMIME MAN

THERE are probably few Londoners who have not heard of that sinister person, the earnest student of the drama; there are, I suspect, very few people who have ever seen him in the flesh, and it would be a difficult matter to tell the enterprising foreigner where he was to be met. I have looked for him in the gallery on first nights, and only discovered a number of bright-eyed youths who refused to pay for programmes, and for the rest displayed a considerable interest in the girls who accompanied them, and a cheerful tolerance of the efforts of the actors on the stage far below. Greatly daring I have ventured among the critics in the stalls, and have heard an admirable discussion on the merits of the latest dancer for my pains. I have met the persons who wait five hours for souvenirs, and the spirited young ladies whose passion for musical comedy brings to mind the worst excesses of the French Revolution. But musical comedy is not drama; nor indeed is pantomime, or my search were ended, for the earnest student of pantomime is no longer a stranger to me.

I first met the Pantomime Man at the dress-rehearsal at Drury Lane Theatre on Christmas Eve. Measured by time this was a serious business, and it was natural that two adults, marooned in a turbulent sea of children, should exchange confidences and criticisms. My new acquaintance, like many great men, wore insignificance as a disguise, and beyond admiring his childlike enthusiasm I did not find him in any way remarkable. He looked shocked when I left after five hours of it to keep another appointment. Afterwards when I came to realise the extent of the experience on which his judgments were founded, I was glad to remember that he had applauded the visible portions of the giant, and had gazed in gaping astonishment at the cascade with its succession of floating nymphs. At one stage of the performance he turned to me and cried, "This is better every year, sir!" and on the whole gave me the impression that he was an unsophisticated lad of some five-and-forty years.

Nor did I see any great reason to change this opinion when I met him a week later in the vestibule of the Lyceum. I was accompanied by two small nieces, whose failure to believe in fairies had not prevented them from insisting on seeing the harlequinade, which, as the Pantomime Man told me in a rapt whisper, he also would not have missed for worlds. He agreed that the principal girl was a charming Cinderella, and then I told him the criticism of my younger niece on the famous crystal slipper; that it was big enough for a giant or giantess, always excepting, of course, the reticent monster at the Lane. He nodded his head shrewdly. "Of course you're right," he said, "but wasn't it pretty when they lit it up with electric lights!" As we drove off I noticed that his eyes were still aflame with reminiscent splendour.

Naturally I hardly expected to see my genial enthusiast again, and of course, for otherwise this essay could not have been written, I did meet him again. A music-hall comedian of genius who was taking a busman's holiday, had brought me to a box at the new Wimbledon Theatre, and the first person I saw in the stalls was the Pantomime Man gazing at the principal boy with merited adoration. Between the acts I went down to speak to him, but he was by no means surprised to see me. "I see your tastes are like mine, sir," he said simply; "I even venture to suppose that you would agree with me that the whole future of the drama in England rests with pantomime?"

I shook my head at this astonishing heresy.

"Reflect a moment," he said earnestly, "and you will find that the drama, what is foolishly called the legitimate drama, is lacking in joy. Sane men and women go to the theatre to be merry, and in that mood they are pleased by the same things as children, colour and movement, dancing and noisy, jolly singing. Where will you find these on the stage, save in pantomime? Comic opera has been contaminated by exotic sentimentality, musical comedy seeks to purvey a nebulous eroticism. The musical halls are incoherent and oppressed by a forlorn desire to improve the minds of their audiences. I hate all these things. When I go to the theatre I want something brighter and more mirthful than life, and I find it here."

I sought to express my admiration of his eloquence with a comprehensive nod. "And how often do you go?" I asked.

"I have been to the pantomime once or twice a day during the season for two-and-twenty years," he replied, "and I have found something to please me in every one of them. For instance, when I saw this pantomime at Nottingham last week——"

"At Nottingham?" I interjected, overwhelmed by his confession.

"Yes, the same pantomime but presented, of course, by another company. Well, they had a Scotch ballet with all the different tartans, you know, that was quite astonishing. Now here they have a dancer, who will amaze you. She is hardly more than a child and yet every step she takes convinces me that life is a joyous thing. Then there are some gay little atomies from Manchester. You have seen some more of them at Drury Lane, but I think they are even better here."

"What's the best pantomime you have ever seen?"

The Pantomime Man looked at me with a quick smile. "Do you know," he said, "I have sometimes asked myself that question, and always found it difficult to convince myself that the latest was not also the best. But there was a pantomime that I saw two or three years ago at Tunbridge Wells, performed by a small touring company of about twenty-six persons, that has made a lasting impression on me. Especially I recall a comedian who sang one of those interminable Somerset reaping-songs, and appeared to have attained to the summit of agreeable irresponsibility. Then, as we were speaking of Drury Lane, I used to enjoy the little pantomimes the children of that theatre used to take on tour; but I find that nearly all pantomimes reach a high level of accomplishment."

"And what do you think of children's plays?"

"*Alice in Wonderland* is really a pantomime and a very good one. You have seen it, of course? *Peter Pan* is too sentimental, and I like the *Blue Bird* still less. It may be wise, but there is no magic in it. It is a pity that such a beautiful setting should be used to convey philosophic platitudes to an audience of disillusioned adults."

I realised that my friend's enthusiasm carried with it its due proportion of prejudice, so I returned to our flock. "You must find the jokes of the comedians a little wearisome after a while?"

"I have failed to make my position clear to you," said the Pantomime Man quickly; "it is not the jokes that attract me in pantomime, but the spirit of joy on the stage and in the auditorium alike. Look here," he went on earnestly, "they are going to ring up in a minute and I cannot talk now. But if you will accompany me on my round for a week or two, I shall be delighted to convince you of the soundness of my attitude towards English dramatic art."

For a moment I hesitated, but it is to be feared that I have outgrown the primitive craving for desperate adventure. As I shook my head the curtain rose, and I saw the Pantomime Man pass forthwith into another world. I slipped back to the box, abashed as one who had declined an invitation to join an aeroplane expedition to the South Pole. As I watched him dreaming in the stalls, it seemed to me that in some way the Pantomime Man was a pathetic figure. But what would you have? Solitude is the abiding-place of the great, and Englishmen especially must expect to be lonely in their enthusiasm.

T

BEDLAM IN 1823

WHEN Charles Reade wrote *Hard Cash*, he painted, no doubt truthfully enough, a very unpleasant picture of the asylums of the day, and one might well have thought that so much earlier as 1823 a still more dreadful state of things would have existed.

So, at least, it was with us, until quite recently there fell into our hands a copy of *Sketches in Bedlam*, written by Dr. Haslam, but published anonymously in 1823–4.

The sub-title of the book is "Characteristic Traits of Insanity," and it is rather given up to a study of the inmates than of the system; but indirectly we get a very fair glimpse of the place at the time, as well as a liking for the cheerful sympathy which Dr. Haslam evidently felt for the patients.

There is no doubt that if the doctor is correct—and there seems no reason to suspect his statements—discipline was then rather lax than severe at "Bethlem Hospital," though this did not reach the strange heights of the Norwich Lunatic Asylum, where about six years before a lunatic had obtained possession of a *scythe* and slain the steward.

Yet we read of a criminal lunatic breaking seventy panes of glass in the dining-room windows, guarded by a strong iron lattice-work, by standing on a form, and prodding through the meshes with the handle of a wooden spoon held in his teeth; of another patient being permitted habitually to eat pebbles, coals and pieces of leather in his gruel; of an officer inmate who spent a pension of seventy pounds a year on "trifles, apple pies, and various kinds of pastry," and of the patients passing their evenings in singing, dancing and theological discussions.

In truth this does not sound over-strict, and perhaps the doctor was right when he wrote of one patient, that "the only prominent symptoms of insanity now apparent is (sic) to get out from here."

And if witty society is a comfort it was not lacking in this Elysium. "He was thought to be mad this time," said one lunatic, "only because nature had furnished him with more discernment, reflection and fancy than his neighbours, and he had not prudence to conceal them; therefore he was found guilty of common-sense and sent to prison"; and again, "All London should be a Bedlam in order to restrain its mad inhabitants, one-half of whom were too mad to perceive the madness of the other half."

This is admirable and must be matched with the gentlemanly instinct of the patient, who would ask the keeper to put the handcuffs on him, for then, as he said, "He had liberty to do what he pleased"; or with the philosophy of the madman, who "committed no violence except now and then breaking a window, and occasionally tearing his clothes, which he said he was obliged to do, 'the time being now come.' " Even the religious maniac was able to write, that we ought "to know that the most distinguished geniuses are liable to egregious and most reprehensible feelings," though it must be confessed that the society of one "whose favourite topic is damning the King and his Ministers" would become rather tiresome.

Wealth was not wanting in this pleasant social circle, for one gentleman owned every house he had ever put his foot inside, while another was in a position to give his son on his marriage "a fortune of 957 millions of money, besides some loose silver he had in his pocket, and four pennyworths of halfpence." It is disappointing to learn that the son was a profligate fellow, and all this money soon went. There were also in the place several queens and princesses and a daughter of no less a person than Jove. This lady, who had no little strength of character, would when displeased with her august parent look upwards and exclaim: "Joe! Joe! do you think this right? Is this justice? Is this justice? Is this justice, Joe?" This has a modern ring.

Yet, though we have so far dwelt on the cheerful side, and this is the side our author evidently preferred to write about, even his light-hearted pen cannot at times avoid a touch of pathos.

The poor savage fellow crying repeatedly, "Why do you keep I here? You have no business to keep I here!" And the sailor who felt so much compassion for the victims of the cruel surgery of the day, with its cuppings and bleedings, poor infants he would call them, and say, "They should not serve you so, 'tis cruel, and I am sure you did not deserve it." Or the woman whose sole answer to all questions was, "For ever and a day as the boy sold his top"—is there not a sentimental satisfaction in the thought that they are long since free?

Though this book, being dedicated to the governor of the asylum, must be taken as a partisan account, it is still noteworthy that there is no mention of the whip in the whole work, and that it was not apparently the custom to put a patient in chains until he had made at least one murderous assault on his companions or keepers. And but for one jarring note of a savage patient being fastened to the coal-chest in the basement gallery, it must be confessed that Bedlam appears to have been managed, in 1823, with a very high degree of sympathy and kindness towards its unhappy inmates.

THE INVALID

It has been a painful journey. First the dead weight on your mind of something the matter with you, some mysterious visitation of the unseen gods, that has troubled your brow, perhaps, for many months. Then come the doctors, with all their magic mastery of the things they do not say, and you find suddenly that you are in bed and ill. At first you struggle against the spell and take an interest in the deeds of the outside world; but every day there is a shrinkage, till the morning comes when the world for you is bounded by the four walls of your sick-room, and that little patch of eventful sky that shows through the window.

In this small space you watch without interest the spectral shapes that come and go, forms of men-folk who shuffle uneasily from foot to foot, knowing not what to say, and finally leaving the room with honest relief, forms of women-folk who play with your pillows, and pass from spot to spot with a strained quietness, which irritates the petulant mind of the invalid ten thousand times more than would the din of a boiler-maker's factory.

But these are small things compared with the wonder that is yours when you realise that the foot which stirs the counterpane at the bottom of the bed belongs to you. Do you not remember that worst day of all, when, your hand being on the pillow before your eyes, you moved your fingers slowly in simple changes, and marvelled as at some strange live thing; while all the while you had a dim consciousness of your mind existent at some great height and burdened with deep and fearful thoughts of nothing?

So pass the days, confused and unreal as dreams, without
a dream's excitement; but the nights, those long sick nights
without an end, there is the rub. Then does your mind
sink from the vague elation of the day to cower tortured
in your weakling frame, then do you know that your head
is hot and your body aching, and that sleep the desirable
is not for you.

And now come the soft cool hands to turn your pillows
and touch your brow, the last defence of your boastful
manhood gives way, and you become as a little child that
thinks not but loves to be soothed.

Thus the black hours, and yet it seems but a little while
before the sky in your patch of heaven has blossomed from
winter to summer, and from the outer world there comes
to you unheeding, the word that you are better.

Yet when you are propped up in bed, a pleasant relief
from the permanent prone, and then moved to the window,
and one fine day, best change of all, supported, swaying
and shawl-swathed, to the garden, even your quenched
spirit remembers something of life, and draws in with
the untainted air the joy in the world that was yours
before.

Now you have reached that pleasant land which lies
beyond the dark gates of sickness and can only be reached
that way—the Land of Convalescence. The birds fight in
the cherry tree and the insects hum incessantly among the
flowers, the big blue sky looms overhead, and on the placid
lawn you sit, feeble, pale, unintellectual, and divinely
happy.

Every now and then you realise this and smile with an
inane sweetness; if people address you, you mutter in-
anities. Perhaps you have forgotten how to smile or speak
sedately, or you are too happy to pose as wise, or the sky
is too blue. But however it is, you only wish to be left

alone, to sit blinking by the hour like a great dog, and soak in the sun.

If only time would stop! There would be your Paradise without a burden. But even while you sit the sun flashes round the heavens and the day is gone. You will not stay convalescent. You must needs get well. And with returning health come returning duties. The world's business has to be managed, the earth must revolve once in twenty-four hours, and it is your task to see that it does it. It is, alas! the task of all men. And so you gather up your knapsack and fill it with stones and are off once more on your haphazard course.

Folk will stop you as you go, and sympathise with you concerning your recent troubles, and you will smile pensively, murmuring that you had rather a bad time. But not a word will you say about those golden days in the garden, for you are only an honest man and no saint.

And if the world is sorry for us, why, faith! we are sorry for ourselves.

THE CLERK IN ART

IT may fairly be said that there is no modern profession so completely neglected by Art as is that of those who have "thrust desks into the pits of their stomachs" and devoted themselves to the quill and the ruler, the day-book and the ledger. Our novelists find them dull, our dramatists undramatic, we may search the walls of our art galleries in vain for their likenesses and those of their offices—the rooms with the green lights and the long mahogany desks. Yet it may well be that now that our writers and painters are in danger of exhausting the possibilities of the old blusterous well-defined types, the soldiers, the company promoters, the detectives, the hooligans and all the rest of the too familiar puppets, they may turn their eyes on the City and write of the great and wonderful people who fill its streets.

To the shallow-minded these thousands of clerks may appear uninteresting, their lives as uniform as their clothes, their minds incapable of the psychological subtleties which we are taught to admire, but a black coat may hide a tragedy and paper-cuffs surround the wrists of a thief; Romeo may flaunt it as an ink-smudged office-boy, Juliet tap a typewriter in Queen Victoria Street, and Pan himself startle the serenity of an insurance office on a bright spring morning. This is scarcely to be wondered at, seeing that outside the great republic of letters there is no profession which draws its members from so wide a range as that of the clerk. In one office you will find the failures of a dozen Public Schools, the successes of a dozen Board Schools, the son of a general on half-pay shares a desk with the son of a labourer, a lad of eighteen who is already earning more money than his father. Barristers without briefs, actors without engagements, who have drifted into the comfortable security of a regular income, hard bearded men from the provinces who are going to get on, callow youths from the suburbs who will accomplish nothing, the offices gather them in and the word 'clerk' covers them all.

Thus it is that under one roof, in one room perhaps, you find men of widely different birth and education sitting down for life to perform kindred tasks for a common authority that yet affects their temperaments in a widely different way. The boy from an elementary school, to whom we have already referred, is well content to be obedient in exchange for a position which already represents success to him and his connections; but the Public School boy, whom tradition has taught to regard the clerical profession with contempt, is frequently embittered by a sense of failure which shows itself in an attitude of resentment towards his seniors and his work. And it is noteworthy that as a general rule the men who occupy the best positions are drawn from neither of these classes; the ambitions of the former are well and quickly satisfied, the latter are too proud to be desirous of success in a walk of life which they tread unwillingly. It is from the private schools, for the most part, that the successful clerk is drawn.

Again, beyond these two broad distinctions of birth and education there are the no less important differences of character and mind. You find the man who for ten years has ordered daily two recent novels from the library, who yet has never read a book to its conclusion, and beside him a man who, being the office caricaturist, rose one hot conquest day and beat his neighbour's head against the wall because he could not catch its likeness. One, scoffing gravely at authority and order, is loved by his seniors and juniors alike; another, always friendly with the head of his department and noisily cheerful with his colleagues, awakens in these latter only a polite mistrust. This lad with his hair as long as he dares to grow it conceals half-finished verses beneath his blotting-paper and troubles editors; another is wise in cricket and football, a friend of pugilists and the captains of sailing barges.

So when you approach them you find that they vary as other men do and are no less interesting. Even as other men, they are born and marry and die, none the less that their office (keen for its reputation) expects them to do these things in a certain ordered manner. One quality perhaps they have in common that is lacking to men of other professions—a certain fatalism born of the certainty of their employment—forty years' work perhaps, and then in many cases a pension.

A baker may change his employer or his shop, a candlestick-maker may become an electrical engineer, but the clerk is always a clerk, and he must not resign his post, for probably he will never get another. Only boys fresh from school are wanted in all City offices nowadays, and the experience that a man may have had in one office is a purely local thing at best, of no use to any other firm.

So it may be that they are a little hard and unsympathetic in their view of life when compared with such a man as a struggling tradesman who launches his ship bravely every morning. As a class, they miss the humanising effects of that poverty which marches arm in arm with hunger. Their meals, they feel, are assured, the rest is only a matter of their holidays and their hobbies. The social questions that trouble most of us at one time or another interest them hardly at all, and it is doubtful whether there may be found any body of men so pro-

foundly ignorant of the politics and the government of
their country. Financially they are uninterested, for only a
minority are taxed other than indirectly. Patriotism is for
them but a jest, for how does their country's pugnacity
affect them? "It won't alter the rises," is a sentence that is
often on their lips. And yet, granting this, and granting
that their lives and the places in which they live them are
frequently superficially uneventful and uninteresting, it
must be owned that the place that City life has occupied in
English art is disproportionately small.

For, as we have said, within the lifelong prison of four
walls, doing the same work and living in the same atmosphere you will find every type of man, you can see character meet character in strife and in friendship. Leaning on
those desks and stirring amongst those musty ledgers,
boys grow to men and pass presently with the rest, and
through those grimy windows young eyes have seen the
spring. If these things be dull and uninteresting, then
would the silence of our wise men be justified, but we
know that they are not.

Where is the great novel, the great play, the great picture
that has drawn the life of the city to us? We ask in vain,
even though many of our novelists, poets and playwrights
served more or less an apprenticeship in the City. They
have told us the joys and sorrows of ships, of slums, of
palaces, of great armies, they have sung to us of forests and
rivers and starry heavens, but, as we hold, the finer task
still waits for the hand of a master.

THE ROMANCE OF DRINK

WE were colloguing the other day at a certain tavern, and the conversation turning on Romance, somebody asked what was the most romantic moment in a man's existence. To which one replied, "When he drinks his first champagne."

Now this is just, but it is not concerning such insidious tipples that I purpose to spin out my paper.

The wines—whether of France, Spain, Madeira, Australia (England, says the cynic), whencesoever they are sprung—shall have no place in this my paper. Even if by such an omission I do a mortal injury to my first and last love, brown sherry. (Ah, sherry! always so good, whether as plain sherry, sherry cobbler, sherry and bitters, or what you will!)

For to-day I sing of our British drinks, by which I neither refer to the home-made wines of the farmhouse, cowslip, ginger, rhubarb and what-not, nor yet basely to those bastard liquors, whose accents betray the Cockney, even while they sport the labels and crowns of their fair French namesakes.

No, I refer to our two national drinks, English ale and Scotch whisky. Respect for the always too tender feelings of the Sister Isle, and possibly the patriotism inherited from an Irish grandfather, would fain have me add Irish whisky to the roll of honour. But whether that worthy ancestor of mine was a teetotaller, or whether those finer shades of the man that constitute the palate have failed to come down to me, I know not. For I do not like Irish whisky and I shall have none of it.

On the whole, I do not believe my grandfather could have been a teetotaller. English ale and Scotch whisky. Scotch whisky. English ale. Do not the very names taken repeatedly make you thirsty? Taken conjunctly make you drunk?

Do they not suggest to your imaginative eye the picture of a tavern? Not a red plush and electro-plate monstrosity, if you please, nor yet marbles. But rafters, black low ceilings, oak panels, old oak chairs, a wide old fireplace, everything old except the barmaid, and she is young and beautiful.

What says the poet?

> Surely such pleasures would be his
>   Who would Elysium find,
> Where every maid a barmaid is,
>   And every barmaid kind:
>
> Where drink is not esteemed a sin,
>   No virtues mar the beer,
> And taverns cry, "Come in! Come in!
>   All are good fellows here!"

In such a tavern nobody can help drinking, nobody can get drunk. The very æsthetic passions that invite him to quench his thirst simultaneously charge him not to exceed his limit. Poor soul! if that limit be but a short one. A misanthrope is a person who cannot take his liquor. A poet is a person who cannot quench his thirst, drink he never so deeply. Be it beer, love, whisky or sunsets, he never has enough. Not even of praise.

Perhaps you know the lines beginning:

> I cannot work to-night,
>   My thoughts are on the wing,
> I cannot read, I cannot write,
>   I only want to sing,
>   Dear, have you heard me sing?

You will remember how the unhappy lover runs through the whole gamut of things he cannot do. Walk, sleep, hate, smoke, and the rest, until he comes to the last verse:

> I cannot drink to-night,
>   Ah me! that is a lie;
> For since I could not stay Love's flight,
>   I've put ten whiskies by,
>   Whiskies and sodas by!

That is the point. The drink did two good things for him, you see. It satisfied him when all other occupations or amusements had failed, and it stopped his writing of verses.

It will be observed that he blended or mingled his whisky with aerated waters, a very commendable practice.

Patriotism should not be permitted to interfere with our drinks. And with regard to hot-weather drinking there is one point to be noticed. English beer, on the whole, does not ice well. It is apt to be flat.

Now, there is a certain brand of German beer, Münich, to wit, that, when the day is very hot and the poet very thirsty, touches perfection, and sets him emulating Hans Breitmann. But as you love yourself and your country, drink it not in English taverns, even though your heart yearns for that faintest kiss of onion that raises this beer to such heights. Was it not Stevenson who bracketed the onion and the nectarine as the best of Nature's fruits?

One feels inclined to adapt Whistler, and ask, "Why drag in the nectarine?"

But I wander from my tipple.

There are two ways of drinking among decent people.

The one is the social way among friends, which involves much merry converse, and plentiful interchange of tobacco pouches, accompanied by moderate potations.

The other is the solitary way that marks a certain age in youth. When you creep humbly into the same bar every evening, crouch up in a corner by the counter, and gazing in a shy and hopeless admiration at the magnificent lady behind the bar, soak steadily for the whole evening to justify your existence, until to your disordered vision the bar is full of charming replicas of the beloved one.

At this age you are greatly shocked at the free-and-easy way in which the other customers address your angel, and you probably pity her because she is so young.

Behind your back she calls you the funny little boy who gets so drunk.

Much has been written and much more will be written about barmaids before they are abolished by a moral County Council.

And rightly, for not even the London policeman can exceed them in interest. For it is owing to their influence that London has its salons after all; salons of wit, laughter, youth, high spirits, tobacco smoke, and Lord knows what, all in one. Salons where many a man is an unconscious Omar, nearly every man an unconscious poet, and all men are at their best. It is here that London makes up its mind. What play is worth seeing, what horse is worth backing, which of them is guilty, how she died, why, how, and wherefore everything. The man in the street of whom we hear so much is the man in the bar. And it is the barmaid who shines on him there like a lovely summer sun, inciting him by her beauty to fresh intellectual effort, lighting his way with her charms through hitherto unexplored regions of the mind.

People generally express a shocked surprise when they hear that someone has married a barmaid. For my part, I wonder why everybody does not marry a barmaid.

They are so lovely and so wise.

They stand for years behind the biscuit boxes, and all the time they are imbibing wisdom hot from the cow. Fresh from the minds which beer and whisky have incited to give of their best. A barmaid wife should not drink because she has seen so much of it, should not smoke because nobody would be surprised if she did, should not be unfaithful because she knows (who better?) where it ends.

Marry a barmaid, and you marry all the wisdom of London.

I have said above that there are two ways of drinking, the solitary and the sociable. But the subdivisions are very numerous. There is the drink hasty that speeds you on a journey, the drink divine that sends you to your bed, the drink maudlin at a poor man's funeral, the drink joyous at a rich man's wedding, the Charles Dickens drink at Christmas, the Charles Lamb drink on New Year's Eve, the drink medicinal when you have got wet, the drink magnificent when you are hot, the drink damnable that an enemy stands you, the drink ironic that you stand an enemy, drinks— drinks without number.

Only Rabelais could enumerate a tithe of them.

Drinks are the commas in a sociable man's life.

There be some, surely they are Philistines, who hold that drinking good strong wholesome liquors is unnatural; who would have us quench our thirst at the nearest water-tap, and go on our way rejoicing, with gratitude in our hearts for that poor, thin fluid.

Unnatural! Why, doth not the very sun in his strange carryings-on in the heavens remind us of our dear potations? Hark to the poet.

> To make our pleasures surer
> The sun doth on us shine,
> Rising like Angostura
> And going down like wine.

As if the righteous old fellow had passed all the night in his cups, and had to take bitters of a morning before he could eat his breakfast.

Of course, there is a serious side of drinking, pleads youth never so wisely.

The day comes when you have married your barmaid and you have to choose between the society of your wife and the society of the tavern, between domesticity of the fireside with the cat on the hearthrug, and the comradeship of the stars with the dome of St. Paul's in the foreground.

Concerning the rights and wrongs of the question it is somewhat hard to judge, from the glorious freedom of un-married life. On the one hand lies beer, on the other the woman, and it is not given to all of us to combine them like Omar to make our earthly Paradise. I recall some verses that give one point of view well enough.

> The soft white hand of woman
>   Set with little pink nails,
> The curling handle of a clean pint-pot,
>   And beer in pails.
>
> The soft red mouth of a woman
>   To kiss and say Amen.
> The cold round edge of a clean pint-pot
>   To kiss again.
>
> The soft bright eyes of a woman,
>   The salt, salt tears that set 'em,
> And once again a clean pint-pot
>   In which one may forget 'em.

He, you see, chooses the pleasant path.

Yet I am not sure that the meek endurance of the tyranny of the hearth does not, on the whole, breed the more lasting contentment.

But lo! I grow prosy, and I seem to hear you saying: "Friend, this fellow irks me, come and have a drink!"

U